Praise for

Kiss the Ring

"*Kiss the Ring* is a fast, hard-boiled urban tale. The elements are all there: explicitly detailed sexual acts, drug use, mystery, and murder. You'll find the prose strong, the premise compelling, and a cast of dynamic, well-developed characters. Enjoy the ride. This is a surefire winner, as is Mink's Real Wifey series."

—*Ebony*

"This crisply written urban thriller from Mink (*Real Wifeys: Hustle Hard*) introduces a street-savvy protagonist, Naeema Cole, who is both a villain and a heroine . . . Fast-paced action, sizzling erotic sex, and a heartwarming kick-ass heroine will have newcomers and urban fiction fans alike eagerly awaiting Naeema's next escapade."

—*Publishers Weekly*

"Mink writes with street flair while sliding in a few erotic sex scenes, yet her tale is one of hard-boiled noir. Naeema plays the noble soul seeking the truth, determined to right all wrongs, and she's willing to off anyone who blocks her path. Sex, bloody violence, betrayal, and a crackling mystery come together in a resounding crescendo of a finish. Take a bow, Meesha Mink, this one's a winner."

—*Library Journal* (Top Pick of the Month)

Praise for

Real Wifeys: Hustle Hard

"A well-laid-out plot spiced with wild sex moves Mink's story right along. Readers will keep turning pages to see if Suga succeeds as she moves toward redemption. Mink's books are the real deal."

—*Library Journal*

"Mink's energy and grit make it a fun read."

—*Juicy Magazine*

Praise for

Real Wifeys: Get Money

"Mink's brisk combination of insult, profanity, and pop culture is what street lit is all about . . . Another powerful story of women orbiting the hip-hop world . . . Luscious is both a villain and a heroine whom readers will embrace. Order in anticipation of high demand."

—*Library Journal*

"Unexpected story lines . . . very realistic . . . a quick read with an engaging main character."

—Huffington Post

Praise for

Real Wifeys: On the Grind

"Marking her solo debut with this new series launch, Mink (coauthor of *The Hood Life, Shameless Hoodwives, Desperate Hoodwives*) gives Kaeyla a snappy and profane voice laced with sarcasm. She's a charismatic woman, both vulnerable and tough. Female readers will love her, but men may want to check their own woman's purse for Taser wires. Load your shelves with multiple copies."

—*Library Journal*

"A gritty new urban series with a down-and-dirty intensity that's heartbreaking."

—*Publishers Weekly*

"The Real Wifeys series tells the tales of strong female characters who overcome obstacles while standing by or getting over the men that they love."

—AllHipHop.com

ALL HAIL THE QUEEN

AN URBAN TALE

MEESHA MINK

Touchstone

New York   London   Toronto   Sydney   New Delhi

Touchstone
A Division of Simon & Schuster, Inc.
1230 Avenue of the Americas
New York, NY 10020

First Touchstone trade paperback edition February 2015

TOUCHSTONE and colophon are registered trademarks of
Simon & Schuster, Inc.

For information about special discounts for bulk purchases,
please contact Simon & Schuster Special Sales at 1-866-506-1949
or business@simonandschuster.com.

The Simon & Schuster Speakers Bureau can bring authors to
your live event. For more information or to book an event contact the
Simon & Schuster Speakers Bureau at 1-866-248-3049 or visit our website
at www.simonspeakers.com.

Interior design by Akasha Archer

Manufactured in the United States of America

10 9 8 7 6 5 4 3 2 1

Library of Congress Cataloging-in-Publication Data
Mink, Meesha.
  All hail the queen : an urban tale / Meesha Mink.—First Touchstone trade
paperback edition.
      pages ; cm
1. African American women—Fiction. 2. Attempted murder—Fiction. 3.
Revenge—Fiction. 4. Newark (N.J.)—Fiction. 5. Urban fiction. I. Title.
  PS3552.R8945A79 2015
  813'.54—dc23
                                    2014038803

ISBN 978-1-4767-5535-9
ISBN 978-1-4767-5538-0 (ebook)

For those people with big dreams
and the inner hustle to make it happen . . .

ALL HAIL
THE QUEEN

Prologue

*M*urder was nothing new to her.

Naeema "Queen" Cole had given birth to one life but had taken many more than that in the name of revenge. Still, the first loud echo of a gun being shot into the night caused life's motion to slow down.

POW!

"Tank!" she cried out from her spot in the crowd in front of the movie theater as the bullet entered the shoulder of the man she loved.

His body jerked as he fell forward, closing the double-parked SUV's passenger door from the bullet's force.

POW! POW! POW!

She gasped as each bullet pierced his flesh. His thigh. His stomach. His chest.

The crowd lining the streets outside the theater screamed, ran, or ducked for cover. Naeema climbed over the red velvet ropes that corralled the movie premiere's onlookers. Her heart pounded as she rushed across the short distance, not caring if more bullets flew as she reached Tank. She caught his bloodied body just as it slid down the side of the car. Her knees gave out under the weight of his tall, solid frame but she did not—would not—let him go.

"Help! Somebody help," Naeema screamed, looking

around at those people still boldly standing around staring down at them.

"Na," Tank moaned, turning his face against her body as he winced in pain.

Love for him filled her and she felt breathless with emotion. Naeema pressed her lips to his sweating brow. "I'm here. I got you. I'm here," she assured him in a fervent whisper against the backdrop of the sirens growing louder in the air.

She clasped the side of his face as she looked down into the pain flooding his dark eyes. She bit back a gasp at the sight of the handprint she made against his cheek. The blood on her hands from his soaked shirt was sticky, wet, and warm. Tank's blood signaled his imminent death.

"Please God, no," Naeema begged in a whisper, nearly choking at the thought of losing him. Tears filled her eyes blurring her vision.

She reached up with one hand to pound on the passenger door as she fought to remain rational and not let panic diminish her senses. She needed help. Tank needed help.

The driver's seat of the double-parked SUV Tank exited was still empty but the local rap artist, Fevah, he was hired to protect and her entourage of three friends were still all inside. "Open this fucking door," Naeema roared, pounding hard enough for darts of pain to shoot across her entire hand.

Anger was an added layer to the myriad of emotions engulfing her as the door remained closed to them but she was flooded with relief as an ambulance screeched to a halt behind the Tahoe. She pressed kisses to his face. "Hold on,

Tank. Don't you dare leave me now," she whispered in his ear in the moments before they took him from her.

As she sat in the street surrounded by the blood of the man she loved, her soul wavered between feeling as empty as her arms at the thought of losing him forever and a fiery anger that would only be quenched at finding out who shot Tank and why.

Whoever the guilty party was just invited hell into their lives.

1

Two months earlier

"*A*in't you gonna call the police?"

Naeema shifted her eyes from the items—*her* items—scattered about her living room and over to the blood still lightly oozing from the busted lip of the gruff man in his late sixties. Just minutes ago she had returned home to find her home had been broken into and Sarge on the floor, struck down by the thief during his escape.

"I'll get you some ice," she said.

"No," he said abruptly, dabbing at his swelling bottom lip with a wrinkled handkerchief from the pocket of his military fatigues.

The man hadn't seen a war in over thirty years but he stayed dressed for combat.

With one full-circle turn Naeema was confident nothing of value had been swiped. Although the house had five bedrooms and three full bathrooms with both a semi-finished attic and basement, her entire life was contained to the living room, with clear paths to the first-floor bathroom to the left and the kitchen to the right. It would take more money than she could save cutting hair to do anything beyond the elbow grease she put into cleaning the rooms of every disgusting remnant of the squatters who had lived in it all those years after her grandfather died. All those years she neglected it.

"No, Sarge," she said, finally answering him as she tapped the gun she held against her thigh and released a heavy breath. "Looks like you stopped them before they could take anything."

"But—"

"You know I don't fuck with the police," she said, her voice hard and unrelenting.

He grunted.

It was funny how that one sound from the grumpy army vet was brimming with judgment and recriminations that she didn't miss. Naeema had come to know him very well since they'd become unconventional roommates almost two years ago. After leaving her husband, Tank, and the home they shared she returned to the two-story brick colonial where her grandfather had taken her in after the death of her single mother. It was abandoned and closed up by the city but Sarge had taken refuge in it from living on the streets. She allowed him to remain, not able to bring herself to evict the wild-looking man in the filthy army uniform. She had known firsthand during her wild teenage years what it felt like to not know where her next meal would come from or if she would have a roof to sleep under that night.

Sarge was slow to speak but when he did spare her a few words they were either funny or bizarrely insightful—and sometimes both. She had come to love the ornery old man—and she suspected that he cared for her, too—although she wouldn't dare tell him so.

Naeema put her gun back in its hiding place in the ash

trap of the fireplace on the far wall of the living room before wiping her hands over her shaven head as she continued to take in the chaos the thief left behind. "I guess I better clean all this up," she said, her voice showing the lack of enthusiasm she felt about dealing with the mess.

"You got it."

That was a statement and not a question. Of that Naeema was sure and she was able to smile even in the midst of her anger. When she first moved in with Sarge she had to convince the man to take advantage of the bathroom in the basement and that had taken some serious cajoling and then flat-out demanding. She wasn't shocked in the least that he wanted no part of helping her clean.

Naeema picked up her mattress from where it leaned against her dresser and plopped it back down atop the box spring on the full-sized metal frame in the center of the room. She quickly snatched the brightly striped comforter set and the floral sheets off and left them in a ball in the center of the bed. There was no way she was going to sleep on them knowing a stranger had manhandled her bed.

Next, she bent down to pick up one of the frames holding a photo of her son, Brandon. Her anger returned in a rush at a piece of the shattered glass that tore the paper of the photo, making a white fleck on his cheek. Brandon was dead. Killed at just fourteen years old. She found vengeance—and some relief of her guilt for giving him away as a baby—when she sought and killed his murderer eight months ago.

She hadn't laid eyes on her son in nearly all his fourteen years. The pictures were a connection to the young man she grew to know during her weeks living under the alias of Queen as she moved among the band of thieves he called friends. One of whom had proven to be more foe than friend.

And she had proven to be the killer's judge, jury, and executioner.

Fuck it and fuck him.

After she picked up the broken frames and removed each of the nine pictures depicting Brandon from kindergarten to eighth grade, she scooped up all her panties from the floor before tossing them back inside the large plastic container where she had kept them. "I don't even feel right putting these on ever again," she said with a twist of her mouth, rising to set the container back upright.

Naeema bent again to stand her nineteen-inch flatscreen television back up. "No good son of a thieving bitch," she snapped, eyeing the jagged crack across the screen.

She dropped to a knee to reach over and plug the set back in.

"I love you, Steebie—"

Naeema rolled her eyes at the rerun of *Love & Hip Hop Atlanta* playing but Joseline's image was fractured by the crack in the screen. She cut the set off before lifting it to where she always sat it atop the container—a makeshift TV stand.

She looked around the room at the rest of her things scattered about and her eyes fell on the stairs leading to the second floor, wondering if the intruder had violated her privacy up there as well. She rarely ventured up there. Her wedge sneakers pressed a shard of glass and snapped it in two against the faded wood floor as she moved across the room to stand at the foot of the stairs. She flipped the switch, brightening the dusty glass-covered light fixture on the slanted wall covered in faded blue-and-white-striped wallpaper.

Ain't shit up there to steal.

She was halfway up when she stroked her palm with her fingertips, wishing she held her gun. She couldn't explain the fear that caused the soft, short hairs on her head to stand on end. The drawn-out creak of one of the steps didn't help at all.

"Aight, Naeema, get your shit together," she reprimanded herself, dashing up the rest of the stairs.

As quick as a booster trying to make it out the door of a store without getting stopped, Naeema stuck her head inside four of the five bedrooms and quickly lifted the light switch to fight the darkness caused by the boards on the windows. In each there was more of the same. Empty room. Faded and peeling wallpaper. Dull wood floors. Memories of better days.

At the bedroom just off the top of the stairs, Naeema leaned in the doorway as she flipped the switch. *If these walls could talk.*

There were many a night she had starting smelling her own ass and thinking she was grown enough to either sneak out or sneak boys in during those late hours when her grandfather slept. He wrongly assumed that the room closest to his master bedroom would help him shelter and protect the preteen who came to live with him after her mother's death, but he overlooked the closeness to the stairs that had become her escape route to freedom. Wildness. Boys. Sex. Drugs.

Naeema couldn't do shit but shake her head. She once rejected everything her grandfather offered that she needed like love and stability. Back then the room with the pink and white walls with teddy bear stencils was worse than any jail cell on *Orange Is the New Black.*

"Just young and dumb," she said with a heavy release of breath before turning off the light and walking across the open hall to the closed door leading to her grandfather's room.

She reached for the clear-glass door handle but her hand paused just above it, her long stiletto-shaped nails causing a claw-like shadow against the wood. In all the years she lived with her grandfather he had always taught her that his bedroom was off-limits.

"A man deserve some privacy in his own house," he said.

Naeema had pushed the limits on many things but she never fucked with crossing the threshold into "his" space. Not once. Even when she returned to take over her claim on the house after his death she had pressed Sarge to clean out any sign of the vagrants that had squatted.

Naeema forced herself to grip the knob, turn it, and then push the door open wide. "Shit!" she swore as a mouse jumped from the windowsill, raced along the wall, and disappeared under the closet door.

She made a note for Sarge to lay out more traps and poison. The fight against mice and roaches in the hood was an everyday struggle. That was one war Naeema was determined to win.

With her focus off the rodent, it sunk in that her grandfather's room with its dark green walls was the only one with the windows uncovered and the glass free from the harm of rocks thrown by bored children. She knew it had to be because the room was on the side of the house where there was only a small backyard cushioning it from her next-door neighbor's.

There was dust and some minor clutter in the corners but as with the other rooms it was empty as well. Naeema closed her eyes thinking she could almost smell her grandfather's aftershave above the stench of uncirculated air and mouse droppings. Almost.

She turned, closing the door behind her.

Naeema didn't bother with the bathroom or the trapdoor leading to the attic. She quickly descended the stairs and cut off the lights. The upstairs was even more of a reminder that she had to find the time and the money to finish renovating the house. It was barely a step above the shitty dump the squatters wallowed in.

At the sound of tires squealing loudly on the asphalt outside she moved to open the front door, turning the knob and lifting the door to unjam it from a botched job by a bootleg handyman she hired to hang it. *You get what the fuck you pay for.*

Standing on the top step she looked up and down the length of the slanted street. The sun had faded and there was just barely a breeze in the June air. Nearly every porch was occupied by residents thinking they could escape the heat of their homes. *Maybe someone saw something.*

People in the hood barely missed a damn thing but it was a toss-up whether they gave enough of a shit to "snitch." Hood politics were legendary. Naeema came down the stairs feeling ready to risk it. There had been at least a dozen or more break-ins on the street for the last couple of weeks, and that had to be enough to make someone speak up about seeing someone running from her house.

She reached the bottom of the steps and took a moment to smile in pride at the gate to the fence now reattached and hanging properly. One lost wrestling match too many with the gate that used to swing with the same abandon of a sweated-out track of a weave from a woman's head. Just no structure. No control. Plain disrespectful.

Now just a thousand other things to do on my list.

Closing the gate behind her and hooking the new bright aluminum latch to the pole, she glanced over at the small brick house to her right. She hadn't seen her neighbor Coko in more weeks than she could count. Maybe even months. The lights were on in the house so someone was paying the bill but Coko had not appeared recently. The young woman had long since succumbed to a heroin addiction that left Naeema having to help her last year after finding her passed out on her porch from an overdose.

Turning away from the house, she went walking up the street with long strides meant to defeat the steady incline and make sure it didn't defeat her. She moved past the few porches that were empty and stopped at a powder blue two-story colonial with white shutters.

A tall, slender light-skinned woman with a wild, curly, bright red Afro glanced up from the head of the preschool-age child sitting between her freckled knees on the step. The little girl offered her a welcoming smile. The woman did not.

She bristled at the coolness. *Fuck I do to her?*

When Naeema moved back into the house and set about making it livable she knew she didn't bake brownies and visit her neighbors for introductions. Hell, she doubted she could point any of them faux, suburban living asses out in a lineup but instant hostility? Taking a deep breath to keep from getting to the woman's level, she forced a smile.

"How you doin'?" Naeema began, placing her hands on her hips. "Someone just broke in my house and I wondered if you saw somebody running away? I live in—"

"Nah. I ain't seen shit," Freckles said, with one last hard look and an eye roll.

At the sound of a chuckle, Nacema looked up and spotted a man sitting on the porch in a kitchen chair leaning against the siding. One of the white pillars nearly shielded his presence. His eyes shifted down to take in her thick thighs in the black high-waisted leggings she wore with wedge sneakers and a tank top tied beneath her full breasts. He twisted the toothpick in his mouth from side to side, enjoying the view, and Naeema knew he was the reason for the woman's instant animosity. His disrespect. His past—or current—cheating. His shit done to her. That was their bullshit. Not hers. *Fuck 'em.*

Naeema kept it moving.

"He ran around dah corner."

Naeema stopped and looked down at the little girl who was still pointing down the street. The opposite direction Naeema was moving.

"Shut your ass the fuck up," Freckles snapped at her, tugging roughly on the girl's hair and popping her cheek with the back of her hand causing tears to fill the whites of her eyes.

Queen's anger sparked and she balled her right hand into a fist as she raised it from her side.

"What the fuck wrong wit' you, yo?" the man on the porch roared, jumping to his feet to rush down the stairs and grip the woman's red Afro in his hand to tug at just as roughly.

Queen uncurled her fingers and lowered the hand she was just about to swing against the woman's freckle-covered neck. Instead, she turned and crossed the street needing to be out of their space for her anger to ebb. On any other given day Queen would straight snap on a man abusing a woman—especially in front of a child—but in that moment she didn't give a shit. He could straight deliver a *Mortal Kombat* punch to her ass and she wouldn't blink.

Ignoring them, she turned and looked down toward Eastern Parkway. The traffic on the one-way boulevard flowed steadily and she knew the thief was long gone. All she wanted was a clue as to how he looked. Any little clue to help her hunt him down and then beat his ass down.

No need to keep going that way. His back would be to them.

Heading back down the street she locked her eyes on an eight-unit apartment building. The porch was crowded with a dozen teenage boys all posted up without a care in the world. She walked up to them and her eyes narrowed as she watched a young girl in booty shorts and a tank walk out onto the porch and take a blunt from the mouth of one dude, hit it, and then turn to blow a stream of thick smoke into the mouth of another just before she kissed him.

Naeema frowned a bit as she got closer and saw that although the girl's thick body said eighteen her face revealed she was no more than thirteen. A baby trapped in a grown woman's frame. That didn't bode well for a young girl without much sense to know better. Naeema knew that shit first-hand.

Her steps faltered as the girl turned and walked inside the apartment building. Every boy watched her movements with their eyes before their bodies followed as well. One by one each disappeared from the porch into the building. One by one.

Naeema shook her head. It would take a fool—and she was far from that—to know their plans included entering her. Violating her while she took their sex like a compliment. One by one. "Shit," she swore.

She continued down the street and then took the steps by two before she pushed the front door open and paused before entering the hallway. It was unlit and the darkness offered some coolness from the heat and sheltered the bodies now gathered in the corner with their backs to her.

"Damn that bitch can take a dick, yo," one of the voices said.

"Hurry up, yo. I got next in the pussy," said another voice.

Naeema pressed her eyes closed as she felt taken back to a time and place where she was the young, dumb girl in a small room with one bed and a line of boys waiting to fuck. One by one.

She pushed the door open wider and the band of sunlight streaming in widened. The boys at the rear of the semicircle, who were of various heights and weights, glanced over their shoulders. Their faces were a mix of guilt and annoyance. Naeema didn't give a fuck.

As the boys' urgent whispers began to rise in the air she jammed a thin and less than welcoming rug under the door to keep it open. "Get out. All of you," Naeema said, her voice showing her aggravation that she even cared to stop the train.

"Who dat?"

"I don't know that bitch."

With an eye roll and a heavy breath Naeema came striding toward them, pushing the sweaty and musty bodies out of the way. She turned up her nose at the smell of the girl in the air. It wasn't pleasant and in the heat of the hallway it was even worse.

A thin boy was between the girl's open thighs as she lay on the floor. He hadn't stopped his awkward rutting in the commotion. The girl looked up and their eyes met in that quick second just before Naeema bent down to grab the teenager by his neck and the rim of his pants, which were down just below his flat ass.

With one solid grunt she yanked him out of her pussy and onto his feet as he hollered out, "What the fuck!"

"Get up," she said to the girl still lying on the floor with her legs spread wide like the arms of a cult leader preaching to his followers.

BAP.

"Ow," Naeema yelled as a hit landed across the side of her face sending sharp darts of pain behind her eyes and her mouth.

"Damn!" someone hollered out.

The footsteps of some of the boys flying out of the hall echoed.

Naeema felt herself sway on her feet but she fought to stay up on them. *Oh shit, I got hit.*

"Why you hit her, Tee-Tee?" the girl asked.

Naeema stiffened her back, wiped her mouth with the back of her hand, and then looked over at the teenager still standing there. Five others stood with him. She didn't know if they were enjoying the show or were ready to pounce. She got her mind-set focused on the latter.

I ain't no killa but don't try me. Well, I sorta am a killa. Anyway . . .

She fired off a round of punches to Tee-Tee's smug face like it was a speed bag in a boxing gym. When she caught the sudden movement of someone in her peripheral vision she instinctively turned and delivered a solid gut punch that sent the short, squat-looking boy to his knees as he fought to reclaim the breath she knocked from him. Just as quickly as she turned back and grabbed Tee by the throat he tried to deliver another blow.

Silly rabbit . . .

She grabbed his arm and whipped his young buck ass around to slam against the wall as she twisted his arm behind his back.

He released a high-pitched scream that would put a soprano to shame.

"Anybody else wanna try me?" she said, locking eyes with each one to let them know she was ready for them. She even leveled a hard look at the girl, who stood there with her booty shorts and underwear down around one ankle.

No one said a damn thing. *Good decision.*

With a grimace she jerked Tee-Tee from the wall and pushed him across the distance into the opposite one. She waited to see if he was ready for some more.

He shifted his eyes away from her. He wasn't.

Naeema turned and the remaining boys stepped back, making a path straight for the ajar front door. She headed right for it, ready to feel the sun and get some fresh air. Just before she stepped out onto the porch she turned and pointed her finger at Little Miss Hot Ass. "Let me holla at you for a minute," she said to the young girl, pausing just long enough on the porch to take a deep inhale.

For the moment all thoughts of the man who broke into her home were set aside . . . but just for the moment.

2

"*N*ow," Naeema said with emphasis over her shoulder before jogging down the stairs and crossing the street to make her way to her house.

She didn't come to a stop until she was in the house and standing with her dick pipe in her hand after searching through her clothes strewn all over the floor. There was a small chip in the tip of the lifelike dick that gave the smooth black finish a white spot. It was slightly imperfect but at least it was still in her possession . . . unlike the half-ounce of weed that had been in the shoebox with it. *Good shit too.*

"Thieving ass," Naeema muttered darkly, wanting nothing more than to pack the hollowed out balls of the pipe with a good chunk of top-grade medicinal Blueberry Yum Yum weed and then suck the fruity-tasting smoke through the hole in the tip.

She didn't have a health problem and her doctor knew nothing about that particular medicinal healing. She just preferred the medicinal strains to the bullshit sold on the street that was more stems and nasty-ass mold than anything. Medicinal weed had elevated the game and Mook had the best connection to a dispensary out of Los Angeles.

She walked out onto the porch with her dick still in her hand just as Little Miss Hot Ass made her way across the street with clear attitude on her face and in the back-and-forth motion of her hips as she strutted. *Fast self.*

Naeema sat down on the top step on the porch, sitting her pipe behind the column as she pulled her cell phone from her bra. She dialed. It rang just once.

"Yo, whaddup sexy," said the voice coming through her cell phone.

"You. You know that. Twenty-four seven, love," Naeema said in a soft, sexy voice. "When can you get here?"

"On the way."

Yes. Yes. Yesssss.

"I need—" she stressed.

"I know what you need."

Yeah my motherfucking weed.

Every bit of that convo had been as fake as a five-dollar pack of weave and filled with enough codes for her weed connect, Mook, to know how much weed she wanted to buy. Just in case the feds were ear hustling.

"Aight," Naeema said, ending the call.

Beep.

The girl stepped up onto the sidewalk and Naeema motioned with her fingers for her to come closer. "What's your name?" she asked her, sitting the phone down on the step beside her.

"Mya," she said as she opened the gate and then closed it behind herself.

"Where's your mom?" Naeema asked.

"She works at night."

Humph. I ain't judging . . . but I'm judging.

"What were you planning on getting out of that . . . besides a wet ass?"

The girl remained silent.

Naeema patted a spot on the step.

Mya glanced back over her shoulder.

Naeema followed her line of vision. The same remainder of boys was sitting on the porch of the apartment building waiting for her. To them Naeema had just hit a PAUSE button and not STOP.

They raggedy-ass train was all the way off the tracks and they ain't even know it.

"You remind me of myself a long time ago," Naeema began, looking away from the teenage boys. "I had to learn that little boys think with their dicks and not their heads and for damn sure not their hearts. No matter how many of them you let run up in you—run a train on you—they will never respect you or love you for that."

Mya was a pretty light-skinned girl with bright eyes and jet-black hair she wore pulled up in a short tail more suited for a pig than a pony. Her edges were thick and dry and the ends of her hair just as thirsty. Her pink tank was so old and worn that the edges were torn and dark from constant wear. Her cutoff shorts were two sizes too small.

Naeema knew the girl was doing the best she could with what she knew to do. She hated to judge her mother right off the bat but it was hard not to.

"They just my friends," Mya said with a one-shoulder shrug.

Naeema fought not to grimace at the plaque lining her teeth at the gum line.

"Don't think you so smart that you do dumb shit and don't even know it," Naeema said. "Your friends don't fuck you in groups on a dirty floor in a hot-ass hallway . . . or anywhere else for that matter."

"But—"

Naeema held up her hands and locked eyes with her. "But nothing. My grandfather used to tell me that little boys would use me for sex like I wasn't nothing but a walking piece of pussy. I never forgot the words but I never listened. Trust me more than I trusted him when I tell you the same damn thing."

She leaned over and gripped the teenager's round chin in her hand. "They'll run right through a pretty girl like you."

Mya leaned her head back just enough to break Naeema's hold but her eyes were filled with the direction of her thoughts as she shifted them over to her "friends" across the street.

"Besides . . . if you're too young to know how to wash your ass you are definitely too young to be giving up that ass."

Mya pressed her knees together and tucked her hands under her arms after she crossed them over her chest. Her eyes filled with tears.

Naeema smiled at her trying to soften the harshness of her words. The world was harsh and the road she was traveling offered no softness. She was saying to Mya how she wished someone had laid shit out for her. Even her grandfather hadn't kept it one hundred with her. Hard and to the point. It was difficult to miss something smacking you dead in the face. Plus with all the attitude she was toting on her shoulders a little humbling was just what she needed for an attitude adjustment.

She's a young girl already smelling like an old whore and that shit needs to be handled.

"A woman has to wash and apply deodorant once a day, Mya. Sometimes two," Naeema said, cushioning her tone. "If you need soap or deodorant and stuff . . . or you just want to talk, my door is open."

Mya nodded and offered her a hesitant smile.

Naeema spotted Mook's nondescript dark burgundy Honda Civic. It was at least ten years old and looked like it was held together with wire hangers and prayers. Just like the phone call, the car was a front to keep him below the radar as he operated his hustle. "You go on home, Mya," Naeema said. *Deuces.*

"What's your name?" Mya asked as she rose to her feet.

"Naeema."

"That's your boyfriend?"

Naeema shifted her eyes from Mook climbing from his car. "No," she said with emphasis.

"Yeah, he don't never stay long when he come to your house," Mya said, glancing back over her shoulder.

"Oh so you nosy too?" Naeema asked.

Mya just shrugged one shoulder.

"Bye-bye."

"Bye, Miss Naeema," she said, before jogging down the steps.

Naeema rose to her feet as Mook walked through the opening in the side of the fence next to the asphalt drive. He looked exactly like his name. Odd. His face was long and thin but his eyes, nose, and lips were big. He was well over six feet but walked with his shoulders slumped like he didn't have a bit of motivation. *Another front.*

Mook climbed the stairs and sat down on the step beside her pulling his hand from his pocket to settle behind her. It lightly brushed her ass. "What's good, Naeema?" he asked with a lick of his perpetually dry lips.

"Don't get fucked up, Mook," she warned, side-eyeing his J. J. from *Good Times* remix-looking ass.

He laughed. "I would love to get fucked, Naeema," he said, knocking his knee against hers.

She locked eyes with him. "I said fucked up. Big difference," she told him, rising to her feet to adjust her leggings, fully aware that her ass and thighs were in his line of vision.

"Damn, Naeema. Don't do it like that," he said, as she wiggled her bottom and pulled the leggings up higher. "You been teasing me for the longest."

And tease is all it will ever be.

Naeema was more than willing to leave Mook's odd-looking ass horny and hot if it got her a discount on her weed.

She focused on Mya walking up onto the porch of the apartment building where she lived and easing past the teenage boys still waiting on her. Naeema smiled when Mya shook her head at something one of them said before she walked into the building and solidly closed the door behind her. Moments later the boys threw their hands up in disgust—and probably disappointment—as they came down the porch and went walking down the street and eventually around the corner.

Not one dared to glance over in her direction.

"Sheee-it, I'll double you up if you just let me smell that fat motherfucker," Mook pleaded.

She looked down at him as he continued to stare at her

ass as he licked his bulbous lips. "Double?" she asked with an arch of one of her well-shaped brows.

I just dropped a hundred last week and that stash is deep in the lungs of the fucker who robbed me. Now I can get a fucking BOGO deal . . . for a sniff?

Mook jumped to his feet and towered over her as he claimed every inch of his full height. His face was excited that she even considered that shit. "Damn right. Whassup?" he asked, cocking his head to the side and holding up his large hands.

"Just a sniff, Mook," she agreed, bending to pick up her pipe and the bag of bluish-colored weed he dropped from his hand when he first sat down beside her. "I got robbed and my weed got lifted. That's the only thing giving you life right now."

. "Well, God bless that thieving motherfucker then," Mook said, comically bugging his eyes out even more.

Naeema turned to walk to her front door and he followed close behind like her shadow. "Weed first," she said over her shoulder before pushing the door she left slightly ajar.

"A businesswoman. No problem," he said, turning to rush back down the stairs.

Naeema turned and leaned in the doorway with her arms crossed over her chest. She shook her head as he pumped the air with his fist and did a little dance at the bottom of her porch like his ass won the lottery or some shit.

She looked up and down the street and then over at the apartment building near the corner. She did a double take to see Mya sitting in a second-floor window with it pushed wide open, her chin in her hand as she openly watched Naeema. The teen waved and smiled at her. Naeema forced an uncomfortable smile and waved back.

Turning and walking into the house, she tossed the pipe and the weed on the bed and then headed to the left of the living room, past the stairs, and a little ways down the hall to the first-floor bathroom. Naeema had no worries about her pussy smelling offensive but she was always serious about her hygiene and after a long day of work barbering she figured the very least she could offer Mook for his hundred-dollar sniff was sweet-smelling pussy. She lowered her leggings and thong bikini to her knees. As she ran the water and added a good dollop of pear-scented Bath & Body Works beneath the stream, she ran her fingers across her cleanly shaven mound and then held them to her nose.

Nothing but the faint aroma of the fruity-scented wash she bathed in that morning. *Completely fuckable.*

Quickly she turned the water off and plunged a clean washcloth in the sudsy water now filling the sink for a ho bath.

Ho.

Naeema lifted her head and faced herself in the mirror as she gripped the edges of the porcelain sink. She saw the softness of her close-shaven head framing her face and highlighting her high cheekbones, full mouth, and almond-shaped eyes with lashes that most chicks had to pay good money to have. She saw she was pretty . . . but she also saw more. *I'm better than that.*

Here she was, a grown-ass woman about to sell a sniff of her goodies for a bag of weed. It was a tough pill to swallow that she was still doing shit she pulled in her teens. When she was young and dumb. Just like Mya.

And the truth of her fucked-up hypocrisy first nudged at her long before she checked her reflection. Seeing Mya looking at her was the true mirror for her ass.

"Fuuuck," she swore, shifting her eyes away from a reflection she wasn't ready to face.

Naeema emptied the water from the sink and tugged her bikini and leggings back up over her thighs, wide hips, and ample bottom.

When she walked back into the living room Mook was posted up by the door waiting for her.

"They really tossed your shit up," he said, holding up the half-ounce of weed before tossing it over to her across the room.

Naeema caught it easily with one hand and pressed it against her nose to deeply inhale the scent with a moan that echoed the excitement of the pleasure point in her brain before throwing the small sack back to him. "Sorry, Mook," she said as he caught it between his large hands with his long, narrow fingers.

He looked regretful as hell. "Damn. Curved," he said.

Naeema reached in her bra and pulled out the fold of money she kept there. She peeled off two fifty-dollar bills and pushed them into his pocket—a little too deeply. Her mouth shaped into an "O" in surprise as she accidentally stroked the side of his dick. Even at rest she could tell that what God didn't bless his ugly ass with in the looks department was made up for in dick.

Both ugly and skinny dudes always packing. Always.

Fuck around and run up on the dick of a mofo that was ugly and skinny? Listen . . .

Quickly removing her hand as Mook shifted his hip to press his dick against her touch, she leaned past him to open the door. "I was just playing, Mook. I shouldn't have fucked with you like that," she said.

"One of these days, Naeema, your thicky-thick fine ass gon' slip and let me hit and—"

"And if I did it wouldn't be in exchange for a damn thing," she stressed. *A sniff? Maybe. Sex? With Mook? Hell nah.*

Although it had been a minute since she and Tank cooled off and she hadn't had a good dicking down since then. That little accidental rub of Mook's dick had awakened her clit from hibernation. *Thump-thump. Thump-thump.*

"Bye, Mook," Naeema said, pressing her hand to his thin chest to give him that little extra nudge he needed out to the porch as she used her free hand to politely pluck her package of weed from his hand. With a smile and extra flutter of her long lashes, she eased the door closed already lifting it so the warped doorjamb didn't stop its smooth flow.

Turning, she eyed the mess she still had to handle. "I need a little motivation," she said, crossing the room to pick up her dick pipe to carry into the kitchen.

Naeema backed against the door Sarge hung after happening upon her naked in the living room/bedroom. The door was so clearly a mismatch to both the kitchen and the living room. Not that it mattered. The once orange walls were now white and the dull walnut cabinets were painted black, but the yellow appliances were still relics that didn't have anymore get up and go to work regularly than a wealthy man. The pale yellow, mint, and white linoleum had seen better days . . . thirty years ago and the small second-hand dinette set she purchased to replace the one she shot during a rampage over her son's murder was straight out of the eighties. The big brown swinging door stuck out but it served its purpose.

She chuckled at the memory of Sarge finding the initiative to get something normal done. That was saying a lot for an oddball who'd rather cook food outside on a cheap-ass grill barely big enough for two full-sized pieces of meat when there was a kitchen at his disposal. *Cracky ass.*

She hated to even take a guess what he was doing in that basement where he dwelled. Nothing would surprise her.

Shaking her head, she quickly washed the dick with dish detergent and rinsed it before drying it with paper towel. Back in the living room she politely prepped and then loosely packed some of that good-good in the balls of her pipe and then lit that motha with a deep sigh of anticipation. The first inhale from the glossy tip was so long and deep her breast rose high in the air as she let it fill her lungs. Tilting her head back to the ceiling she licked her lips before pursing them to release a stream of thick smoke. "Yesss," she sighed, as the smoke continued to swirl in the air above her head like clouds.

Naeema kicked her sneakers off and folded her legs Indian style as she lowered her head and raised the dick to her mouth to suck the whole tip into it. With a little giggle she circled the smooth ceramic with her tongue like it was real . . . and pulsing . . . and able to fill her mouth with cum and not just smoke.

Her nipples hardened into tight buds as she took another long toke. "Shit, I'm. Horny," she said, the smoke leaving the corners of her mouth as she spoke.

Her clit was all the way awake now. *Thump-thump.*

Weed made her horny.

Smoking weed out of a big black dick that was lifelike made her horny.

Not getting dick on the regular made her horny.

Hell ugly-ass Mook made her horny.

Something had to give.

"Fuck *that* shit," Naeema swore, rising to her feet to walk across the room and sit the pipe on the fireplace mantel.

High *and* horny led to bad sex decisions. All. The. Time.

Naeema set about cleaning up the aftereffects of the robbery. As she was throwing all her beloved stretchy, latex-infused garments in a pile to be washed it suddenly hit her that Tank never showed. She had no doubts that Sarge's snitching ass had called him. There were many times she threatened to stop putting minutes on the old man's cell phone after yet another discovery that the NNN—Naeema News Network—was putting out regular updates.

A mix of anger and hurt swirled. Naeema pulled out her cell phone but the pointed stiletto shape of her nail shadowed the touchscreen as she floated her thumb in the air above it. *Nah. No. Fuck him. Shit. Triple fuck his ass.*

But still the phone was in her hand and her thumb was ready to swipe.

No matter any bullshit going down between them Tank always came when he was called. Always. Whether the call was made by her or a nosy old man in the basement who she knew was just looking out for her.

Maybe this time we're done for good.

She bit her bottom lip as she finally tossed the phone away onto the middle of the bed. The seesaw had to stop one day because continuing on like this was pure madness. Still . . .

Naeema ignored the dick she was smoking from and the real-life one she was missing as she finished setting the living room back to her idea of normal. As she picked up a pile of DVDs that she had stacked on the corner of her dresser, she was surprised and pleased to find her iPod. She hardly ever listened to it but it was nice to know it wasn't stolen.

Knock-knock.

She glanced over at the front door as she wrapped the earbuds around the iPod and then set it atop the stacked plastic containers next to the broken television. She moved over to one of the living room windows and pulled back the sheer curtain and the blinds to look onto the porch. Night had just begun to darken the skies and Naeema had forgotten to replace the bulb in the fixture on the porch but she could clearly make out Mya standing there.

I done started some shit now.

With a roll of her eyes she moved toward the door but stopped to turn and race back to the fireplace to pick up the dick pipe. "She's seen enough dick today," Naeema muttered, hurrying to sit the pipe on the kitchen table before rushing back to finally open the door.

She bit back a smile as Mya just breezed right on in, leaving Naeema in a cloud of some sweet, overpowering perfume that made her eyes water just a bit. "You busy, Miss Naeema?" she asked, now dressed in a black T-shirt and SpongeBob sleep pants.

Naeema fought the urge to ask if she bathed and then

soaked herself in cheap perfume or if she just bathed in the perfume. "Actually you are just the person I want to see," she said, shutting the door.

Mya glanced at her over her shoulder. "This is a big house. Why you sleep in your living room?" she asked, making a face that showed her confusion as she moved around the bed and to the dresser against the far wall.

"Same reason you ask a lot of questions . . . because I want to," Naeema said, coming over to take the stack of Brandon's photos from Mya's hand.

"He's cute," she said.

"Was. He *was* cute," Naeema corrected her.

"Was?" Mya asked.

"Someone broke into my house and I wondered if you saw anyone running from my house not too long before I came over to your apartment building?" she asked.

"I saw a dude running but I don't know if he came from your house."

Naeema pierced the young girl with her eyes. "Did you see what he looked like?"

Mya shook her head. "Kinda but not really. He ran by so quick."

"Would you recognize him if you saw him again?" Naeema asked, her heart pounding as she felt her adrenaline racing. She was like a beast on the chase in the wild.

"I ain't no snitch," Mya said, sounding reluctant and slightly apologetic like she didn't want to let Naeema down . . . but she would.

Hood politics.

Naeema shook her head. "Listen, I will show you a picture of them on my phone and you tell me yes or no. Plus, snitching would involve the police and I can *promise* you, Mya, that calling the police is the last thing on my mind," she said, hoping her tone wasn't too ominous. She didn't want to scare the kid or let on that she may very well hold the fate of a man getting seriously—like *seriously*—fucked up in her little hands.

///

$\mathcal{N}$aeema removed the cape from her client's shoulders with one hand and brushed away any stray hairs from his neck and shoulders with the other. "There you go, Diego," she said, turning the chair for him to face one of the mirrors lining the walls behind the stations of A Cut Above barbershop. She held up a large hand mirror behind him giving him a view of the back of his head in the reflection.

"Yo you the best, Naeema," he said, his voice low enough for just her ears amidst the noisy backdrop of the men gathered in the shop.

"Thanks," she said, thinking that his deep voice and that sexy mix of his Puerto Rican and East Coast accent was almost dope enough to make her forget he was one of the biggest heroin hustlers in the tri-state area. *Almost*.

Naeema was far from innocent. Hell, she had bodies. Last year she committed crimes ranging from robbery to murder as she hunted down her son's killer—and she would do it again. And she wasn't one to knock someone hustling but it was hard to overlook the effect of heroin on the city she loved. That shit was on the streets hard in the nineties and now it was back badder and more lethal than ever. Working in a barbershop meant she got a level of news about the ins and outs of the streets that the police and the press would love. Motherfuckers were really dying—killing to get it or overdosing from it.

Their eyes briefly met in the mirror but Naeema just gave him a slightly playful expression before she spun the chair and then walked behind it to busy herself cleaning up her station before her next client. She heard him chuckle low in his throat behind her. Diego Martinez knew he was fine—tall, fit, and sexy. Broad shoulders. Narrow hips. Slanted eyes and full, suckable lips. Dimpled chin. Tattoos. Even the faded scar across his left cheekbone. Just blessed. Fine and fuckable. He *knew* that shit. And he was just as clear that if maybe he pressed a little harder he could find out if she lived up to the sex appeal she exuded without even trying.

The chuckle was a reminder of that. Slightly mocking.

Naeema knew she was a hypocrite. To her Mook and Diego were dealers but not on the same level. So no matter how fine Diego was she couldn't overlook he was hood-rich off heroin. Mook had a better chance with her than Diego and *his* chance was minuscule to fucking none.

"Here you go."

Naeema turned and extended her left hand as he reached out to press money into it. His black eyes were almost possessive as he took in the fit of the jeans on her ass and hips. Like he owned it and was sitting it up on a shelf until he felt like playing with it. *Negro please . . .*

He stroked her palm with his thumb.

"I'm married. Remember?" Naeema said gently, trying to tug her hand free.

He held it tighter and turned it over to stroke her bare ring finger. Another chuckle and shake of his head. "Take it light, Naeema," Diego said, before taking a step back from her as he released her hand.

Something about the final look he gave her made a shiver race up Naeema's spine. She couldn't quite place it as desire or fear. He was built to deliver both.

Naeema slid the money Diego gave her into her back pocket knowing without looking that it was a crisp hundred-dollar bill. Diego had money to burn and dropping a bill on a ten-dollar haircut meant nothing to his pockets. Leaning onto the back of the barber chair she watched through the front windows of the shop as Diego moved like a star through the crowd of dudes that always hung out in the parking lot of the small mini-mall that housed the popular barbershop, a liquor store, and a beauty supply store—all owned by her boss, Derek Majors.

Her eyes narrowed as she watched Diego walk his sexy ass to his convertible Benz boldly double-parked on the busy street. He knew no one would mess with it. He stopped just before he climbed behind the wheel to look back toward the mini-mall. Her eyes followed his line of vision and she frowned a little as Davon "Murk" Grant strode across the lot to greet Diego. Naeema eyed the two men. Both were big-time dope hustlers in and around the city. Their conversation barely lasted a minute before Diego walked away to climb into his car and speed off. Murk moved to a car and soon drove off too.

Probably cooking up some shit to flood the city with more dope.

Naeema didn't give zero fucks about either one of them, their hustles, their wives, their sidechicks, nor their kids if they had any. *Fuck 'em.*

She eyed her boss, Derek, as he came down the stairs from his second-floor office. He worked the room like a two-bit politician looking to charm votes and give empty promises of shit never to come.

He eyed her as he walked out the door. She eyed his slick ass right back.

His office was in the barbershop but he posted up in the liquor store. Rumor was he was fucking the hell out of the new cashier he hired, who was more ass than brains. She fought the urge to be Petty McBetty and give his wife an anonymous call to catch his cheating ass. She wanted to but she didn't. The cashier wasn't the first and probably wouldn't be the last of Derek's sidechicks.

He was a well-dressed man with money trying to trick himself into believing he wasn't ugly. He was born that way and would die that way and the in-between was nothing but cash and ass flow. Shit he could control.

Who gives a fuck?

She had to remind herself that she didn't. She didn't have the time to keep tabs on someone else's husband when she still hadn't heard from her own. Her feelings were hurt that Tank didn't show up to check on her.

Damn.

She blinked her long lashes, hating the tears that rose up as she pulled on each of her fingers as she continued to stare out the window at the busy traffic on one of the dozens of streets leading into downtown Newark. People in a constant state of go. Working, moving, riding, walking, fighting, grinding, partying, chiefing, fucking. Doing anything to keep from thinking. Worrying. Dealing.

Between the disrespect of the robbery and being hurt to

the blow of Tank not turning up, Naeema felt tension spread from her nape and down across her shoulders. The shift had come quickly. Her emotions were visceral. They pierced her.

She released a heavy breath as she rubbed her fingertips over the full-sleeve tattoo on her left arm made up of her son's yearly school pictures from kindergarten to eighth grade interwoven with a large cross, roses, and scrolls. Feeling that same haunting darkness come over her at the thought of his death and her guilt, she curled her fingers into as much of a fist as she could to break the pull. She had enough weighing her down.

"Yo Naeema, we need a woman's opinion."

Shifting her eyes from the street she found nearly all of the men in the shop looking at her. As always, the shop was loud and raucous but Naeema felt right at home even as the lone female. It had been that way for the over ten years she had been cutting hair there. She enjoyed the fellas' conversation, which could go from politics to street gossip in no time at all. In time they got used to her and held nothing back. They all thought of her as their sister and on many occasions she had to either defend or just enlighten them on the female point of view.

But she wasn't in the mood for that shit.

"Nah, miss me with it this time," she said, rubbing her hands over her shaven head before looking back out the window at everything and nothing.

"PMS," someone said over the fray—someone new or extremely motherfucking bold because Naeema's temper once stoked was infamous.

But she wasn't even in the mood to curse out whatever lame-ass fool just tried her.

"Yo, Naeema, you ready for me?"

She looked over at one of her regular clients rising from his seat in the waiting area. She bit her bottom lip and continued to gently tug on each of her fingers as she looked back out the window, back at the men laughing and talking, and then back to her client. Her eyes shifted from one to the other and the other. Again and again and once more.

Fuck this shit.

Naeema grabbed her knock-off studded MCM bag from the small closet on the barber station and snatched off the leopard print apron she wore to shove it in its place before she turned and just rushed toward the door. She felt someone grab at her arm but she jerked free of their loose grip and crossed the lot to where her motorcycle sat.

She slid on her hot pink helmet and cranked the bike to reverse out of the parking spot. Sitting low in the seat she guided it toward the crowd of hard-faced dudes in white T-shirts smoking freely on stuffed Philly blunts. She revved the bike and they finally parted to allow her to accelerate forward. Her boss suddenly stepped in her path and Naeema rolled her eyes as she easily steered the bike to the right of him and sped out of the parking lot.

She enjoyed the feel of the air against her body as she dipped and weaved in and out of cars, New Jersey Transit buses, and even children playing in the streets enjoying their summer. She didn't stop until she turned down a long, wide alley off Broad Street leading to a blacked-out glass door with the word BOXING in large red block letters. She parked her bike in between two vehicles that lined the brick wall of one of the buildings that flanked the alley.

Nothing but a workout could help get her mind right. Release. Process. *I'm ready to hit some shit.*

She entered the gym, her eyes taking in the two large boxing rings in the center of the room where men sparred and then the weight equipment and boxing equipment lining the walls. The sounds of fist hitting flesh or boxing equipment echoed in the thick, musty air of the facility that was nothing but the bare essentials. The black paint on the exposed brick walls was peeling. Flyers announcing upcoming boxing events were haphazardly hung. No frills. No fuss. Just working out through boxing.

She loved it.

In the days since her most recent breakup with Tank she had come back to the gym to be trained and keep her shape. Fat ass? Thick thighs? Hips? All cool. A gut to go along with all of that? *No haps.* She wanted to keep it more along the lines of Amber Rose than Luenell the comedian. Especially in the body-conscious clothing she favored.

Naeema rushed into the female locker room glad that she paid the monthly fee to rent one of the bright red lockers lining the walls. She took a quick shower and changed into a bright yellow sports bra and leggings.

"Naeema!"

She had just exited the locker room and looked up to see her trainer, Rocko, motioning for her from the front ring. She moved toward him. She didn't have an appointment and her plan was just to get out her emotions by getting into some work on the treadmill and then one of the speed bags.

"You feel like a quick sparring match?" he asked, sounding like the beloved guido that he was with bulging muscles, a deep tan, and jet-black moussed hair.

She eyed a woman in the corner of the ring getting her gloves laced up.

"I don't know," Naeema said, her reluctance showing.

Rocko gave her a playful wink and another wave. "Just a little light workout," he said.

Naeema gave him a friendly smile that didn't reach her eyes. In fact, he was irking her nerves. She didn't enjoy having to decline an offer more than once.

"Find me somebody with some fight in 'em, Rocko," the woman said, turning to lightly pound her gloves against each other. "She don't want to fuck with this."

Naeema narrowed her eyes. She didn't know if it was a bad coincidence or divine intervention. "You sure you want to fuck with that?" she asked, continuing forward and climbing up into the ring with ease.

Rocko nodded. "Naeema . . . Ashley. Ashley . . . Naeema."

They gave each other a head nod in greeting.

"Just a little lightweight spar, ladies," he said, suiting Naeema up in gloves and a head guard.

They squared up in the ring with Rocko standing between them. As soon as he stepped out of the way Naeema swung and delivered a feather-soft blow to Ashley's shoulder.

"Good, Naeema," Rocko called from somewhere outside the ring.

Naeema didn't know and didn't care. She was focused. And she didn't miss the spark of anger in the woman's eyes. Naeema brought one hand up to block a right punch the woman threw and followed with a right of her own that the woman leaned to the left to avoid.

A blow to her right side caught Naeema off guard and she released a stream of harsh air at the pain as she doubled over. *Shit!*

"You all right, Naeema?" Rocko called out to her.

"Damn, my bad," Ashley said, sounding apologetic.

Naeema cut her eyes up at her as she slowly straightened her body. She tilted her head to the side as she spotted the woman was happy as shit no matter her fake-ass words. With a nod of understanding, Naeema took another deep breath before she delivered a roundhouse kick to her side that toppled the woman off her feet and down onto the mat with a loud THUD.

"Damn, my fucking bad," Naeema said mockingly.

Ashley jumped to her feet and came running across the ring at Naeema.

"Fuck!" Rocko exclaimed.

Naeema locked her left leg and swiftly raised her right catching the bitch midstride with a kick against the side of her head guard.

WHAP.

Wrong day. Wrong chick to try.

Rocko jumped between them just as Ashley swung. Her blow landed against Naeema's right temple.

"La-dies," he exclaimed in disbelief. "What the fuck?"

Tank trained her for every possible scenario and her instincts kicked in as she dropped down to a squat and leveled a leg sweep to Rocko that laid him flat on his back with a look of surprise. She rose, jumped over him, and delivered a round of blows to Ashley with a swiftness that caught the woman off guard.

"Ow," she cried out.

Naeema shut the woman's mouth with an uppercut and then delivered three swift kicks—one to her thigh, then her hip, and then her upper arm. She finished her with a gut punch that sent her tumbling back onto the mat again.

Naeema was about to land dead on her ass and fuck her up some more when someone caught her from behind locking a strong arm around both of hers. She tried a couple of moves to break free but each challenge was met with ease.

"Stop it, Na."

Only shock at the sound of *his* voice stilled her. And sent her heart pounding like crazy in her chest.

Tank.

Her entire body felt a new level of awareness. Every fine hair on her body stood on end and her pulse raced. *Thump-thump.*

She wanted to let her body go slack in his arms and just be held by him.

Her anger came back full force. "Let me go, Tank," she said, as he carried her out of the ring.

"You aight, Ashley?" Rocko asked, helping the woman to her feet where she wobbled back and forth like her focus was shot to hell.

"I guess you shouldn't have fucked with it," Naeema called over just before Tank carried her toward a long hall at the rear of the gym.

"Put me the fuck down, Tank," she said, even trying to

jerk her head back to butt against his as she futilely fought against his strength. His might. His will.

Tank owned and operated his own security firm specializing in bodyguard services for politicians and celebrities. Staying fit and being prepared to fuck someone up was his business and his body was built to succeed at it. He could easily be mistaken for a power forward on a professional basketball team. Tall, muscular, strong. He handled her with an ease where other dudes would struggle.

"Stop acting the fuck up, Naeema," he said, his deep voice hard with anger.

And with that ease he opened the door to one of the cedar steam rooms and stepped inside, finally releasing her as he leaned back to pull the door securely closed behind them as the steam swirled. Naeema tumbled to her knees but hopped right back up on her feet to stand before where he stood with his arms crossed over his chest in the sleeveless navy tee he wore with basketball shorts.

For the first time in weeks Naeema laid eyes on her husband, Lavarius "Tank" Cole. Just fine as fuck. She forced herself to look away from his Laz Alonso–like goodness. It was too much. The steamy heat. His looks. Her anger at him. Her disappointment in him. Her love. Every pulse in her body throbbed. Including the one between her legs. *Thump-thump. Thump-thump.*

Grinding her teeth, Naeema locked eyes with him again. Their faces were just inches apart. "Let me out," she said, her teeth clenched.

"What was that all about?" he asked.

"None of your fucking business . . . that's what," she said. "Nothing about me is your business."

"How many times have I heard that?" he asked, his voice mocking.

"Let's fix it where you don't have to hear that or anything else I have to say ever again, Tank," she snapped. "Go file the papers and be on your way."

They hadn't spoken in weeks and their most recent attempt to reunite had ended in a fiery argument over . . . over . . .

She couldn't even remember. The thing was a disagreement over something as dumb as the time a TV show came on and could quickly escalate to them bringing up old arguments and old hurts. Molehill to mountain. They argued just as hard as they loved and that seesaw of making up and breaking up continued.

It had to stop.

"You aight?" he asked, his voice deep and strong.

"I'm straight," she said, her voice cool. "Just as straight as I've been since the last time I spoke to you."

His body stiffened. "You told me to stay the hell out of your life and that's what I did," he reminded her.

She thought he would never let her down. He would always come when he was called—whether by her or the nosy old man who lived in her basement. Until last night.

"Fuck you," Naeema said, reaching a fist to her mouth to pull the end of the ties of the boxing glove with her teeth.

He grabbed her hand and began to undo the ties for her.

Naeema snatched her hand away and hit him soundly in the arm. "I don't need you for nothing," she snapped.

Tank's eyes got bright with his anger. "Man, fuck you, Naeema," he said.

Her eyes flared and she hit him again. And again. And again.

Releasing a breath filled with all his aggravation, Tank grabbed her wrists in each of his hands and pushed them behind her back. "Stop," he said, his voice low.

She hated the tightness in her throat and the tears filling her eyes. She bit her bottom lip and fought against him.

"*Stop*, Na," he said.

She looked up to lock eyes with him. "You didn't even show up last night after the robbery," she said softly, her voice filled with disappointment and hurt.

Love could strengthen or weaken you and in that moment Naeema felt defenseless.

"When do you not show up for me?" she accused.

Tank looked incredulous. "When I get tired of you telling me you don't need me, Naeema," he admitted.

She looked away from him. The truth was hard to face. She clung to her independence like a motherfucker, but she knew he was there as her safety net. There were times during one of their long separations that she knew he was seeing another woman but she would hop on the phone and call him from that woman's bed if there was something she needed—be it as simple as changing a fucking lightbulb to fucking her. But she always made it clear she didn't need him.

"We got back together and you wouldn't even move back home or let me move in with you," he said. "Hell, you barely wanted me to spend the night."

Oh yeah. That's what that last argument was about. Naeema closed her eyes and her lashes lightly brushed the tops of her cheeks.

"I had one of the fellas patrol the neighborhood and I

called Sarge every hour to check on you," he said. "Today I
went over while you was at work and got some fingerprints."

Naeema dropped her head against his sweat-soaked
shirt. Tank. *Her* Tank. He was *that* dude. "I hated knowing
somebody was in my house and mixing all through my shit,"
she admitted. "I barely slept all night and when I did I had
crazy-ass dreams."

He released her arms.

"And every time I woke up I would hug the pillows and
sit and wish you were there," she admitted, as he removed
the gloves from her hands. "I was so pissed and so fucking hurt you didn't come to me. My whole day has been
fucked."

"And that's why you beat that girl's ass like that," he
asked with a half-smile.

"Mostly."

"Good thing I came by to drop off my ad looking for
a new guard for my team," Tank said. "I trained you too
good."

Naeema nodded solemnly as she looked at him. Her
breath came in these little-ass gasps that mirrored the
steady, fast pace of her heart. Quick and shallow. "Tank."

His eyes dropped down to take in her partly open lips
before shifting to take in the heat of her eyes. "No," he said,
lifting his hands to her shoulders to gently push her back a
bit from him.

"Tank," she said again, licking her lips and tasting the
salty sweat on her skin as she reached out and grabbed the
damp front of his T-shirt in her fist. She laughed as the back
of his sneakers hit the door as he tried to retreat from her.
She had him between a soft and a hard place.

With a flirty look at him she turned and pressed her ass back against him before bending over to grab her ankles as she grinded against him as the steam continued to press against their bodies. Naeema felt her nature rising. It had been so long since she had some. Even the feel of the sweat dripping down the valleys of her body was turning her on. Her nipples were hard. Her clit was aching. Her pussy was wet.

Tank had no choice but to prepare to be sexed.

She turned and got on her knees. His hard dick was pressed against his shorts and eye level with her.

"I'm seeing someone, Na."

"So," she said, reaching under the hem of his shorts to stroke the smooth skin of his hard dick.

Tank had one of those big, pretty dicks. Evenly proportioned. One smooth color. Perfect shiny tip. Thick. Long. Even his balls hung just right.

He caught her hands in his just as she was about to free his dick from his shorts and stroke that pretty motherfucker with her tongue. "She's out in the truck," he added quickly.

Naeema froze.

Say what now?

Naeema stood up. "Wow. Curved by my own husband," she said.

Tank reached for her.

She sidestepped his touch. "Can I go enjoy my workout now?" she asked, not looking at him.

"Na."

"Please. Ain't this shit embarrassing enough for me?" she snapped.

Tank dropped his head and sidestepped to avail her of opening the door to the steam room to exit.

Naeema walked quickly down the hall toward the two main rings. "Sorry," she shouted to Ashley, who was on the treadmill, as she sprinted past and headed straight out the door.

With one look back over her shoulder to see Tank coming down the long hall, Naeema upped her speed to a full run to reach his blacked-out Mercedes Sprinter van. She opened the door and hopped up into the driver's seat just as she saw Tank reach the door of the gym. *Fuck youuuu.*

Naeema allowed herself just a moment to let it marinate that the woman sitting in the passenger seat was a white woman. *Really, Tank?*

"Who are you? Is this a carjacking?" the pretty blonde asked.

Naeema locked the doors and reversed out of the parking spot before accelerating forward down the wide alley. She barely checked traffic before she made a right to enter the flow of it.

"Excuse me?" the woman said with attitude reaching over to tap Naeema's arm with a long nail painted bubble-gum pink.

Naeema gave her a sidelong glance that was thorough enough for the woman to quickly remove her finger. "Look here, Barbie."

"My name's not—"

"I'm Tank's wife, Naeema, and that fact makes this van just as much mine as it is his—"

"His wife," she exclaimed.

"That's right. I don't really care who you are or what you are or what you want to be. I only have one question for you. Where do you want me to drop you off: at home, the nearest bus stop, or a cabstand because your time chillaxing with *my* husband ceases today. Clear?"

She nodded and bit the tip of her nail. "Uhm, cabstand please."

"Smart girl," Naeema said, before steering the luxury passenger van toward Newark Penn Station.

4

Bah-dup.

Naeema activated the alarm on Tank's Sprinter, which she parked in her driveway. She felt anxious at the stunt she pulled. She was curious as fuck what his reaction would be. She knew he was probably blowing her cell phone up but it, along with her keys and street clothes, were still in her locker. *Fuck it.*

She wasn't worried about him being stranded. He would just call one of his workers or use friends to bring him one of several vehicles he owned. Or his own key to the bike she left behind—the bike he purchased for her for one of their anniversaries. She knew he would not leave the bike at the gym. Nor would he dare mess with calling the police and she was sure he chilled once he spoke to Blondie to make sure she was alive and well.

"BeckySusanMeghan is lucky she got a ride and not an ass whipping," she muttered as she jogged up the stairs.

The loud blare of someone laying on their car horn caused her to stop and look over her shoulder. A white Cadillac did a slow roll up the street as its driver, a light-skinned dude with cornrows, leaned out the window showing off a mouthful of gold grills.

Naeema glanced down at the sports bra and leggings

that served no real purpose in covering her. She met his leer and he finally faced forward with a shake of his head meant to compliment her and then accelerated forward. She wasn't embarrassed by her body or the attention. She was well aware she had the kind of body selfies and bathroom pics on Instagram were made for. First J-Lo and then Beyoncé made fat asses popular for mainstream America but brothas, Latinos, and country white boys *been* down.

She shifted her eyes over to the apartment building where Mya lived. Both the porch and the window were empty. Last night, in between dodging a hundred and one questions from the nosy teen, Naeema had quizzed her to push forward memories of the burglar. She had felt relief and guilt after finally urging her back across the street to her own place. The relief? Mya talked too damn much and asked way too many questions. The guilt? She wasn't blind to the sadness the girl carried. It was there in her eyes, in the way she carried herself, and in the way she so instantly clung to Naeema.

In her life she knew that kind of sadness her damn self all too well.

With one last look she turned her head and continued up the stairs. She opened the metal mailbox attached to the brick wall and removed her mail.

"Shit," Naeema swore as she reached for the doorknob. Her keys and her cell phone were back at the gym.

So busy trying to fuck Tank that I fucked myself.

She hit her knuckles against the door.

Knock-knock.

She shook her head, knowing it was a complete waste of time. Sarge would never hear her down in the basement and the doorbell was just one of a gazillion things on her list to have repaired.

Shit.

Naeema rattled the keys in her hand as she jogged back down the stairs with her mind set on knocking on the back door until Jesus carried her home or Sarge was able to hear her over his loud television playing in the basement. She was halfway down the stairs when she turned the keys over in her hand and looked at them.

How could I forget?

She smiled as she recalled a clear memory of her pushing the silver key across the kitchen table with the pointed tip of her acrylic nail to Tank sitting next to her as they ate breakfast before heading out to work. He had eyed her in surprise before nodding and then leaning over to press a kiss to the back of her neck. Her invite. His acceptance. Their compromise to his request for them to live together again.

The concession didn't last very long.

But there, nestled between the keys to his Harley Davidson and the Sprinter were three house keys. She turned and headed back up the steps to the front door, trying first one key and then another.

Click.

The relief felt good as she turned the knob and lifted the door before pushing it open with a nudge from her bare shoulder. Going from the outdoors inside offered her body no relief. Even the house seemed to sweat, letting off the smell of old wood. The heat pressed back against her body as she walked through it to turn on the portable air-conditioning unit. The battle between a lower light bill and coming home to a cool house was nonstop.

She flipped through the stack of envelopes as she stayed posted up in front of the AC. "The fuck?" she said, holding up a bright red envelope addressed to Ezra Manigault.

She had no idea who or what Ezra was.

Setting what looked to be an envelope containing a card onto the mantelpiece, Naeema continued shuffling through the bills and mailers as she crossed the scuffed, faded hardwood floor to the kitchen. Pushing the door opened she sat the stack on the counter along with Tank's keys. The door leading down into the basement was slightly ajar. "Sarge," she called out, washing her hands at the sink before she opened the fridge.

She wasn't much of a cook and never claimed to be. And without AC in the kitchen the last thing she planned on doing was turning on a stove to kick the temperature up to the level of pure hell. "Sarge," she called again, looking over at the open door.

It was quiet. Too damn quiet.

Naeema shut the fridge and left the kitchen to retrieve her gun from its hiding place in the ash trap of the fireplace. Her adrenaline kicked in like a motherfucker as she checked to make sure it was loaded with a full clip. She held it at her side in her right hand as she walked back into the kitchen. Quickly she checked the back door. The lock was intact and none of the glass was broken.

She opened the door leading into the basement wider and started down the stairs. The second step from the top lightly creaked under her weight but she didn't stop. Her heart pounded as she said a silent prayer that Sarge wasn't hurt again *and* that the robber had returned. She wanted to trap his no-good ass in that basement and wear him the fuck out for violating her home.

But first things first.

She wished she had turned on the light at the top of the stairs. She hadn't been in the basement since she first moved in. There was just enough light coming from the small windows along the top of the walls to make out a figure lying on the floor next to the twin bed pushed against the wall. She paused at the foot of the steps and looked around the entire area for possible hiding spots.

When she was sure no one would jump out and grab her from behind she made her way over to him. "Sarge," she said, gently pushing his shoulder to ease him onto his back.

"What?" he snapped suddenly, his gruff voice irritated because she awakened him.

Naeema yelped and jumped in shock, falling back onto her ass, her hand hitting the concrete. She accidentally pulled the trigger. A spark of fire lit up the dimness.

POW!

"Shit," she and Sarge both swore.

Bits of sheetrock burst from the bullet hole.

Naeema carefully set the gun on the floor. "Oops," she said.

Sarge glared at her the entire time as he struggled first to his knees and then to his feet as he held on to the mattress on the bed for support. "Oops my ass," he snapped. "Me and you and *that*"—he pointed to the gun—"ain't gon' make it."

Naeema rose to her sneaker-covered feet before she bent down to pick up the gun to make sure the safety was on. "I thought we got robbed and you were hurt again," she said, reaching up to drag her fingers across the ceiling as she felt for the light fixture and then pulled the string dangling from it. "Why were you on the floor?"

"I gotta pay rent to have some business you're not in?"

Naeema's hand hit the bulb. It felt loose in the socket. She turned it tighter and the basement lit up with light. "Yup," she said, completely joking.

Sarge grunted.

She bit back a smile as she looked around the basement and sniffed the air. She had always assumed that with as much time as Sarge spent down below that it would smell like feet and ass, but there was a slight tinge of pine scent in the air. She'd also assumed it would be a pigsty. It wasn't.

The twin bed was made with the covers pulled tight across it and a flat pillow perfectly square with the red-and-blue-painted headboard obviously meant for a toddler's room and not an old man's domain. It was all her money could buy back then and she hated to think of him sleeping on the floor on a bundle of old blankets that she had to beg him to let her wash.

The same blankets on the floor beside the bed she now knew he never slept in.

Just like he refused her offer to use the kitchen upstairs to cook the cases of canned food against the wall. She eyed the small grill in the corner by the stairs.

As she took in the small bathroom missing the door he used upstairs to divide the kitchen from the living room, she said a prayer he at least used the toilet and not a fucking bucket or some shit.

Even his clothes—either military or work uniforms—were stacked inside a large plastic bag sitting on the second-hand dresser and not inside the drawers. She rolled her eyes and threw her hands up in the air when he didn't open the door to the fridge but instead bent to open a dingy cooler and pulled out a can of beer. She shook her head.

"Sarge, why are you still living like you're on the street?" Naeema asked, as he leisurely scratched at his raggedy silver beard before repeating the action on his ass.

"Me and mines," he said.

In the corner was a small tent. A fucking *tent*.

"What's that, your guest room?" she snapped.

"You and yours," he said, pointing upward before he opened the can and took a deep sip.

She fought the urge to fire a bullet dead through the middle of the can. Her aim was that damn good.

As he released a satisfying sigh and a small belch, Naeema turned and crossed the basement and stomped up the stairs. "I can put you out, old man," she said over her shoulder.

Sarge just chuckled, knowing she didn't mean it.

His cell phone rang.

She paused on the stairs.

"Looking right at her," Sarge said.

Tank.

"She did what now?" Sarge exclaimed before he released a howl of laughter. "No shittin'?"

Naeema continued up the stairs.

"What we gon' do wit' her?"

"Not a damn thing," she called down the stairs before she smiled as she entered the kitchen and closed the door.

Naeema heard the roar of her motorcycle as she sat inside the rear of the Sprinter. She knew it well. Just like a mother knew her baby's cry.

She arched her brow and lowly slid the robe she wore from her body, as she looked straight through the tinted windshield at Tank turning onto her drive. His face was lined with annoyance.

She moved her nude body to the front just long enough to flash the headlights of the vehicle against his body. He just sat there with the motor still running and stared straight into the windshield.

Can he see me? Can anyone see me?

Naeema moved back deeper into the van as she glanced up and down the street.

Shit. I don't care.

Tank climbed his big sexy ass off the bike and continued to stare into the Sprinter as he walked up the drive and along the side to open the passenger door and climb inside. His eyes widened a bit at her sitting there naked as all get out with one foot propped up on the back of the plush leather seat to the left of her. His view dead up the middle aisle of the seats was clear.

And so was hers.

Anger still creased his fine-ass face. *Humph.*

She propped her other foot up onto the seat to the right of her and eased her hands down her legs to gently press her knees wider apart before she shifted them down to spread her lips and free her clit.

Tank averted his eyes.

She arched her back, pushing her breasts forward as she watched him through half-closed lids with a moan.

"Where's my fucking keys, Naeema?" he asked, ignoring her and climbing over into the driver's seat.

She knew this man that she spent the last eight years of her life loving—maybe not consistently living with—but always loving. Just as surely as she knew he was the man to call to bury a body and get rid of a gun, she knew he would bring her motorcycle back; she knew he was not as mad as he put on; and she knew he would not deny her anything—including his dick. Especially that.

"That's fucked up what you did, Na," he said, rising up out of the seat just enough to pull another set of keys from his pocket.

Naeema stiffened. "Are you mad about this van or your bitch?" she asked.

He started the engine. "Man, fuck her. You don't fucking want me but you don't want nobody else to have me. That shit's childish as fuck, Na."

"Oh I want you," she said.

Tank looked into the rearview mirror. "I'm going home. Put your clothes on and get out, Na," he said, turning his head to look out the driver-side window. To avoid the sight of her. The temptation.

Naeema was selfish and she knew it. She clung to it like a shield, refusing to go back to a time when she put everyone and everything before herself. To the point of being used as a cum bucket by horny little boys and perverted older men. To being thrown out on the street while pregnant by her baby's father and still living every day waiting for the no-good motherfucker to call her and say come home. Following her friends' actions because she was afraid to lose them.

She was selfish as hell. Now. She had been through some shit and the love she had for Tank scared her. She meant to keep him near but not too close. Dangling on a string. And it wasn't right. It *was* fucked up. But she loved him too much to let him go for forever but was afraid to love him any more than she already did.

And in that moment she knew he'd want promises she couldn't make and she wanted the kind of explosive, back-breaking, sore-pussy-making sex only he had the power to lay down.

"I'm pulling the fuck off, Naeema," he warned, allowing himself one quick glance back at her.

Her horniness trumped his hurt feelings. She was wrong but in that moment she didn't give a fuck and a half about being right.

Just selfish as hell.

Fuck it.

He accelerated the van forward and steered to the left of her bike before checking for oncoming traffic and turning to drive up the street. "I'm headed to a job, Naeema," he said, his eyes on the road as he drove.

She shifted her body to the edge of the seat and moaned loudly as she slid her middle finger inside her pussy as she lightly gripped one of her full breasts to shift up high enough for her to lick her brown, taut nipple.

She felt the vehicle jerk and she pressed her feet against the back of the seat to keep from rolling forward. Tank's eyes were on her in the rearview mirror and she knew her move had made him hit the brake.

"Naeema!" he said sharply.

She rolled her hips as she slowly pulled her finger out to stroke her clit and then suck her own juices from her finger. "Hmmmmmm. Good," she said, the slight scent of her soap still clinging to her fingers from the shower she took after leaving the basement.

She knew his eyes were on her in the rearview mirror just as much as they were on the road ahead as he drove. Her heart pounded fast as hell. Her nipples were hard. She was wet. Her clit was swollen in heat against her fingers. The idea of him watching her as she played with herself kicked shit up a notch.

If he waited much longer to give in to temptation she wouldn't need him at all.

She pressed two fingers against her clit and licked her lips hotly as she moved her fingers in circles with just the right amount of pressure. She released a tiny cry of passion as she shivered. The anticipation was building like a mother-fucker and she felt that thrill of the moments just before a climax exploded. "I'm gon' cum," she purred, gently stroking one of her nipples with her thumb as she squeezed the soft flesh of her breast.

Tank looked over his shoulder.

Her thick thighs shivered as she arched her back.

"Stop," he said, bringing the van to a stop in the middle of a side street before he rose and came toward her. His hard dick pressed against his shorts leading the way.

She released a breath through pursed lips and held her

hands up like he was robbing her. "Come get the best pussy you ever had," she told him, watching as he jerked down his shorts and fell to his knees between her open thighs. "The best you will *ever* have."

Tank held his thick, long dick in his hand, stroking the base of it with his thumb as he looked down at her spread before him. Waiting for him. "You want this dick? You gon' get this motherfuckin' dick," he told her, anger still edging his words. "Turn the fuck around."

Eager like crazy Naeema twisted on the seat and got on her knees with her titties pressed against the cool leather as she looked out the tinted rear window. Tank filled her with his dick in one strong thrust. She gasped and closed her eyes. "Yes," she whispered hotly, fighting the urge to bite into the leather headrest.

Tank climbed up onto the seat behind her putting his knees on either side of hers as he wrapped his arms around her body to stroke her clit with one hand and palm one of her breasts with the other as he fucked her deeply. Roughly. Swiftly.

The sound of each stroke smacked loudly.

Bap-bap-bap-bap-bap.

The soft hairs surrounding his dick tickled her ass.

Bap-bap-bap-bap-bap.

Naeema cried out. He wouldn't let up.

Bap-bap-bap-bap-bap.

"You want this dick?" he asked thickly before sucking and then lightly biting her shoulder.

She nodded.

"Uh-uh. No. No. No," he said, stopping mid-stroke.

Bap-bap—

"You want this fucking dick?" Tank asked, pressing his lips against the side of her face as he stroked her clit.

The sound of someone laying on a horn sounded off.

They both looked out the rearview mirror at a line of cars behind them.

"I want that dick. Give me that fucking dick," she said, in between deep pants as she worked her pussy walls to grip and then release his dick.

Bap-bap-bap-bap-bap-bap-bap-bap-bap-bap.

Her body jerked forward against the seat with each hard thrust as she watched through glazed eyes as the cars began to go around them.

Bap-bap-bap-bap-bap-bap-bap-bap-bap-bap.

"FUCK YOU!" someone yelled as they passed.

"Too late," Naeema said with a smile as she closed her eyes.

"Damn right 'cause I'm fucking the shit out of your hardheaded ass right now," he said before licking the corner of her mouth.

Naeema gasped.

Bap-bap-bap-bap-bap-bap-bap-bap-bap-bap.

They both cried out as they came together. Fast. Fiery. Furious.

Many things between them changed from day to day but their love and their chemistry—their connection—never changed. Never.

"Damn, Na. Damn," Tank moaned as he exhaled short bursts of air against her neck.

"I know," she said, her breathing mirroring his. "I know."

* * *

Naeema sat up in bed, the sheet falling to her waist as she looked around Tank's bedroom. Something had awakened her. The room was dark except for the light from the television. Her eyes landed on the open bedroom door. Her brows dipped as she frowned.

Tank had to indeed rush home and prep for a bodyguard job after they finally got their shit together in the van. With nothing on but her robe, she agreed to stay behind at his house. And she could have sworn that Tank shut that bedroom door after he showered, got dressed, and left.

Right?

She bit the tip of her nail as she replayed the hours since Tank left.

"I took a shower," she said softly. "Did some sit-ups. Called Sarge's crazy ass. And watched all those reality shows 'til I fell asleep."

She never left the bedroom.

Right?

Kicking the cool sheets off her legs, Naeema climbed from the bed naked and walked into the hall. The fine hairs on her body seemed to stand on end and she rubbed her thumb across her palm wishing she had her gun in her hand.

Calm down. It was probably a noise on the TV.

The robbery last night had fucked her up. She knew she was being hypersensitive and shit but she still walked through the entire house and checked every bedroom. In the living room she moved to the window and peeked out the curtain. She leaned in closer when she thought she saw a shadow move across the porch.

"You up?"

Naeema gasped and whipped around with her hand raised.

Tank turned up the dimmer switch. He frowned a bit as he eyed her. "You aight?" he asked.

Naeema made a fist and lowered her arm. If she had a gun in her hand Tank would have been shot. "Did you just get here? Because something woke me up," she said.

He nodded and removed the black short-sleeved V-neck T-shirt he wore. "Yeah, I came in the back way," he said, flexing his toned arms in the black wife-beater he wore before he sat down on the brown leather sectional.

Naeema came over to sit down beside him. She was a strong woman—a take-no-shit-from-no-one woman—but in that moment as Tank pulled her head down onto his chest she was happy for his strength. His protection. "That robbery really got me fucked up, Tank," she said.

He kissed the top of her head and rubbed her thigh just below her ass. "I still got one of my guys patrolling the neighborhood. Whoever it is won't get in your place again."

Naeema nodded and tilted her head back to look up at him. "I want to know who he is. Okay?" she asked softly.

The one-word question held so many expectations of Tank.

"Okay," he agreed, shouldering them well.

5

Two months later

$\mathcal{N}$aeema looked down at the blunt she was smoking and twisted her mouth upward. She hated it. The high wasn't the same for her. The cigar paper added another level to the shit that was just unnecessary for her. And just because she knew how to split, fill, and lick a blunt didn't mean she wanted to. She especially didn't fuck with it with others. *Fuck passing around something somebody else rolled with their spit. Miss me with that germy shit.*

She tapped the ashes into a glass she was using in place of an ashtray. The door to the suite in the Renaissance Hotel opened and Tank paused in the entrance to take in the sight of her sitting on the edge of the bed in nothing but a lace strapless bra, matching thong, and black patent leather heels as she smoked. She smiled at him as she released a stream of smoke through her nose. As he shut the door she stood up and offered it to him.

Tank shook his head. "Not when I'm on duty," he told her.

"Where'd you go?" Naeema asked, sitting back down and crossing her legs.

"I have to check in and out with you?" he asked, his tone tinged with sarcasm.

Naeema made a face. "I don't shadow you like that so don't flip on me with no bullshit, Tank," she said, eyeing him.

He said nothing.

The last couple of days his mood swung between short tempered and distant. Both were a hassle to her life. "Come chief wit' me," she offered again, holding out the blunt. "You need it."

He glanced up at her briefly as he checked his phone.

She shrugged. "I know Sarge threw my pipe out," she said. "Probably used it for batting practice or some shit."

Tank dropped his iPhone onto the bed beside her and started to undress. His face was pensive as he looked off into the distance.

"Tank, yo, you heard me. I said I know Sarge threw my pipe out," she repeated. "Tank."

"Huh, bae?" he asked, turning his head to look at her.

"Sarge. My missing pipe."

He balled up the T-shirt he wore and tossed it into his open leather duffel bag on the luggage rack by the door. "Leaving it in the kitchen was crazy," he said.

Naeema nodded. She'd retraced her steps and the last time she could remember seeing her weed pipe was the night of the robbery when she took it into the kitchen just before she let Mya in. She could only imagine what all Sarge had to say when he came upstairs to a ceramic dick sitting on the table. She laughed before she took another toke and held it as she eyed Tank. "Buying an even bigger one to replace it is the real pissing contest," she said.

Tank smiled but it didn't reach his eyes.

Man, fuck it.

Naeema walked out onto the balcony overlooking the bright lights and fast-moving energy of Times Square. The city's sounds were alive and popping. Tank was in town to supervise the security detail for platinum rap artist Fevah during the premiere of her movie *Killer Eyes*. He invited Naeema along and they were planning on spending the weekend together.

She gave zero fucks if someone could see her. She turned and leaned back against the balcony as she eyed Tank in nothing but his boxers as he removed everything from the pants he just took off. Through the haze of smoke Naeema took in his body. The way he moved. His tattoos. The swing of his big dick. His everything.

And it all said motherfucking boss. He was a man in control.

But she knew *she* could make him lose it.

"Who's working with you tonight?" Naeema asked, holding the blunt between her fingers as she took in the way his dick was thick even at rest.

"Yani's escorting Fevah and her entourage in," he said, moving over to the safe to unlock it and remove his weapon.

"No Grip?" she asked, surprised that his right-hand man wasn't in attendance.

"Nah, he's out of town," Tank said, as he checked the Glock with speed and skill before setting it on the bed atop his outfit for the night. "That's why I'm driving them all there and back."

Tank's vehicles were all bulletproof, providing an additional layer of protection that he worked hard to provide for his clients. It was his job to make sure nobody got fucked up. He did it well. What security he couldn't provide via his licensed gun, his bulletproof vehicles, and his team he was able to provide via his training in hand-to-hand combat.

"Well, thank you for getting me in to see the movie," Naeema said. "I don't have to fuck Fevah up for doing you a favor on some ill shit. Do I?"

Tank leveled his eyes on her. "When we're together we are together," he said.

Naeema released smoke through her lips. "Just make sure all the females you work with know that."

"They can't make me fuck 'em, Na, and I'm not looking for no pussy."

She gave him a look that said *You better not be.*

"You grabbed the wrong damn shirt," Tank said, holding up a light gray button-down shirt.

"You're just driving," she said, knowing he favored wearing either all black or navy when he was on duty.

"Yeah you right," he said, glancing up at her.

He did a double take. "Damn you look sexy as shit, bae," he said.

Naeema arched her brow and tilted her head in a nod of thanks before she held the blunt to her mouth and took another toke. Her head was freshly shaven. Her makeup was beat with smoked-out eyes, long mink lashes, and a bright red lipstick that made her mouth plump. Large fake diamond studs in her ears. Her full-arm tattoo sleeve. The sexy lingerie. The five-inch stiletto heels. Her vixen body. All with the bright lights of Times Square as her backdrop as she smoked a blunt.

Tank looked meaningfully down at his dick.

Her eyes followed his. It was hard and long and pressed

against his boxer briefs and pulled the waistband away from his body. *Well, damn, somebody's in a better mood.*

Naeema dropped the half a blunt and then pressed it beneath her shoe before she walked back into the room. She grabbed Tank by his dick with one hand and an armless chair with the other. She pulled both out onto the balcony. "Sit," she said as she bent slightly to tug his boxer briefs down around his thighs before he did. The rim caught on his dick as she did causing it to spring back and forth like a diving board.

"You wild, Na," he said, reaching up to smooth his hand over his Caesar as he shook his head in wonder.

"You ain't new to this," she said cockily, straddling his hips as she stroked the back of his head with one hand and his dick with the other.

Tank's sexy eyes were on her face. "You a bad bitch, Na," he said, before dipping his head to suck her nipple through the lace as she rose up on her toes to pull her thong to the side and lower her pussy down onto his dick.

"You best believe it," she told him as she pressed her feet against the wall on either side of him and leaned back to circle her hips and then glide them back and forth as she straight took care of the dick.

"Fuck," he swore, looking down at her breasts and her hard nipples pressed against the black lace as she rode him. He looked down at his dick wet with her juices as it disappeared and reappeared with each of her strokes. "Who pussy?"

"What it say?" she asked him thickly before letting her head fall back as she reached up to tease her nipples as he supported her with his hands gripping her hips.

He looked down at his name tattooed across the plump bald mound. The sight of it made his dick even harder.

Naeema moaned at the slight change.

They weren't new to it at all and neither gave a fuck if they were putting on a hell of a show for anyone. In that moment it was all about them and nothing else mattered. Seriously.

Naeema glanced down at her watch as she stood among the crowd outside the movie theater in anticipation of the red carpet arrivals of all the celebrities attending the premiere. She wished like crazy that she wore something besides the gray cotton spandex jumpsuit she wore from Lucki Charmz. She loved the outfit she bought from one of her favorite on-line retailers but having strangers brush up against her bare back was really pissing her off. August heat was warm even at night and being pressed between hundreds of sweaty bodies wasn't helping a damn.

"Come on, Tank," she said, tired of listening to Fevah's newest song "The Hottest" blaring around them on an annoying-ass loop. Between that and trying to block out a group of females running their mouths nonstop she was about to go crazy.

"I'm the hottest chick in the game . . ."

Naeema rolled her eyes.

"Is that Fevah?"

"Who the fuck is that?"

"How you late to your own shit?"

She could take the endless questions of the women over one of them giving a detailed, tongue-smacking retelling of catching her man, Laranz, getting blown by her cousin.

"I'm the hottest chick in the game . . ."

With another roll of her eyes she checked her watch again. She had the tickets to enter the premiere in her fake Louis Vuitton bag, but once she arrived via the car service Tank hired for her she remained outside with the rest of the onlookers because she wanted to see Fevah's arrival more than she wanted to see her movie.

And she really could care less about the Brooklyn-born rapper that was taking hip-hop by storm. She wanted to make sure the cute girl with the waist-length weave and plastic surgery–created body wasn't feeling her man. She wanted to lay eyes on them and see their interaction for herself. *Fuck that movie.*

She glanced over at the paparazzi and the TV cameras lining the red carpet as A-list to C-list stars posed for pictures or to answer questions fired at them by entertainment reporters.

The crowd began to stir and Naeema saw a lot of the reporters and paparazzi turn to look down the length of the red carpet. She turned to the left just as Tank's all-black Tahoe came up the street and pulled to a stop at the beginning of the red carpet.

Naeema blocked out the crowd's rising murmur as they wondered if it was finally the arrival of their beloved Fevah. She bit her lip and rose on the black wedge sandals she wore as Yani climbed from the passenger seat and Tank came around the front of the SUV to talk to him.

Yani opened the rear door and helped a small white woman in her forties out first. She announced to the entertainment reporters that Fevah was about to hit the carpet. *Final-fucking-ly.*

The crowd began to scream at the top of their lungs. Naeema pushed back as they all seemed to swell forward. "Damn, chill the fuck out," she shouted over her shoulder.

The security lined up along the length of the rope holding back the crowd began to hold up their hands. "Stay calm, people. Everybody relax," they commanded.

Naeema turned just as Yani stepped onto the curb to talk to the white woman as Tank walked his sexy ass to the rear door. He reached for the door handle and looked back at Yani and the woman Naeema assumed to be Fevah's publicist for some kind of go ahead.

The crowd continued to roar as the swell came forward again. Lights from what must have been a million camera phones were already clicking away around her. Naeema kept her eyes locked on Tank as she gritted her teeth and pushed back against bodies, scents, and voices. Shit.

He nodded at them just before he opened the door and stepped back. Fevah smiled and waved as she turned on the rear passenger seat to exit.

POW!

"Tank!" His name tore from her like a roar as his shoulder jerked back from the force of the bullet. The weight of his large frame pushed back against the passenger door, closing it.

Her eyes widened. Her pulse pounded. Her knees went weak.

Life moved in slow motion before her. Slow and torturous.

POW! POW! POW!

The bullets pierced his flesh and forced his body against the passenger door, and seemed to pierce her soul as well.

The crowd lining the streets outside the movie theater screamed, ran, or ducked for cover. Naeema climbed over the red velvet ropes corralling the movie premiere's onlookers. Her heart pounded as she rushed across the short distance, not caring if more bullets flew as she reached Tank. She caught his bloodied body just as it slid down the side of the car. Her knees gave out under the weight of his tall, solid frame but she did not—would not—let him go.

"Help! Somebody help," Naeema screamed, looking around at those people still boldly standing around staring down at them.

"Na," Tank moaned, turning his face against her body as he winced in pain.

Love for him filled her and she felt breathless with emotion. Naeema pressed her lips to his sweating brow. "I'm here. I got you. I'm here," she assured him in a fervent whisper against the backdrop of the sirens growing louder in the air.

She clasped the side of his face as she looked down into the pain flooding his dark eyes. She bit back a gasp at the sight of the print she made against his cheek. The blood on her hands from his soaked shirt was sticky, wet, and warm. Tank's blood signaling his imminent death.

"Please God, no," Naeema begged in a whisper, nearly choking at the thought of losing him. Tears flooded her eyes blurring her vision.

She reached up with one hand to pound on the passenger door as she fought to remain rational and not let panic diminish her senses. She needed help. Tank needed help.

The driver's seat of the double-parked SUV Tank exited was still empty but the local rap artist, Fevah, he was hired to protect and her entourage of three friends were still all inside. "Open this fucking door," Naeema roared, pounding hard enough for darts of pain to shoot across her entire hand.

Anger was an added layer to the myriad emotions flooding her as the door remained closed to them but she was flooded with relief as an ambulance screeched to a halt behind the Tahoe. She pressed kisses to his face. "Hold on, Tank. Don't you dare leave me now," she whispered in his ear in the moments before they took him from her.

As she sat in the street surrounded by the blood of the man she loved, her soul wavered between feeling as empty as her arms at the thought of losing him forever and a fiery anger that would only be quenched at finding out who shot Tank and why.

Naeema struggled to her feet and looked down at the warm, sticky blood coating her hands. She looked up and then held her hand up to cover her face at the bright lights of the cameras beginning to point in her direction. The barrage of questions being shouted at her blurred into a roar.

The sirens blared as the ambulance raced by.

Tank.

She turned to follow it with her eyes. *What hospital? I don't know which hospital.*

She scooped down to pick up her purse and raced around the vehicle.

"Yo."

She stopped and looked across the wide expanse of the hood at Yani running over to her. "Don't come near me. Stay the fuck back," she told him, slamming her hand against the hot hood before pointing an accusatory finger at him. "Don't fuck with me, you punk-ass bitch."

Something in her face must have hit home for him because he backed up.

Not once during the melee had Yani gotten close enough to the scene for Naeema to even remember he was there. She gave him one last glare and then jerked the driver's side door open to climb onto the seat.

"Who the fuck are you?"

Naeema gripped the wheel and shifted her eyes from the bright red rear lights of the ambulance to the three women sitting in the SUV's backseat. The one in the middle with a waist-length black weave with burgundy tips was Fevah. All three were crying, shivering, and clutching one another's hands.

Naeema could care the fuck less . . . or at least she wanted to.

She looked at them and back to the red lights of the ambulance getting smaller in the distance. *Fuuuuuuck.* "That's my husband that was shot," she said, turning back around to accelerate the SUV forward. "I have to get to the hospital."

"Wait . . . what?"

Naeema flexed her shoulders in irritation as she sped like crazy to catch up with the ambulance. *I should have rode with him. Why didn't I ride with him? Tank, please hold on. Please.*

"I want to go home. Take me the fuck home," Fevah said, hitting the back of Naeema's seat.

Naeema lifted one hand from the wheel long enough to shoo her words away like aggravating flying pests.

"TAKE. ME. THE. FUCK. HOME."

Naeema's lips tightened in anger. She opened the armrest and pulled out Tank's Glock. She pressed it between the wheel and her hand as she continued to dip and weave around the traffic, as she stayed pressed to the ambulance's tail. "My motherfucking husband was shot trying to protect you and I am going to the hospital," she said, her eyes shifting to them in the rearview mirror and back to the busy traffic-filled street ahead of her. "Either shut the fuck up or get the fuck out. Choice is yours."

The three women all resumed their crying.

The ambulance breezed through a red light. Naeema stopped just long enough to check for oncoming traffic before she ran it. *Tank. Please hold on.*

POW! POW! POW! POW!

She blinked with each echoing memory of gunfire.

Her eyes dipped down to the blood on her hands. She bit her bottom lip as a tear raced down her cheek and salted her mouth.

"I'm the hottest chick in the game . . ."

At the ringtone, Naeema took her eyes off the bright lights of the hospital up ahead in the distance to look at Fevah in the rearview mirror as she answered her iPhone.

"Yes, I'm still in the SUV."

The ambulance made a sharp left and Naeema followed.

"They canceled the premiere?"

POW! POW! POW! POW!

Naeema flinched again.

"Tell the police I am safe and we're pulling up to—"

"Bellevue Hospital," Naeema provided as she eyed the sign on the corner detailing directions to the medical center.

"This shit is crazy, yo," Fevah said to whomever was on the phone. "I could've died tonight."

"Word," one of her friends co-signed sadly.

Naeema pulled the SUV into a parking spot next to the ambulance.

"The fuck we gon' do now, Fevah?"

"They sending a car for me."

Naeema gripped the door handle but she stopped at the loud snorting coming from the rear of the SUV. She glanced back just as Fevah sniffed again and pinched her nose before she passed a thick glass vial of coke to one of her friends.

Coke was meaner than weed but Naeema wasn't judging a damn thing. Right then she would gladly smoke a fat blunt to ease all the emotions beating her the fuck down.

"Nobody followed us. Stay in here. It's bulletproof," Naeema told them before she took the keys out of the ignition.

"You know y'all fired, right?" Fevah asked, wrapping her fingers around the vial.

"Bitch, please," Naeema drawled. "You know we quit, right?"

She grabbed her bag before she rushed from the car just as the EMTs lowered Tank's stretcher from the ambulance.

POW! POW! POW! POW!

"How is he?" Naeema asked, as she slid her bloody hand into Tank's as she ran alongside the stretcher inside the emergency room's open double doors.

"Alive . . . barely."

Tank's face was covered with an oxygen mask and there was an intravenous line in his arm. His eyes were closed.

His breathing was slow and labored. Blood soaked his clothing and the stretcher. The bullets tore jagged holes in his flesh.

"Tank, I'm here," she said to him. "I'm here, baby."

She felt someone undo her hand from his. She held the fuck on even as her body went weak with fear and her shoulders sunk as she cried.

"Ma'am, please. Let go of him."

Nacema uncurled her fingers and moments later their touch was broken. She stumbled backward as she watched him until the doctors and the stretcher disappeared from her view behind double doors. She trembled and felt as if she stepped out of her own body.

She couldn't wrap her brain around never seeing Tank alive again.

"No. No," she gasped. "No."

POW! POW! POW! POW!

She squeezed her eyes shut but then opened them quickly as the image of Tank's shooting began to replay against her closed lids. Clear. Vivid. Brutal.

Tank was shot.

She bit her bottom lip to keep from screaming at the top of her lungs with all her fear and rage.

Tank was shot.

She felt her knees go weak and she didn't stop her body from sliding down the length of the wall until she sat on the floor with her feet spread wide.

POW! POW! POW! POW!

Naeema drew her feet in and wrapped her arms around her chest. She sat her chin in the groove between her knees and closed her eyes. The image of Tank's body riddled with bullets was replaced with the graphic scenes of her son's body from the crime scene photos. Scenes of his brutal death.

I can't lose Tank too.

She stroked the wide gold band of the ring she wore— her son's ring. The same ring she made his killer kiss in the moments just before she shot him to death without remorse. She looked down at the ring now covered with the blood of the man she loved.

Tank's shooter would pay too.

She rose to her feet and took a seat in one of the waiting room chairs.

In the midst of her misery her anger gave her strength. Not much. But some. Enough. For now.

6

"Tonight, the shocking attempt on the life of Chasity Williams—better known as platinum-selling rap artist Fevah—has rocked the entertainment world. While arriving here at the Ziegfeld Theater for the premiere of her first major film, the vehicle Fevah was exiting was bombarded with gunfire and her bodyguard was shot and critically wounded during the incident. He is currently in surgery at Bellevue Hospital Center with no recent updates on his condition. Police are investigating the shooting but have no leads on just who wanted the popular hip-hop star's light put out far too soon. This is Maria Vargas reporting for WCBL Live 8 News . . ."

Naeema closed her eyes and pinched the bridge of her nose. The shooting had been at the top of the news for the last six hours since it happened. Every broadcast. Every channel.

She was tired of looking at Fevah fans laying out flowers and teddy bears at the sight of the shooting as though the bullets intended for her had actually pierced her flesh and left her on a surgical table for the last six hours.

Two police detectives had been to the hospital to question her but for Naeema it was more about finding out what they knew. So far she could fit it all inside a motherfucking thimble.

The door to the small waiting room opened and six men filed in. Every last one had a powerful presence even as their expressions were tight with the same anger and pain she felt. She eyed each one. Quari, Kyle, Linx, Frasier, Darren, and Amir. Tank's team. All except Grip, who was on his way back from his mini-vacation, and Yani, who was smart to stay away. When those bullets starting flying his whack *on-duty* self flew in the opposite direction. *Fuck his lame ass.*

Amir sat Tank's duffel and her overnight case next to her feet. "Thanks," she said, giving a small smile to the dude who was built like a linebacker for the National Football League.

"No problem, Naeema," he said.

She had sent him to the hotel to gather their things and check out.

The men all took a seat and looked at her.

"What's going on with Fevah?" she asked, staring off at a crack in the paint on the wall as she used her thumb to turn her son's ring on her finger.

"She hired a new security team and they wouldn't let us in to question her," Linx said, his blue eyes almost clear enough to be turquoise.

Naeema felt her gut burn with anger. "I guess Tank taking her bullets as she shut the door to protect her hip-hop-pop ass wasn't good enough," she said, biting her bottom lip.

"Exactly," one of the men agreed.

"Who?" Naeema asked. "Who did she hire?"

"I'd have to find out," Linx said, looking disappointed that he couldn't provide an answer to a very simple question.

Naeema said nothing as she looked away from the stout white man with a blond buzz cut. She knew he would get the answer and just because she asked. Tank was their boss—their leader—and she was his wife. Their deference for Tank transferred to her because they knew her well and they knew she wanted the gunman—or gunmen—just as badly as they did. If not more so.

She looked at Frasier—a light-skinned man with a bald head, freckles, and a beard.

"The police did a damn good sweep of the scene and nothing was left behind. They have all the bullet shells," he told her.

"Where were they?" she asked, her look intense.

"The markings on the ground say it was someone right in the crowd," Frasier said. "I texted you the pictures."

Naeema nodded. She wasn't ready to see them yet.

"We have to find out who wanted Fevah dead," she said, stating the obvious. "And I could care less why. Like seriously I don't give fuck if they want her dead because she shot their mother. I don't give a fuck."

The men fell silent and all shifted to some sort of comfort in their seats.

"And let me make something clear," Naeema said, eyeing each one with eyes cold enough to chill them to their bones. "Tank would take a bullet for any of you and if your asses won't do the same then you'll be on the outside looking in just like Yani."

"But Yani said—"

Naeema sat up straight in her chair and pierced Amir—

the newest member of Tank's staff. "I don't give a flying fuck what his punk ass said. I was there," she said, her eyebrows dipping with her anger. "If you want to sacrifice you're motherfucking job to protect his then have at it, Amir. The floor is yours, my hitta."

From the corner of her eye she saw a couple of the men slightly motion with their heads for him not to fuck with it.

"Nah, I'm good," Amir said.

"Good," she stressed, keeping her face stoic even as she felt a wave of tears creep up on her. These men respected her but she knew they expected to see some sign of weakness and she absolutely refused to fulfill any fucking dreams. She'd save her tears for when she was alone.

> *"And in local news Councilman Victor Planter is being heralded for a recent move that would bring a significant number of needed jobs to the city of Newark. The councilman made a stipulation clear that bids submitted for construction within city limits must include an agreement to hire local workers from the city. Many residents hope other politicians follow Councilman Planter's lead and prove that the residents of Newark and their well-being matter beyond just the revitalization of the downtown area. Councilman Planter had this to say today at a groundbreaking for a new hotel in Newark . . ."*

"That shit sounds good on paper," one of the men said.

Naeema glanced up at the bald-headed, dark-skinned black man in a suit speaking on the television.

"I'll have to see it to fucking believe it," Quari said. "Plenty of brothers want and can use that work."

"Plenty of white brothas too, Quari," Linx said. "We *all* are struggling right now."

"Right. Right."

Naeema said nothing as the news moved to the shooting. They were running the story into the ground. She was pressed to get her thoughts together. To get her mind right. Every question had an answer. Every lock had a key. It was all about making the connections. Putting it all together. And above all—for her following her instincts. They hadn't failed her yet since she learned to respect them.

To help weed out her son's killer she had to go undercover as Queen using wigs, a fake-ass background, and plenty of lies. For months she lived among a band of thieves and got so lost in the game that she didn't know if she was coming or fucking going. She doubted she needed to go that deep with it but she was pretty sure that Queen could come in handy again.

"Text me Fevah's address and don't worry about contacting her directly again," Naeema said, going back to twisting the ring on her finger.

I got it.

"We did it, Mrs. Cole."

Naeema looked up at Tank as they stood together on a white sand beach in the Bahamas under the floral-covered altar with the gentle breeze causing the white material draped across the top to billow in the air.

"Yes we did," she said, thinking her husband looked hella good in his khaki linen suit with a cream silk V-neck tee.

She smoothed the hand he didn't hold over the waist of the ivory lace bustier dress she wore. The halter top with the back out and the hem just below her ass was wild for a wedding at a church but it was just the right fit for a man like Tank and a woman like Naeema on a beach in the Bahamas. Just the two of them.

Their union was all about Jay Z and Beyoncé's "Bonnie and Clyde," Method Man and Mary's "You're All I Need," and Biggie's "Me & My Bitch." Any of 'em could have been their theme song and right then, just moments after getting married, they both felt like they could say "fuck the world" because they had each other's back like no one else could.

Tank tugged at her hand as he turned to walk down the aisle that she walked toward him just minutes ago. With one last look at the turquoise water Naeema followed behind him with her straw high-heel sandals in her hand. Her shoulder-length ebony curls bounced and the long gold beads she wore hit against the shorter necklaces nestled in her cleavage above the sweetheart neckline. When she stumbled Tank stopped and scooped her thickness up into his arms to carry her the rest of the way down the aisle.

"Mrs. and Mr. Cole," she said, reading the words tattooed on her left ring finger. It had been worth the pain to brand herself his and only his. He had the same tat. They'd gotten them done that morning before heading out for the flight to the Bahamas for their intimate wedding weekend at the Atlantis.

Fuck rings. Rings could be removed.

Naeema pressed a kiss to his smooth cheek. She shaved

him last night as she sat naked in his lap. "You can put me down, Tank," *she said as he continued across the beach with her in his arms drawing the stares of the few people they passed.*

He shook his head. "Never. I always got you, Naeema," *he said.* "Always."

That look in his eyes when he said it and the feel of the strength in his arms as he held her took Naeema's breath away. There was a time she thought a man would never respect her enough to wife her and now she had one that made her believe that for forever and a day she could rely on him.

"And I got you, too," *she swore, stroking his mouth with her thumb before dipping her head in close to kiss him deeply.*

"Always?" *he asked in that hot little space between their mouths as they paused in their kissing.*

"Always . . ."

"Mrs. Cole?"

Naeema blinked as she was brought back to the present by the nurse standing in the waiting-room entrance. "Yes?" she asked as all the men rose to their feet.

"Your husband is out of surgery and the doctor will be out in a moment to update you," she said, placing a hand to her chest as though all the men staring at her made her nervous—in a good way.

Naeema rose to her feet. "He's alive?" she asked, her heart pounding.

The nurse nodded. "Yes."

Thank you, God.

"When can I see him?" Naeema asked, fighting back tears of relief.

"He's in post-op but we have his room ready if . . . if you want to clean up," she offered gently.

Naeema looked down at her blood-stained clothes and nodded. Up until that moment, not knowing if Tank was at least alive, Naeema hadn't given a fuck about leaving that hospital to change clothes. She tucked her pocketbook under her arm and turned to get their bags.

Amir and Linx already had them in their hands.

Tears swelled up and Naeema dropped her head as she fought not to let a tear fall. She didn't have family. Her grandfather died years ago. Her son was murdered. Her husband was fighting to live. Sarge never left the house and she wouldn't ask him to. She didn't really fuck with female friends anymore.

In that moment these men were all she had and she was grateful for them. "Thanks," she said, blinking her lashes like crazy as she shook her head.

No one said anything but they all stood there waiting for her to make the next move for them to follow. She released a long breath through pursed lips before she turned and followed the nurse out of the waiting room with her head held high.

The men all followed close behind.

Naeema glared across the bedroom at Tank sitting on the edge of the bed in nothing but his boxers. She barely had on much more in her bright green lace teddy. They both were pissed the hell off.

Naeema was hot as fish grease because Tank was just get-ting home after they just argued the night before about the same shit.

Tank was furious because he was tired and just wanted to come home to a happy wife and some sleep—neither of which panned the fuck out for him.

From her spot leaning against the wall by the window she pulled back the wood blinds to look out at the cars parked on the street outside the row of brownstones in New-ark's University Heights section. She arched a brow to see a man and woman climb out from the backseat of a SUV. Both brows dipped when the man went into one home and the woman went into the one next door. Both were married and living with their spouses.

Out the corner of her eye she spotted Tank lying down on the bed.

Never had they argued so much as when he started his own business two years ago. Her disappointment fueled every bit of it. She thought things would get better when he focused less on being a bouncer and more on security. Shit didn't change. Still late nights. Still disrespecting bitches.

She never caught Tank cheating but he was a man like any other man and how much temptation could any man take?

"I can't do this anymore, Tank," she said.

Before the words fully left her mouth he swore under his breath and sat back up. "Naeema, could you finish whatever the fuck is bothering you this time so I can carry my black ass to sleep."

His annoyance hurt. "This time but same old shit, Tank," she said, wishing he could understand that she just wanted to be heard. She just wanted him to respect how she felt instead of letting it go in one ear and out the other like she didn't have shit to do but find things to argue about. She just wanted to know he cared enough to give a fuck.

"Okay. I'm wrong. I'm sorry. I ain't shit," he said, looking over at her. "What else, Naeema? Because all these bills can't get paid off your arguments every damn night . . . or cutting hair."

That stung like a motherfucker and she felt it deep in her chest.

Another old argument.

"It's over, Tank," she said, her voice barely above a whisper as she wiped away the tears she didn't even know were falling at first. She shook her head with regret before she pushed off the wall and walked to the bedroom door.

"Yeah right," he said, lying back down on the bed.

She stopped to look back at him, her hand on the door. He lay on his back with his arm across his eyes. She bit her bottom lip and closed the door before making her way to the guest bedroom.

She lay across the top of the bed and held her hand up to look at it in the moonlight. The tattooed wedding bands had faded in time. Just like the peace in their relationship.

Naeema thought of the house she grew up in when she was living with her grandfather. She checked a few months ago after another heated argument and it was indeed hers. Funny how she ran away from that place so much growing up, too young and dumb to be grateful.

And now she was running back to it . . .

Naeema blinked and the memories of their breakup

faded as she looked over at Tank lying in the bed. She stroked his hand with her thumb as she rose to her feet and stepped closer to the bed to bend down over him. "I'm here, Tank. I'm here. Right by your side. And I love you. Please . . . please don't leave me here all alone," she whispered. A tear fell from her eye and down onto his cheek.

The doctor explained the bullet to the chest had caused major blood loss and led to Tank going into cardiac arrest during surgery. He was lucky the bullet entered his lower chest and not his heart. The doctor successfully repaired the damage from the bullets but Tank remained unconscious and she had no idea if he could hear her but she wasn't willing to let the words go unsaid.

She looked up when the door to his hospital room opened. "Grip!" she exclaimed, instantly feeling some of the burden was lifted off her shoulder as she eyed the tall, bald-headed man. "Can you believe this bullshit?"

He hugged her briefly to his side. Her head just barely reached his chest. "I wish I had been there, man. This shit is crazy," he said, his voice deep and rich with his East Coast accent.

"I want Yani fired," she said, her eyes on Tank's face.

"Done," Grip replied without hesitation. "I don't blame you for leaving his ass there."

"Fevah switching to a new security team gives off the impression that Tank failed," she said, reclaiming her seat but holding on to Tank's hand. "We have to stay on top of all the clients right now to make sure that when he recovers his business ain't went to shit. You know?"

"I got it, Naeema. Trust me."

And she did.

"Seeing him get shot right in front of me was so fucked up," she said, her voice low.

"It couldn't have been easy seeing all that blood stain his shirt."

"It wasn't. It was horrible," she said.

POW! POW! POW! POW!

She flinched.

"We'll get to the bottom of it, Naeema," he promised. "You have my word."

"Would you stay here with him 'til I get back?" she asked.

Hours had passed since Tank came out of surgery and the fellas had long since left her alone and by his side. She was reluctant to leave but she had to. Tank was the first person to teach her it was best to strike while the iron was hot.

"No problem. I know you been here since last night. Get some rest," he said.

Naeema nodded as she stood and moved past him to walk to the door. "I should be back in two hours tops," she promised, giving Tank one last glance over her shoulder.

"You good."

With a nod Naeema left the hospital room. She stopped at the nurses' station long enough to leave her cell phone number and let them know she would be away for a couple hours before she made her way down the hall to the elevators. She was plotting.

Sleep was the last motherfucking thing on her mind.

Naeema found the parking lot where one of the men had left the SUV after getting it cleaned. She was thankful when she unlocked and opened the door that the smell of blood was gone. *Tank's blood.*

She used OnStar to locate the nearest hair supply store and maneuvered through the busy New York traffic until she turned off the street and into the parking area in front of a large store. Before she left the vehicle she dug her phone out of her bag and called Sarge.

"Yeah," he said, gruff and rough as ever. "Y'all okay?"

"Yes. We're better—not our best—but better," she said. "He's out of surgery but unconscious and they're just trying to get all of his vital signs stable."

Sarge released one of his infamous grunts.

"Is everything good at the house? Are you eating?" she asked, biting her full bottom lip.

"Take care of you."

She nodded as if he could see her.

"And leave this thing up to the police, Naeema," he added.

"I can't, Sarge," she replied, refusing to lie. Not to him. Their odd-ass bond was way too real for that shit.

"Listen to an old man that seen shit, done shit, and knows shit. Leave this be. You won't get lucky twice."

She knew he was talking about the shit she'd seen, known, and did to bring down her son's killer.

"I'm gonna stay in a hotel near the hospital but I'll come and check on you during the week," she said.

"Check on me?" he balked before he grunted yet again.

Naeema fell silent and let her head fall back against the leather headrest. She was tired as shit but there was no time for that.

"You can't save the world, little girl."

"Maybe not the entire world but definitely those in my world—including you, Sarge," she stressed before she pulled the phone from her ear and ended the call.

Beep.

Naeema got out of the car and adjusted the fit of her clothes as she made her way inside the store. "Can I see your wigs please?" she said to the Asian woman who walked up to her with a ready smile.

"Right this way," she said, heading toward a long wall with multiple shelves holding faceless wig heads with wigs on them.

Naeema followed behind looking around the massive store taking in everything they offered—including wash-and-wear clothing that was more stretch than anything. *Just the kind of shit I love.*

"Human or synthetic?"

The last thing Naeema needed was more wigs. She had a container of selections back at her house in Newark. All colors. All lengths. All styles. All textures. She wore her hair close shaven but on the days she felt like long hair she taped a wig on and kept it moving.

"Synthetic," she said without a doubt.

"Over here. Over here," To Wong Foo said, pointing to the majority of the wigs.

Naeema looked up and quickly made a choice. "Number twenty-three in black," she said.

"Wow. Quick," the store owner said before heading into the storeroom.

Naeema quickly made her way over to the area where she saw the clothing. She snatched up a lime green dress with cutouts along the sides and found a pair of twenty-dollar black sandals. The store owner brought the plastic container holding the wig to the cash register at the front of the store. Everything came to less than fifty dollars.

"You want put hair on now?"

Naeema ignored her and left the store. She climbed into the back of the SUV, thankful for the dark tint as she quickly pulled off her clothes and shoes. The dress wasn't made for panties and she was glad she used Tank's hospital room to take a quick shower. Shoving all her clothes in the plastic bag she hurried into the dress and sandals and finger-combed the short bob wig once she slipped it on her head.

She exited the back of the car and walked back across the lot to the store.

"Look good. *Very* good," the store owner said, eyeing the slits on the side of the dress that exposed Naeema's cinnamon brown skin.

"Makeup?" she asked.

"Do it for the Gram!" the woman said holding up a cell phone.

Naeema held up one finger, blocking her shot. "Don't fuck with that," she said, her voice hard and meant to show she would throw that phone against the wall with a quickness if she even tried it.

She lowered the phone. "Makeup in here," she said, pointing to the glass case she sat behind.

Naeema quickly chose a peach lip gloss and gold eye shadow. After tossing five dollars on the counter she used the mirror stand atop the counter to quickly apply the shadow to her eyes and a light sprinkle to her cheeks with her fingertips before putting on a good dose of gloss that left her lips feeling sticky.

When she turned and left the store she could have sworn she heard the flash from a camera sound off. *Fuck it.*

Back behind the wheel of the Tahoe, she cranked the car and headed back into the bumper-to-bumper traffic of the Big Apple as she made her way toward Upstate New York under the direction of OnStar's navigation system.

The hem of the cheap spandex dress kept riding high on her thighs as she drove until eventually Naeema let it be as she tried to come up with a plan during the thirty-mile trip to White Plains.

Naeema wasn't overly religious but she kept sending up prayers for guidance to Father God as the landscape changed from the bustle of the metropolis to the sloweddown pace of the suburbs. She was just anxious to finish up her task and get back to Tank's side at the hospital. She picked up her phone to double-check the signal was still strong in case someone from the hospital called.

"Your destination is on your left."

Naeema eyed the two brick colonial at the end of a long road that switched from paved to flat red-clay dirt. There was a black Range Rover blocking the entrance to the long curving drive leading to the house on the hill. She slowed up, already wishing she hadn't driven Tank's car in case the tag was run. *Think. Think. Think.*

She took one hand off the wheel to quickly reach in her purse for her fake oversized Chanel shades and reapplied the lip gloss as a short but wide black dude climbed from behind the wheel of the Rover. She pulled to a stop just as he headed to her vehicle. Quickly she removed Tank's Glock from inside the armrest and set it on the floor before she climbed out, leaving the driver's-side door open.

Hips and ass don't fail me.

Even as he kept one hand close to the opening of his black blazer to pull the gun she knew he concealed, his black eyes dipped to take her in from head to toe in the dress that was even more revealing than what Naeema usually fucked with.

But she wasn't Naeema. Now she was Queen.

"Can I help you?" he asked, his wide-set nose and flaring nostrils giving him the look of a really big—but really cute—teddy bear.

Naeema thrust her bra-less titties high and his eyes dipped to take in her nipples pressed against the thin material but then he shifted his gaze to the front license tag on the Tahoe. She opened her mouth and then closed it. She kicked out the idea of playing a lesbian wild girl from Long Island—with a fake accent and all.

One run of the tag would reveal that lie.

She quickly skimmed the trees for any video cameras recording her. "I know the bodyguard that was shot last night and I wanted to speak to Fevah. If you could just let her know I'm here," she said, figuring she put herself in enough of a jam to come as close to the truth as possible.

"I can't do that," he said, crossing his hands in front of him.

Naeema pressed her hand against her flat belly, meaning to draw his eyes there. "You can't or you won't?" she asked.

"Both," he said.

Naeema wondered if she wanted to speak to Fevah badly enough to take his big ass down and drive the Tahoe into the Rover to clear the driveway or switch up the game plan. She went for the latter. "Listen, I'm just trying to figure out who is behind the shooting last night," she said, her voice softening as she pretended to wipe sweat from the back of her neck and then the top of her cleavage.

The horny motherfucker didn't miss shit.

And neither did she.

Hook.

"Anything you can do to help me, I really would appreciate it," she said, pulling the edge of the dress from her body as she fanned herself. "I want to find out who it is tried to kill Fevah and shot one of our guys. I want it real bad."

Line.

"I know in this business you must know what it feels like to want something real bad. Like you don't even know how to think straight to get *it*," she said with a hot little emphasis on the last word as she hitched her dress a little higher on her thighs.

She heard that motherfucker swallow.

Sinker.

"I'm on duty," he said, stepping close to her.

Naeema forced herself not to step back.

"But give me your number and when I'm off duty I might be able to help you get some satisfaction," he said, tilting his head to the side as he raised his hand to pull her dress away from her body with his finger and look down at her body.

Men are so fucking predictable.

The shit really irked her nerves how tits and ass always fucked them up. She used it to her advantage but she still had no respect for their weakness.

Naeema gripped his big, rough hand and her dress snapped back to her body like a second skin. "What's your name and number?" she asked, pretending he had a chance in hell when he didn't. "We can meet up and then we'll both get satisfied."

"Cecil. 212-555-3480."

"Talk to you soon, Cecil," she promised before turning to climb back into the Tahoe, which was still running. She gave him a smile before she closed the door and turned around at the end of the road to head back to Manhattan.

A number to a lowly bodyguard babysitting a driveway wasn't shit but right then it beat a fucking blank.

7

*N*aeema was getting anxious as fuck.

"I need to smoke."

Naeema could kick herself for not taking the weed she still had in her carry-on case with her during that long ride to Upstate New York. She could've blazed one and took her time. Now she was wondering if she smoked in the bathroom if she would set off smoke alarms or some shit.

Weed would mellow her the fuck out. Help her think. *Plit-plot.*

She got up from the seat and opened the door to the small, narrow closet where she had stuffed their luggage.

Bzzzzzz. Bzzzzzz. Bzzzzzz.

Naeema frowned and turned to eye her cell phone sitting on the bedside table. It sat silent. *Tank's phone. How in the hell did I forget about that?*

She removed the luggage but didn't see anything beneath them.

Bzzzzzz. Bzzzzzz. Bzzzzzz.

She looked up before stepping inside the base of the closet and reaching on the top shelf to pat it until she felt a plastic bag. Grabbing it, she shook her head at Tank's shoes, his wallet, and his cell phone. The clothes had been cut away from his body for better access to the gunshot wounds.

She took out the cell phone and wallet. The iPhone was locked and the wallet had almost a grand in hundred-dollar bills.

To be honest, she was camping out in his hospital room until the nurses caught on and sent her home because even the cheapest hotel in the area was a hundred dollars a night. She wouldn't spend Tank's money unless she absolutely had to but if the moment arose it was as good as gone.

She dug the Ziploc of weed and blunts out of her bag, rolling it up tight, and moved across the room to shove it and the wallet down into her pocketbook. After taking her seat she looked down at the phone and then over at Tank. Back at the phone. Over at Tank once again.

Sheee-it.

She swiped her thumb across the touchscreen and crossed her legs as she settled back against the chair to try every possible passcode she could think of. His birthday. Hers. Their anniversary. The date they met. The number he constantly played in the Pick 3. Hell, the tag numbers on all his vehicles and her motorcycle. House number. Last four of the house and cell number. Numbers pulled out her ass.

Shit.

She tapped the end of her thumbnail against the phone just as it vibrated.

Bzzzzzz . . .

The phone went dead mid-vibrate.

Fuuuuuuck.

Her fingers gripped the phone tight enough to dent it. She didn't have a charger. She slid the phone in the side pocket of her pocketbook and stood up to stroke Tank's cheek lightly with one hand and take his hand in the other.

She would give anything for him to open his eyes and look up at her. Smile at her. Hell, talk shit to her. Anything.

It had just been two days since Tank was shot. His condition was stable but he was still unconscious. The police had been back in touch with her but they couldn't provide any clues. She felt like there was something else she could be doing other than sitting there waiting on the fellas to bring her bits and pieces of whatever news or clues they swept up from the street. And even that was coming in whack-ass dribs and drabs.

She bent to lightly kiss his lips before turning to scoop up her pocketbook and leave the hospital room. She stopped at the nurses station. "I'm going to go out for a little while," she said to the short, plump redhead looking at her with soft eyes filled with concern.

"Once you leave out you won't be able to get back in downstairs this time of night," she said.

Naeema looked back at the door to Tank's room.

"I'm on duty 'til morning," she said.

Naeema looked down when the woman lightly patted her hand. She eased her hand from under hers.

"I'll keep an eye on him and call you if anything changes," the nurse said, looking apologetic for touching her. "You go get some good rest."

"Thank you," Naeema said. "Please call me. No matter what time."

"I will."

Naeema gave her a genuine smile before she turned and headed to the elevator at the end of the hall. When the doors opened she stepped in and turned as the doors closed behind her. She paced around the four walls like a caged animal until the elevator slid to a stop. The doors opened and four uniformed NYPD officers stood there. Her body went tense as shit.

Naeema didn't fuck with the police. She'd seen too much and even dealt with some bullshit firsthand in the hood to be groomed with mistrust.

The officers cleared a path for her to exit and Naeema did that with a quickness, thinking of the weed she carried. As she left the hospital she took a deep inhale of the summer air as she made her way to the Tahoe in the parking lot.

She looked up at the sound of glass breaking. A tall, skinny dude with a hoodie on had a crowbar raised high in the air above the car he just fucked up. *Fucking stick-up kid.*

Naeema kept it moving minding her own.

"Yo, shawty."

Here the fuck we go.

She ducked to the left between two cars and stayed low as she moved forward toward the Tahoe.

"I just wanted to holla at you, beautiful. Dayum."

Fuck you royally, bastard.

She waited until she was at the passenger door to deactivate the alarm and snatch the door open. She heard his sneakers beating down on the concrete and rushed up into the seat pulling the door closed.

"Unh-unh. Hold up, bitch."

The door was snatched from her hand. Naeema looked into the face of a white boy. She hated that this surprised her.

"Let me get it," he said, licking at his red lips with the tip of his tongue as his eyes shifted back and forth crazy as shit.

"I ain't got it," she said, shaking her head.

He held up the crowbar.

Naeema pulled her right hand from inside the console and quickly whipped out Tank's gun to press against his forehead as she removed the safety and cocked it.

Click.

"Gun tops crowbar, motherfucker," she told him, curling her upper lip as she nudged his head back with the barrel of the gun. "Get the fuck from 'round here."

"Aight. Aight," he said stepping back as he dropped the crowbar.

It clanged loudly against the ground.

"Matter of fact, let me run *your* motherfucking pockets, you thieving little bitch," she said, flashing back on the fucker who broke into her house. "Let's see if you like the other side of a stickup."

"I'm sorry," he said, turning the pocket of his hoodie and jeans out.

All his shit fell to the ground. Crack pipe and all.

"Stomp that stem," she said.

He looked at her and his eyes filled with pleading as he shook his head a little.

Naeema saw the desperation in the depths of his baby blues and his addiction in the yellowed whites. For a moment—not much of a moment—but a moment, she felt so sorry for whomever it was he used to be. Before the drugs. The addiction. "Stomp it," she said.

Again he hesitated.

"Mother, do you understand how bad this shit got ahold of you?" she asked him, her voice incredulous as hell. "You rather risk gettin' shot in the fucking head than stomp that bitch?"

Something in his eyes changed. She didn't know if it was the truth of her words or enough desperation to struggle with her for the gun. "Stomp it," she said again, pushing the gun against his head until it tilted back and he could look straight up at the night sky.

He raised his foot and brought it down on the crack pipe.

She frowned in disgust when a tear raced from his eye. "If you give a fuck about yourself you'll walk in that ER right there and beg them to admit you to their inpatient rehab program, yo. Shit is crazy," she said, keeping the gun to his head but switching her right for her left so that she could crank the SUV and throw it into drive. She took her foot off the brake and rolled forward until his body no longer blocked the door from closing and the gun was pulled away from his head.

As Naeema accelerated forward she watched in the rearview mirror as he squatted and picked up the broken pieces of his pipe. It was one of the saddest things she ever laid eyes on. *God bless his strung-out ass.*

She sped away from the sight of what had to be the lowest point of his damn life. Nothing could go lower but him being straight and sucking dick for dope. Weed was her ultimate and she *knew* she loved that shit too much sometimes.

She didn't even fuck with a blunt after that whole scene and drove out of the parking lot after paying the fee. She put the gun back in the armrest and pulled over at the first dollar store she saw to buy a cheap prepaid phone, a card with minutes, and a phone charger. Back in the car she activated the phone and loaded the minutes.

She quickly dialed Cecil the bodyguard's number on the

prepaid as she picked up her touchscreen to open up Instagram. Earlier today she set up a fake account and followed Fevah's account. Not more than five minutes ago she posted a vid.

"Come out and salute your girl at Club Vixen. Nothing stoppin' my shine. Kno' what I mean. It's going down," she'd said, her makeup, hair, and bodysuit as colorful as a box of Fruity Pebbles.

This bitch picking up the style Nicki Minaj drop-kicked.

"Whaddup?"

"Cecil? This Yummy. From yesterday. The lime green dress," she said, needing to make sure that he wasn't on Fevah's security detail that night and curious if he had any new info to offer.

"Yeah, yeah. What's poppin' lovely?"

Naeema rolled her eyes and looked down as she swiped over to the club flyer Fevah posted earlier. "I was too busy to hit you up earlier but I wondered if you was working tonight?" she asked, looking at the rapper with nothing but her long weave to cover her breasts cut and pasted above a picture of the New York skyline and liquor bottles.

"Nah, I'm off tonight—"

"Hold on one second. I got another call," she said, lowering the phone to put it on mute.

"Yo, I'm a put this call on speaker. Yo. Catch this thotology."

Naeema leaned back a bit in surprise at Cecil talking to someone in the background. "Lame," she muttered.

"I'm a slow walk this ho right over to give me brain, yo," he said, sounding excited.

Naeema arched a brow when she heard them fools dapping each other up. Her intention was just to make him think she got an emergency call and couldn't go through with meeting up. *This bullshit right here . . .*

"Cecil," she said, after taking the call off mute.

"Yeah, Lovely. What it do?" he said.

"Well, like I was saying bumps on your dick is not a good look—"

"What?" he exclaimed.

"You sent me a dick pic and it was bad enough your shit is . . . *limited* and shit but fucking bumps and shit? Nah, I'll pass."

"Yo, what the fuck is going on?"

"Your dick dirty. I don't like dirty dick," she said before smacking her tongue as she drove out of the small parking lot to carefully merge with the New York traffic headed down the FDR Drive to get to Brooklyn.

"Fuck you."

"Didn't you just hear me say no?" she asked. "Lose my number, Dirty Dick. Deuces."

Naeema carelessly dropped the phone in the cup holder. It instantly rang and vibrated. She ignored it as she maneuvered through the traffic. New York was cool but she was ready to get her ass back within the Jersey limits permanently. New York traffic was just disrespectful.

Naeema was glad when she finally exited the FDR and continued on to Club Vixen. She had been to the club before. She parked down the street from it to get in the back and change out of the T-shirt, leggings, and kicks she had on for the dress, heels, and wig she left on the backseat yesterday. She turned on the overhead light long enough to lightly beat her face with makeup. "I gotta go home tomorrow and get some clothes," she said to her reflection in the camera on her phone.

She would have preferred to stroll up to the club with one of her 'fits from her personal collection but the dress and super-duper cheap heels would have to do. She drove closer to the club but still had to make her way up the street alone to get in the short line outside it. She had nothing but her ID, her cell phone, and a hundred-dollar bill in her hand when she would have preferred to have some fire-power. *Just in case.*

As the line moved forward at a snail's pace, Naeema kept brushing the bangs from her eyes with the tips of her nails. The steady bass of the music was sounding off outside the club and she gave a small smile to a group of ladies dancing to the music as they waited in line.

It reminded her of the days she hung out with Sasha and Roz. When she first hooked up with Tank she had let the friendship fall by the wayside. Their friendship symbolized fun times. Wild-ass times. She just couldn't see keeping them and Tank. For her a choice had to be made.

"The one in the black jumpsuit . . . and the one in the red shorts."

Naeema looked up from cleaning behind her rhinestone-covered nails to see a beefy dude wearing a SECURITY T-shirt pulling girls from the line as someone called out orders from inside one of the new Hummers.

She frowned. *What prostitution stroll kinda shit is this?*

"For sure the one in the green dress," the voice said. "And the chick in the white jeans."

Naeema looked on as the Hummer pulled away up the street.

"Right this way, sweetheart."

Naeema looked at the security guard as he unhooked the velvet rope keeping them corralled in line like animals. *Fucking sheep.*

"What's this about?" she asked him as she stepped out of the line.

"The talent for the night asked that you ladies be let in the club. You in or out?"

Naeema nodded as she followed him up the street and into the club. She pulled the long sleeves down on her arm to make sure her tattoo sleeve was covered. She just hoped the "talent"—whom she assumed was Fevah—didn't recognize her from the night of the shooting.

The club was packed and she could see why the line was so long to get in. The dirty version of Bobby Shmurda's song was playing and even Naeema couldn't stop from pausing long enough to catch a few smooth-ass steps of the Shmoney Dance along with almost everybody else in the club.

The security guard glanced back and Naeema reluctantly followed behind him until they reached the area right in front of the stage. Everyone was busy partying but she knew as soon as the show started the crowd would swarm around the stage.

As the musicians took the stage, Naeema fought back a yawn and checked her phone to make sure the loud music hadn't kept her from hearing it ring. It was just after midnight and she was beat. She just wanted to figure out a way to get close to Fevah's cokehead ass.

The music started to play and Naeema turned from looking around the dimly lit club to eye the stage. Sure enough the surge of bodies brought the heat around her like a winter coat would in the desert. Everyone around her applauded and yelled for Fevah at the top of their lungs. *Damn, what they gon' do when she actually step onstage?*

Naeema felt someone palm her ass. Not a rub. Not accidental. She turned but not a soul did a damn thing to reveal they just felt her up.

"I'm the hottest chick in the game . . ."

The lights on the stage dimmed and the crowd went crazy. Fevah truly was on the rise to superstardom and the hometown crowd was acting blessed to be in her presence.

"I'm the hottest chick in the game . . ."

One by one a spotlight lit up her DJ on the turntables, her hype man E-Double, and then her two dancers on opposite sides of the small stage. Then after a drum roll that increased in intensity one final pink-tinted spotlight flashed on the middle of the stage revealing Fevah. She was dressed in a sequined crop top and matching pants. The tips of her thirty inches of jet-black exotic weave were bright fuchsia.

"Ladies," she called out, before holding her rhinestone-covered mic toward the audience.

The women all yelled back.

"Fellas," she called, repeating the mic move.

The fellas stomped, shouted, and barked like dogs.

Fevah laughed and flung back her head before the music played loudly and she was performing her first hit, "Fire."

Naeema, like damn near everyone else in the club, rapped along to the radio hit that pushed Fevah's first release to go platinum. Naeema couldn't deny it was still a banger but she wasn't that gone in the music that she didn't notice there were a dozen or more dudes standing just off-stage. She wondered if they were with Fevah or not. Security? Entourage? Groupies? Or just club workers?

It fucking mattered to her plan to get close to her.

"Now before we get started I want to give one of these four ladies an opportunity to get turnt up with me in the VIP," Fevah said, motioning offstage.

Moments later the same beefy security guard from earlier came to escort them through the crowd and up onstage. She eyed the three other women up there with her. Like her they were all hips, ass, and thighs with clothes to show it off. It was the reverse of Day-Day's line from *Friday After Next* because it definitely was their booty and not their beauty.

Fevah walked over to the turntables covered with a cloth with a sequined-covered caricature of her face to take a sip from a bottle of water.

"Best dancer wins. Y'all get to vote but the winner is up to Fevah. Let me hear some noise!" E-Double said.

"I'm the hottest chick in the game . . ."

Fevah started rapping the words to her newest song and the crowd joined in as Naeema and the three women started to dance. Naeema thought it was odd as hell that Fevah didn't pick men to show out for her and when she raised her hands high above her head as she slowly circled her hips she caught the rapper eyeing the way the hem of her dress rose on her thighs before she quickly looked away like she got caught cheating on a test.

Humph.

While the other women focused their attention on the calls and whistles of the dudes in the club, Naeema turned her back to the crowd and made sure to catch Fevah's eyes on and off as she pulled out some stunt that she knew sent the crowd and Fevah wild. Not even when one of the women dropped on the floor in a split, did a flip, and dropped in another split that sent the crowd crazy did Naeema care.

This chick ain't hunting up no dancer.

Naeema twerked her ass as she caught Fevah's eyes again from across the stage and sucked the tip of her finger before she bit her lip with a bold look down at Fevah's pussy pressed against the front of her sequined pants.

"I'm the-the-the hottest chick in the game . . ."

Naeema smiled and turned back toward the crowd when the rapper stumbled over her own verse. *Shook. Ha-haaaa.*

"Aight y'all. Let's get to the winner," E-Double said, walking up to the woman on the opposite end of the stage who did the splits. "Give it up for—"

"Ursula," she said into the mic when he held it in front of her mouth.

The crowd roared loudly.

"Invette," said the next.

"Georgia."

"Naeema," she said giving another look back at Fevah.

There was no doubt that the crowd was all about Ursula and those splits.

Humph.

E-Double spoke briefly with Fevah and then took three gift bags someone handed him to give one to Invette. Then Georgia. And then Ursula . . . who was shocked.

My gut never lies to me.

"Sometimes less is more, ladies," Fevah said before the

music came up and she began rapping her upcoming single, "Fuck Tears."

The ladies were released back into the crowd and Naeema followed the security guard backstage. Naeema frowned a little. "I thought I was headed to VIP?" she asked.

He shrugged and opened a door with a card with the words "Fevah's Dancers" taped on it. "Last minute she said bring you back here."

After he closed the door, Naeema walked around the room and opened one of the bottles of Fiji water. The loud thumping of the music could still be heard and she used the time to try the doors in the room while Fevah and her crew were making money onstage. One led into a bathroom. The other led into a bigger room where everything was plush as hell. Fevah's dressing room.

The door was yanked from her hand and Naeema tilted her head back to look up at a tall white dude with long blond hair pulled back in a ponytail. "I was looking for the bathroom," she lied, stepping back and pretending to be afraid of him.

He glared and pointed one long finger at the door on the opposite wall.

Naeema turned and headed back across the room. Before she made it four steps she heard the door close and the lock turn. *Shit.* He completely fucked up her plan to rummage through all Fevah's shit for any hints on who wanted the fiery rapper dead.

She didn't even bother going to the bathroom and instead tossed the water bottle in the trash and leaned her back against the wall, feeling the bass of the music beat against her body. She stayed there until the music stopped and the crowd's applause echoed.

Her heart pounded from the lack of control she felt as she waited. She was by no means a lesbian, but if dancing for a crowd and turning Fevah on meant she got at least a few minutes to pick the bitch for info then it was worth it to get to the bottom of who hurt Tank.

The door opened and Fevah came in, locking the door behind her. Two locked doors kicked Naeema's adrenaline into overdrive. "I love your new song," Naeema said, making her voice low and husky.

"Thanks," she said, sitting down on the edge of the black pleather sofa and looking over at Naeema.

"I was so sad to see you almost got hurt the other night," Naeema said.

"I don't want to talk about that," she said.

"Is it safe back here?" Naeema asked.

Fevah stood up and came over to stand in front of Naeema. They were the same height and their eyes were lined up. Their mouths lined up.

When Fevah's hands came up to ease between Naeema's warm thighs she pressed them close, trapping them. *Enough of the bullshit.*

Fevah smiled. That shit was knowing. Too knowing. "It's safer back here than it was the last time we saw each other," she said, easing her hand from between Naeema's thighs to lightly roll her nipple between her fingers.

"So you know who I am?" Naeema said, moving from being sandwiched between the wall and Fevah's closeness.

"It's going to take more than a wig and some cheap makeup to make me forget that body," Fevah said, raising her hands to twist her weave into a topknot. "And since y'all keep trying so hard to get at me I decided to get this shit over with so you and your crew can leave me the fuck alone."

Naeema gladly took off the synthetic wig and let her scalp breathe. "I apologize if we're coming at you but finding out who shot my husband benefits you too and I just want some leads."

"Just like I told the police already, I don't have any enemies. No crazy exes. Nobody I pissed off," Fevah said, sounding annoyed.

"No crazy stalkers?" Naeema asked, crossing her arms over her chest with the wig still balled up in her hand.

"No, nothing crazy," she said.

Naeema walked over to the table laden with snacks and drinks. She grabbed a notepad and pencil she saw there earlier and scribbled down the number to her new burner phone. "If you think of anything else please call me," she said, walking over to hand the rapper the paper.

"I can think of *lots* of reasons to call you," Fevah said, reaching out quickly to stroke one of Naeema's soft, exposed thighs.

"Just info. Thanks."

"You ever got your pussy ate by a woman?" Fevah asked, reaching out to touch her again.

Naeema stepped back out of her reach. *Damn, she pressing like a dude.*

"Once when I was high off of—shit, I don't even remember," she admitted.

Fevah licked her lips. "And?" she asked.

Naeema shrugged. "It wasn't for me."

Fevah laughed and then pulled a vial of coke from inside her top. "She wasn't for you. I am. Trust me."

"I'm good."

"Do you do security work? Maybe you can be my personal bodyguard," she said as she dipped her pinky in the cocaine and dabbed some on her gums. "That's a good cover. I don't like people in my business."

"You do realize that the shooting is all on the news and not once since I've been talking to you have you asked how my husband is doing? No flowers. No calls. No shows. Nothing," Naeema said. "Then you fire him like it's his fault."

"The news updates the story every fucking hour," Fevah said. "So you want the gig or not? You protect me and I'll satisfy you."

"In the words of Kelly Price: I'm booked," Naeema said just before she tugged her wig back on and left the room.

$\mathcal{N}$aeema was anxious to get back to Tank but she was glad she spent what little of the night was left in her own bed. After leaving Club Vixen she called the nurses' station to check on Tank and decided to make the thirty-minute drive back to Newark instead of wasting Tank's money on a hotel. Plus she was able to get some more clothes, check her mail, and make sure Sarge hadn't pulled a stunt that would leave them both on the street—even though she doubted his behind would mind.

Being back at the house reminded her of the robbery but she didn't have the energy to focus on that fool. Almost losing personal items was bad. Almost losing Tank was beyond tragic. No, the lucky motherfucker would get off for now. She had bigger fish to catch and fry.

Knock-knock.

Naeema walked over to the window overlooking the porch but found it empty. She looked back over her shoulder. Sarge. Ever since he put up the door he always knocked before he came into the living room. "Come in, Sarge," she said, stopping by the fireplace to get her gun. It was licensed and she had a concealed weapons permit. She needed her own piece and not Tank's just in case she shot a motherfucker—while protecting herself, of course.

Sarge pushed the door open. At first Naeema saw nothing but the tight, short silver and white twists of his hair looking like a dingy Q-tip. She slid the gun inside the molded case and zipped it closed before sliding it between the layers of clothes in her fake Gucci duffel.

He finally stepped into the living room eating a cold can of baked beans with a plastic spoon. "Just want to lay eyes on you," he said, smacking his lips.

"I'm good," she promised, cutting her eyes up at him as she sat down on the chair before the long mirror in front of the window to do her makeup. "I'll be even better if I could find my weed pipe."

His smacking slowed down as the rest of his body froze and he stared off at nothing.

Naeema was just about to put mascara on her lashes and she dropped her head side-eyeing him faking like a statue or like his ass was invisible or some shit. She pressed her elbow onto her knee and then rested her chin in her hand as she watched him. The smacking stopped and he shifted his eyes over to look at her but shot them back straight ahead as soon as he peeped her sitting there watching him like a hawk. *That pipe was gone. All the way gone.*

"Me and mine," she said, twirling her finger around her. "You and yours. Remember?"

He backed out of the living room slowly, his face and eyes still straight ahead.

Something really bad happened to my damn pipe.

Shaking her head, she finished putting on her makeup and double-checked her lineup and the white fitted jeans she wore with a white tee with huge hot-pink lips stretched across her bosom paired with white high-heeled gladiator sandals.

Knock-knock.

Naeema paused in putting on rhinestone hoops to cross the floor and look out the window. She was surprised—but not really—to see Mya standing there. She'd honestly forgotten all about the teenager the last couple of days. Clasping the earring her heels hit against the scuffed wood as she walked over to open the door.

Mya's hands were pressed to her stomach and her eyes filled with tears. "Ms. Naeema. Can you help—"

Naeema touched her hand to Mya's back and guided her into the living room. "What's wrong?"

"My stomach hurt," she said with a wince. "Feel like somebody stabbing me with a knife."

Naeema let her sit down on the edge of the bed. "Is your mother home?"

Mya shook her head in response before she cried out in pain, clutching at Naeema's hand, which lightly rested on her shoulder. "I don't want her or my stepfather to know," she said, the pain so intense she sounded out of breath as she spoke.

"I thought it was just you and your mom?" Naeema asked, walking over to her dresser to open the top drawer and pull out a bottle of Tylenol.

"My stepdad live with us too."

Naeema walked across the living room and pushed open the kitchen door. It hit against something. Hard. Coming around the door, she put her hand on her hip when Sarge stiffened and looked off at another spot. "I didn't mean to hit you . . . but that's what you get for eavesdropping."

She grabbed a bottle of water from the fridge, removed the top, and tossed it into the trashcan. "The fuck?" she said when she turned to find Sarge now facing the corner still stiff as a statue.

She waved her hand at him dismissively. "Whatever, Sarge," she said, her voice sounding beyond sick and tired of his shit.

"Take this. It's Tylenol." Naeema handed Mya the water and shook two pills out of the bottle. "Go home, call your mother, and then lie down until she comes to take you to the doctor."

Mya just held the bottle in one hand and the pills in the other as she shook her head. "I think I got something, Ms. Naeema," she admitted in a soft voice before she quickly glanced up at her and then back down at her hands.

"Oh," Naeema said. "Oh. Okay."

"I can't tell my mom. Please help me, Miss Naeema," Mya said, crying harder. "Please."

Naeema took a step back, her fingers lightly pressed to her mouth as she ran a dozen different scenarios through her mind. An STD would explain the scent of Mya's intimacy in the hall that day.

"I'll run away before I tell them," she added.

"You have to go the doctor, Mya, and I can't take you," Naeema exclaimed. "If you want I will be there when you tell your mom if that will help."

Naeema looked over her shoulder at the sound of a loud grunt from behind the kitchen door. She swung her head back when the girl cried out in pain.

Shit. She really needs to go to a doctor ASAP.

"Where is your mother?" Naeema asked. "Your stepfather?"

"They not home."

Naeema stepped up close to wipe away some of the sweat beaded on the teenager's forehead. *She needs help.*

Sarge stepped into the living room. "Right is right, Naeema," he said, his disapproval all in the lines creasing his face. "And wrong is wrong."

Naeema bore a child but she never got to be a mother. Not the struggle every day to make sure your child is fed, clothed, and educated. She passed that job to Miss JuJu. Still she knew the black and white of right from wrong.

And she also knew there were shades of gray.

"Let's go," she said to Mya as Sarge released another grunt.

She hurried across the room to grab Tank's keys and her white Gucci crossbody bag. She helped Mya to the door and with one last look at Sarge that showed she wasn't even sure she was making the right decision they left the house.

Naeema was relieved to finally get back to New York and be able to lay eyes on Tank. The steady beeping of the medical equipment flanking the head of his bed was the only sound. He was slightly elevated in bed and his linens were crisp and fresh. His chest rose and fell and if she knew no better she would just think he was sleeping.

She smiled as she walked close to his bed after she set the duffel she carried in front of the closet. "I'm back, Tank," she said, bending to press kisses to his brow. "I'm sorry I was gone so long."

She pulled the chair closer to the left side of the bed and took his hand in her right to stroke gently with her thumb as she used the remote to turn the TV on and lower the volume. As she mindlessly looked up at the television on the wall she tried not to let it sink in that his hand offered her nothing back. Nothing at all. Still . . . she held on.

Even when the nurses or aides came to check his vitals, the hospital cleaning staff came to lightly clean the room, or the doctor came to update her on his status Naeema never let his hand go.

Glancing at the nondescript clock on the wall she used her free hand to pull her cell from the back pocket of her jeans. She dialed the burner phone she purchased. It seemed to ring forever before it was answered.

"Mya, this Naeema. How you feeling?" she asked.

"Much better. I was sleeping," she said, her voice thick with it.

"It's time to take one of the big pills," Naeema said.

"Okay."

"Do it now," she stressed.

"Hold on."

The trip to the doctor had taken the entire morning, lies about being Mya's mother, and a third of the cash from Tank's wallet to pay for the visit and the medicines to cure her of both trich and a urinary tract infection.

"I took it."

"Is anyone home yet?" she asked.

"My stepdad . . . but I told him I had a stomach virus. I got the phone on vibrate."

Naeema grimaced with her guilt. Had she made the

right decision? Was she really a grown-ass woman helping a child keep secrets from her parents?

She could only pray that trusting her gut didn't get her truly fucked up one day.

"Okay, I'll call you back when it's time to take the other pill," she said.

"Okay . . . and thanks, Miss Naeema," Mya said. "And I'll keep my promise. No more sex."

Naeema didn't know if she believed that.

After ending the call she unlatched the crossbody to put her phone inside. A loop of Tank's cell phone charger sprang out. *I almost forgot about that.*

After dropping Mya back home, Naeema had grabbed her duffel from her house—before Sarge could emerge from downstairs with any more disapproving grunts— and went by Tank's to grab his phone charger. She looked around the brightly lit room. The only outlet she saw was above the sink.

Naeema released Tank's hand.

Curiosity was killing the cat.

She plugged the phone up and leaned back against the sink as she waited for it to get enough of a charge to turn on. As soon as the screen lit up she got busy trying to figure out his passcode. She hated that he made it so hard to crack. She even knew the password for his e-mail and online banking accounts—and when she was feeling nosy she logged on and peeped his balances.

Aggravated, she tapped her thumb against the zero four times.

The home screen and all its icons appeared.

"You have got to be kidding me, Tank," she said with a shake of her head but then it made perfect sense. Tank assumed anyone dumb enough to fuck with his phone wouldn't be smart enough to guess a password so simple.

Biting her bottom lip she looked over at him. Truth be told they were honest with each other—probably too honest—and if she had ever simply asked him for the passcode he would have given it to her. And now that she had unlocked it she felt like the worst kind of lame for behaving like the shooting was her opportunity to snoop—when she didn't even have to. They always kept it "one hundred" with each other.

Bzzzzzz.

She looked down at the screen as a text popped up.

I KNOW YOU SAID YOU WERE BACK WITH WIFEY
SO WE HAD TO CHILL BUT I JUST WANTED TO LET
YOU KNOW I'M PRAYING FOR YOU.

"Not wifey. His *wife*, bitch," Naeema muttered.

In the hood those legal papers made the difference.

So Tank put his sidelines and part-times on alert that his number one was back.

He never was the type to play games. He offered up nothing but the truth and it was always up to that person to swallow it or spit it out. He truly was a real stand-up guy. He'd been that way since day fucking one . . .

Naeema climbed from the passenger seat of the turquoise Geo Tracker and then held it forward to let her friend Roz climb from the back as Sasha hopped out of the driver's seat. She paused at the sound of music already filling the late-night air from inside Club Infinity. "They playing our jam," she said, smoothing her hands over her wide hips in the black off-the-shoulder latex dress she wore with patent leather booties.

Cassie's "Me & U" already sounded good as fuck and Naeema partied right there in the parking lot. The blunt they smoked and the Ecstasy they popped had her feeling nice.

"I know them other guys, they been talking 'bout the way I do what I do," she sang along with the music, raising her hands to shake her shoulder-length curly weave.

"Let's get in the club, bitch," Roz said, grabbing Naeema's arm and pulling her behind her.

Naeema and her friends crossed the crowded lot. She paused when she spotted two heads outlined through the rear window of a Honda Accord suddenly become one. She walked up to the car and looked down through the driver's-side window at some chick giving the dude in the driver's seat mad head. She was nasty with it. Spit. Slobs. Deep throats. Licks. All kind of tricks.

She had old boy grimacing and gritting his teeth and grabbing the back of her head.

"Dayummmm," Naeema said, knocking on the glass as she laughed her ass off. "You a bad bitch."

The headmaster looked up with spit all around her mouth and chin.

Naeema gave her a thumbs-up.

"Man, fuck her," the dude said, grabbing the chick's head and guiding her mouth back around his dick.

And she went back at it.

Naeema laughed and clapped as she let them be. She

continued to the open gate of the fence surrounding the parking lot. Sasha and Roz were just ahead getting in the long line leading into the club. Club Infinity stayed packed.

Now Naeema could hear Yung Joc's "It's Goin' Down." She partied her way up the street and in line with her friends. "I want some Henny," she said.

"I want a hard dick to ride," Roz said in her leggings, tank, and thigh-high boots.

"Me too, bitch," Sasha said, dropping it low to the ground and winding it back.

Naeema's co-sign never made it to her lips as they moved up in line and her eyes fell on a tall broad-shouldered dude standing by the entrance with a bright yellow T-shirt with SECURITY written across his chest in black. He was talking and laughing with someone but Naeema's eyes remained locked on him.

Damn he fine. Sexy.

Everything about him. His looks. His build.

Shit.

Step-by-step they moved closer to the door. To him. She half-listened to her friends talking about this and that, but her eyes—her attention—rarely strayed from him. She felt excitement as she got nearer to the door. To him.

What the fuck?

Naeema had seen and had plenty of men in her twenty-some odd years. Fine motherfucking ones. She was used to men.

Oh shit.

Her heart pounded as he looked down the length of the

line and then did a double take when his eyes fell on her.
Stayed on her. Only her. He would look away if someone
said something to him but always his eyes came back to her.
And found her eyes already on him.

Must be the weed and the X.

Right?

"How you doin' tonight?" he asked when she stood be-
fore him, his eyes taking her in from head to toe.

"Better now," Naeema said, offering him a smile as she
looked up at him with her heartbeat. "You?"

"Naeema, let's go," Roz said, tugging at her hand.

She yanked it away.

His eyes dipped to take in the move. "I'm damn good,
right now," he said.

"Man, fuck it. I'm going in," Sasha said.

"Naeema," Roz called.

Mr. Sexy Security moved the metal barricade and
Naeema didn't hesitate to move through the opening to
stand at his side.

"So you're Naeema?" he said.

She nodded. "Good thing I don't have any warrants the
way they yelled out my name."

They shared a look before they both looked away like
third graders with a crush.

The conversations of the last few people entering the
club filled the air along with "Shoulder Lean" by Young Dro
blaring through the open door.

"So are you content, Naeema?" he asked, as the other
security entered the club and he started stacking the metal
barriers.

"Content?" she asked, not sure what he meant.

"You know what I mean," he said with a smile. "Happy. At peace and all that good shit."

"Why?" she said, avoiding the question.

"Your name . . . it means to be content."

The fuck?

"I never knew that," she admitted, looking at him.

"Me either," he said, showing her the phone in his hand. "I looked it up."

He winked at her.

"Still, you taught me something about myself I ain't even know."

"That's what's up," he said.

"And who are you?"

"Call me Tank."

"Tank? Is that your real—"

"Nah."

"You got a girl, Tank?" she asked, feeling nervous as shit when he finished loading the barricades inside the club and came to stand back beside her.

"Nah, but do I have friends," he admitted.

"Friends?" she scoffed.

He nodded as he reached over to wipe at something on her cheek. "Friends. Not a lot but a few. And when I meet the young lady that makes me want to lock it down she will know I never lied to her and the friends are gone because she's my only lady. The truth is always better than a lie. Right?"

Naeema looked up at him. "Right," she agreed skeptically because she had never met a man like him . . .

Naeema smiled at the memory. She had stayed outside

with his sexy ass all night and had no clue or care what went on in the club that night. His conversation had been too good. His sex appeal too good. His looks too good.

That night she skipped out on her girls and she went home with Tank. For the first time in her life she spent all night with a man and didn't fuck. They talked. All night. About nothing and everything.

But that next night . . .

Naeema tilted her head back and fanned her neck as it suddenly got warm.

She looked back down at the message and fought the urge to text or even call the chick back as she powered down the phone, left it on the counter, and walked back over to Tank. She took his hand in hers again and wished like crazy that she hadn't let it all go without a second thought.

She knew she was fucked up. Her way of thinking. Doing. Being. Just fucked.

And he stuck around waiting on her to get her shit together.

She bent and pressed her lips near his cheek wishing he smelled more like himself than the antiseptic smell of the hospital. "I know if you were able you woulda got to the bottom of this shooting but I promise you I'm doing my best . . . it's just my best ain't nothing without you. Bonnie ain't shit without Clyde," she whispered, her throat tightening. "And even though I know you would not want me out there hunting down the dirty motherfucker that did this shit, you would still help me figure it all out."

Another kiss near his mouth.

"Come back to me, Tank, 'cause baby you all I got in this world," she admitted, reaching down to take his hand in hers. "I know I act like I don't need you but I do. Just like I know you need me.

"I ain't got no mother. No father. No son. No grandparents. Nobody. If you leave me too I don't know what the fuck I'll do. I swear to God," she admitted, unable to stop the tears.

Her pain and her fears were in every damn drop.

"It just ain't the same," Naeema muttered, looking down at the blunt she was blazing inside the Tahoe. To her it was a waste of good medicinal weed to pack it in a fucking cigar wrapper.

Still, she blazed. Shoes off, one leg bent with her foot pressed on the driver's seat, SiriusXM's The Heat station playing, the SUV parked in the right direction for her to see the entrance in and exit out of the parking lot of the hospital, but far back enough to handle her shit if the cops rolled up.

Naeema hit the blunt again and leaned her head back against the rest with her eyes closed as she held it in her lungs before opening her mouth to release it. It was the first time she felt relaxed in days. For just a few minutes she was going to allow herself to feel nothing. No fears, tears, sadness, or anger. *I don't want to feel a damn thing but high.*

She took two more strong tokes before she brushed the edge of the blunt against the side of the ashtray and then lightly tapped it to put out the embers. "Whoo!" she said, raising her head.

She felt like she could barely open her eyes. *Fuck it. Why bother?*

She closed her eyes and leaned her head against the

driver's-side window with a little smile. She hadn't smoked since the night of the shooting. She was feeling it.

"I said we load it, cock it, aim and shoot . . ."

Naeema reached out with her finger to tap the button on the steering wheel to raise the volume. There was a song playing that had this 1970s, "listen to it while you shoot up heroin" vibe. She peered over at the digital screen. "'Bulletproof.' Raheem DeVaughn featuring Ludacris," she read.

She never heard it before. Didn't know if it was old or new but she liked that the flow of it was mellow as shit and that's what she needed. Something laid-back.

"I said we load it, cock it, aim and shoot . . ."

She reached into the armrest and pulled out both Tank's Glock and her 9mm. "Load it, cock it, aim, and shoot," she said, pointing the barrel of both guns toward the windshield.

POW! POW! POW! POW!

She winced as the memory of Tank's shooting came back to her with the same fiery flash of a bullet being shot from a gun.

"Load it. Cock it. Aim. Shoot," she said, looking down at the guns in her hands.

POW!

"And shoot," Naeema said softly as she closed her eyes.

POW!

"And shoot."

POW!

"And shoot."

POW!

"Fuck," she exclaimed, feeling her high fade in the truth of what she missed that night.

One shot at Fevah that missed? An accident.

Three additional shots long after the passenger door closed under the weight of Tank's body? Shots that all landed in Tank. Intentional. Deadly intentional.

Naeema felt a chill spread over her body.

Tank was the target of the gunman from the jump.

*N*aeema was breathing hard when she stepped off the elevator and forced herself to just quick-walk down the hall to Tank's hospital room.

"Somebody done blazed 'round this mofo," she heard someone in the waiting room say when she passed.

She made a quick note to change clothes just as she pushed the door open. She paused to find a woman sitting by Tank's bedside looking comfortable. Naeema's eyes squinted when she recognized Tina, the full-figured, dark-skinned cutie that she ran up on at Tank's house last year. The one she slapped down to the floor for her smart mouth. True, she and Tank had not been together at the time but still . . . respect is always given when demanded.

And Naeema demanded it at all times.

"Listen, I was just coming by to check on him because the news was not giving out any more updates," Tina said, holding up her hands as she rose to her feet.

Naeema walked farther into the room but waved her hand back toward the door. "Have a nice one," she said, brushing past the woman to reclaim her spot by his side.

Naeema looked down at his face and her heart truly broke to think someone wanted him dead. The game just completely fucking changed. "Who tried to kill you?" she whispered down to him.

"Kill him?"

Naeema looked up and her eyes glassed over with anger. "Why are you still here?" she snapped.

Tina shook her head and turned up her lips. "There's no need for all that. My fiancé is downstairs waiting on me. I just came to check on a friend," she said.

"Well, your fiancé's a lame to drive you to check on another dude you used to fuck," Naeema snapped. "Now raise up outta here before you need a room of your own. Please believe that was your final warning."

This time she watched the woman until the door closed behind her.

Naeema dropped down into the chair beside Tank's bed. *What do I do next?*

Calling the police was never her first option. The way they fucked over the investigation of Brandon's murder was a prime example. Plus, if she planned to annihilate the shooter then clueing the police in that Tank was the true target was a giveaway she couldn't risk. *Fuck that.*

Call in the team to strategize? *No one would know better than them if Tank had enemies that would strike out at him with murder in mind.*

She eyed Tank lying there, probably the only time in his life he had been helpless. *And while I'm chasing down his shooter who would be here to make sure they didn't finish the job as he lay here unconscious?*

Naeema twisted her son's ring on her finger as she tried her best to think straight through the haze of the weed. *I need help.*

She pulled out her phone and dialed Sarge.

"Yuh."

"Sarge, I need you. Me and Tank we need you," she said, rising to walk over to the window and look out at the traffic.

"What?"

She took a breath and looked up at the ceiling as she lightly kicked the wall with the toe of her shoe. "Tank was the target. I need to look into the who, what, when, where, and why. I can't leave him here alone, Sarge," she said emphatically.

"Call the police."

"No."

"Naeema—"

She shook her head. "Sarge, I am sending a car service to the house to pick you up. Get in the car. I need you to sit in this room with Tank while I handle this shit, Sarge. Do you hear me?" she said, her emotions tightening her throat.

Sarge didn't say shit but Naeema could hear him breathing into the mouthpiece.

"Get in the car. Let it bring you to New York. Come and sit with Tank for me."

"No," he said, his voice gruff, almost like a dog's bark.

"Yes," she stressed.

"Naeema—"

"I have never asked you for anything, Sarge. Not one thing," she said, her voice almost a hiss.

"You ask too much . . . and you know it."

She did. Sarge rarely left the house and then he only ventured onto the porch or into the backyard. She knew she asked a lot of him but it was for Tank and for him she would ask for even more if need be.

She opened her mouth but then closed it, forcing herself to relax. To release. "I need you, Sarge," she said, her voice barely above a whisper and every emotion that swirled inside her was heavy in the words.

She didn't like to ask for help or to plead. She had just given a lot. And he knew that.

Beep.

He ended the call.

Naeema used her phone to look up a car service in Newark and called them. *Sarge better not let me down.*

She grabbed her duffel and quickly pulled out a change of clothes before going in the bathroom to quickly shower. She had just turned off the water when she heard talking outside the door. Quickly wrapping the towel she brought from home around her, Naeema opened the door.

Both Grip and Linx looked over at the door and then looked away out of respect. She stepped back, feeling her anxiety ease. "I'll be right out," she said, knowing the sight of her wet and draped in a towel probably threw them off.

She dried off and pulled on a thong and sports bra before dressing in black leggings and a black T-shirt with JUICY written across it in shiny gold letters. She balled up the clothes she had worn in the empty bag she brought just for that and left the bathroom. "Sorry about that, fellas. I was worried who was out here with him," she said, accepting the seat Grip vacated to bend down and pull on the black wedge sneakers she carried in her hand.

"No problem," both men said.

"Listen, I'm actually glad y'all are here," she said, sitting back up and looking at each of them. "I need you guys to be straight up with me and understand that I need the truth and nothing but."

"You know we will," Grip said, looking down at her from his tall height.

"And whatever we discuss does not leave this room," she added.

The look in their eyes became serious as they nodded their agreement.

"Does Tank have any enemies that you know of?" Naeema asked, reaching over to take his hand in hers. She was thankful for its warmth.

"Naeema, what's going on?" Grip asked after sharing a brief look with Linx.

She looked to Tank wishing he could truly provide some guidance. "I think Tank was the target that night. Not Fevah," she said, her eyes still on him.

"Are you sure?" Linx asked.

She bent her head down to touch it to his hand. "No, but it's something we need to look into," she said.

"I know he testified against Murk last month."

Naeema stiffened as she turned her head to look back at Grip. "What?" she asked in disbelief.

"He saw some shit. This dude is crazy dangerous. It had to be done, Naeema," Grip added.

"Lot of good it did with Grip still on the streets," she said, her voice tight.

Her hand tightened on Tank's. If there was one thing they disagreed on it was the police and the court system. Tank tried to work within their guidelines, then hoped and wished shit turned out right. Naeema didn't fuck with it at all.

Why would he draw fire like that?

Murk was a notorious drug dealer known for heartlessly taking out his competition or anyone who betrayed him. No hit man. No guards. He put the work in himself. He had zero fucks to give.

"And then there's Willie," Linx added.

Naeema shifted her eyes to the bald white man that had more swagger than some brothas. "Willie who? Not Willie Parker," she said, referring to Tank's childhood best friend. *Them two are brothers from two different mothers.*

Or they used to be.

It was true they had fell out a few years back but murder? Nah.

"He's been hounding Tank pretty hard lately about the business being half his," Linx said, his face serious.

Naeema leaned back in her chair and covered her face with her hand. It was too much. In less than five minutes she went from no suspects to two. *The fuck?*

"I need time to think," she said. "Uhm, don't make a move until I call you. Let me sit on all this for a second. Please."

Linx and Grip both moved toward the door.

"No police," she added, dead-ass serious as she looked back at Tank's profile.

She fell quiet after they left, her thoughts scattered but her eyes focused. She didn't even realize how much time had passed until the door opened and she looked over at Sarge standing there. She was glad to see the oddball vet in her life, scroungy hair, worn fatigues, and all. She smiled at him and he waved his hand at her dismissively as he shuffled into the room with a walk only Fred Sanford could replicate.

Naeema was thankful for his cranky ass.

"I'm here," he said gruffly, walking over to stand on the opposite side of the bed to look down at Tank.

"Keep your friends close and your enemies closer," Sarge said. "And sometimes they're one and the same."

Naeema looked pensive.

"Ain't right," he said.

"It's wrong. It's real wrong, Sarge," she said, feeling a coldness flow through her veins that should make a smart foe fearful.

He cast his gray eyes on her. "Two wrongs ain't right though."

Naeema didn't bother to argue the point. She thought her days of pseudo-vigilante justice were done with the bodies she took down in pursuit of her son's killer.

She'd thought wrong.

"You want me to get you something to eat until I get back, Sarge?" she asked as she rose to her feet.

He shook his head and came around the bed to claim the lone chair she vacated. "I brought my own," he said, patting the bulky pockets of his fatigue pants.

She bet good money his pockets were stuffed with those tiny cans of Vienna sausages and baked beans. *Something to blow his ass up. Thank God Tank's unconscious because the farts might send him back under.*

"Be careful, Wonder Woman," he said dryly.

Naeema reached the door and looked back at him. "You mean Foxy Brown, sugar?" she said, playfully imitating the 1970s accent of the character played by Pam Grier.

"You can't keep asking God for forgiveness for the same thing," he called to her.

Sarge knew she had killed in the name of avenging her son.

"Well, it's a good thing I ain't did nothing to need forgiving yet."

With that she left the hospital room.

"Excuse me," Naeema said, stopping at the nurses' station.

A harassed-looking woman with more cheeks than chin turned to eye her. "Yes?" she asked, her tone annoyed and annoying.

For Tank, Naeema. Don't flip. Swallow this one for Tank.

"Uhhm, I just wanted to ask that my husband not have any visitors except my grandfather," she said, using her proper voice and a pleasant smile.

"That's the job of security downstairs. Not mine," she added, turning her back on Naeema.

One, motherfucking two, damned three, shitting four, fucked-up five, slap a hoe six—

"Anything else?"

Naeema opened her eyes and eyed the nurse, letting her ten count to not whip ass end. She glanced down at the woman's name tag pinned to her scrubs. It was turned backward. "You should play the lottery because this is the luckiest day of your life," Naeema said, before lightly slapping the desk and walking away to the elevator.

She had more important shit on her to-do list than to ruin a nurse's day.

Pressing the button to summon the elevator she pulled Tank's cell phone from her back pocket unlocking it and scrolling through his contacts. The doors opened and Naeema looked up to see a Latino brother with tattoos covering his entire neck.

Their eyes met briefly.

Naeema stepped into the elevator and turned, her eyes on his back as he disappeared down the hall. *What if he's a hired goon? What if he's going to hurt Tank right now?*

The doors moved toward each other but Naeema jerked her arms between them and pushed out before running down the hall and pushing the door to Tank's room open as she exhaled in short bursts.

POW! POW! POW! POW!

Sarge looked confused by her reappearance and he raised his arm to turn down the volume on whatever sitcom he was watching on television. "What's wrong, Naeema?" he asked.

She shook her head.

"Is everything okay, Mrs. Cole?"

She turned to find two of the nurses standing at the door. They pushed past her to enter and check on Tank.

"I'm sorry. I just I heard his alarms on the machines," she lied. "My fault."

Sarge squinted as he studied her while the nurses checked Tank.

Naeema turned and walked back down the hall aware of the curious eyes on her. *Get your shit together, Naeema.*

She was thankful to get in the elevator alone and ride down in silence.

Keep your friends close and your enemies closer. And sometimes they're one and the same.

The realest shit ever.

Sarge was an oddball nut who every so often in the midst of one liners and sarcasm would drop knowledge. The moments were rare but always insightful.

As she left the hospital and made her way to the adjacent parking lot, Naeema programmed the address she took from Tank's contacts into the GPS on her phone. She had the directions she wanted in less than a minute.

Behind the wheel of the Tahoe she made her way from NYC to Jersey.

"Your destination is on the right."

She eyed the modest brick home as she drove past it slowly. The driveway and the spot on the street in front of it were empty. It was just nearing late afternoon and the homeowners on the tree-lined block were mostly still at work. Naeema took advantage of this and parked the Tahoe around the corner. After tugging on the Chinese bob wig to cover up her Caesar cut and grabbing her key ring along with Tank's, Naeema walked the distance to the house all easy-breezy like she was a homeowner in the neighborhood just enjoying a friendly stroll.

She walked up to the house and bent to play with the strings on her sneakers to covertly look around and make sure no one was eyeing her from a distance.

I should have waited 'til dark.

She turned and walked up the drive to the side entrance. She was thankful for the tall gate between the homes and the trees partially blocking her from anyone's view from the street. Saying a silent prayer there was no alarm, she used the small metal hammer on her key ring to crack and then break the glass.

She waited before she entered, turning to head back

down the drive and farther down the street before she reached the corner and turned to walk back. *No one home. No police sirens. No inquiring neighbors.*

Naeema quickly turned back up the drive like she lived there as she pulled on a pair of rubber gloves and reached her hand in carefully to unlock the door. She entered via the kitchen and looked around as she moved through the opening to what turned out to be a long hall. Room by room, Naeema searched the house for any hint of betrayal against Tank. She found none and made her way to the living room to sit in the leather recliner, cross her legs, and wait.

The sun faded and the room got dark as hell. Naeema eyed the lights of passing cars flashing against the wall. She hit her stiletto nails against each other. *Click-click-click.*

Naeema appeared to have the patience of Job when instead her anger and need for revenge was slowly being stoked by impatience.

Click-click-click.

The sound of a key turning in the lock caused Naeema to shift her eyes toward the front door. Moments later it opened and the living room was flooded with light as Yani hit the switch and stepped inside his home.

He froze at the sight of her sitting there.

"Come on in, Yani," she said, beckoning him with a quick double bend of her index and middle fingers.

"What's going on here, Naeema?" he asked.

"You tell me," she said.

He stepped into the living room and shut the door. He pulled an office chair from a small hutch in the corner. "How's Tank?" he asked.

"Why did you try to kill him?" she asked.

Yani's ass was about to press into the seat but he paused and lifted his head to look over at her. "Do what?" he exclaimed.

Naeema stood up and sharply extended her foot to his chest to push him down into the seat. It rolled back and hit a curio cabinet causing it to rock slightly as she pressed her foot between his open legs. Yani grabbed her ankle and her calf.

Naeema flicked her wrist to undo the latch on the small but very sharp switchblade on her key ring. "You'd be surprised how deep I can plunge this motherfucker through your skull," she warned, her eyes hard and brimming with her intent.

He held up his hands. "Out of respect for Tank, Naeema, but this is disrespectful."

"Where were you when the shots were fired?" she asked.

"You think someone was gunning for Tank?" he asked.

"Shut the fuck up," she snapped. "Where were you?"

"The crowd went crazy and by the time I was near him you were already there," he said, looking up at her. "I didn't shoot a gun."

"No, but maybe you made sure he was in the line of fire and you wasn't," she said, pushing her foot against his balls. "That's what the fuck it looked like to me."

"Then look again," he said.

"Keep your friends close and your enemies closer. And sometimes they're one and the same," she said, bringing the knife up to lightly stroke his cheek with it.

His eyes darted to the right to eye the knife. The blade's

sharpness seemed to glisten. "Yo chill, Naeema," he said, bringing his hand up to tightly grip her wrist.

She drew her foot back and thrust it forward as she bit her bottom lip in a mock growl.

He hissed at the pain and buckled over.

Naeema withdrew her foot and stepped back. "If I find out you had anything to do with this—"

"I didn't," he snapped, pressing his hand against his injured nuts.

Naeema eyed him.

"You talk about friends and fucking enemies and I haven't talked to nobody from the team since the night of the shooting. Nobody is answering my calls. But they my boys, right?" he asked. "All of a sudden I'm out of a job. That's where I been all day fucking filling out applications and shit.

"Now you in my fucking house thugging out on me like I really couldn't take you if I wanted to," Yani said, rising to his feet.

Naeema squared up.

Yani looked her up and down and laughed as he stayed with his hands pressed to his knees. "I got a jacket—a police record—and I caught hell finding a job in the past because of it," he said, his voice less strained as he rose to his full height. "Tank gave me a job and trained me himself. Helped me to make money so I wouldn't be desperate enough to push dope again. I was able to rent this house and do for my kids. You can believe what the fuck you want but I didn't have shit to do with this shooting, Naeema, and if you try to come at me I will stop you."

She arched a brow before she dropped low quick as shit and kicked the back of his leg to send him down to the floor. She retracted the knife. "I'm not done with this or you," she said. "And remember that Tank trained you but he trained me, too. Don't let my femininity get you fucked up because you think dick trumps pussy every time."

She turned and stepped over him to reach the front door. "Sorry about your side door," she said over her shoulder before she left.

As she made her way down the steps and then down the street she quickly removed her gloves and tucked them in the rim of her leggings. She had hoped everything would begin and end with Yani but she wasn't confident enough in his guilt. *I can't call it. I just can't call it.*

"I love you, Daddy!"

Naeema turned toward the direction of a child's laughter. A man and his daughter were in their backyard jumping on a trampoline. Their faces were both bright with happy times. And love.

She smiled as the little girl's laughter filled the air. *Not a care in the world.*

Those days were long gone for Naeema.

Pushing away her regrets she continued down the street and reached the Tahoe, climbing into the driver's seat. As she turned the corner and drove by the house with the laughing little girl she forced herself not to turn her head and take another glimpse at a past she wished she had been able to enjoy.

She looked at Yani's house though and saw him standing on the small stoop outside the side entrance looking at the damage she left behind. He wouldn't call the police. Men like Yani never did. His mistrust of the police was just as strong as hers.

She put him and the chance of his guilt aside for now.

One down. Two to go.

$\mathscr{I}$t was mid-August and the summer heat was blazing like twenty hells combined but Naeema kept on the short black jacket she wore as she walked inside Lucky Bail Bonds. The little storefront left a lot to be desired. The brown carpet was stained, matted, and filled the entire office with the smell of mildew. Posters of wanted criminals and adverts for legal services were tacked to the fake wood paneling that made it feel like a cave. There was only a desk with two chairs in the center of the room with a dented tan metal file cabinet in the corner and a table against the wall holding a small fridge and microwave.

Willie Parker sat in one of the chairs. He eyed her from behind the veil of smoke filtering up from one of the Swisher Sweets he smoked. Or at least she assumed he did because he had on his ever-present shades. She'd bet good money they were authentic designer brand. Just like his clothes. Willie was a label whore. Always was and always would be. She also knew he still had the cardboard box with a lid that the Swishers came in. She wouldn't doubt his money, his keys, and probably even his piece was in it.

"Stop right there, Naeema," he said, opening the top drawer of the metal desk to pull out something.

A motherfucking Swisher Sweets box.

Naeema smiled and shook her head. Her smile faded when he flipped it open and pulled out a gun that he sat atop the files cluttering his desk. Then he reached under the desk.

Bzzzzzzzzzzzzzzzzz. Clank.

He'd locked the door.

"I ain't trusting you worth a fuck," he said.

Naeema felt a jolt of apprehension but she hid it well as she motioned for approval to sit in the seat by his desk. At his nod she moved closer but before she sat she opened the jacket she wore and removed her 9mm from its holster. She sat it on the desk with the barrel pointed at him before taking the seat. "If your Rick Ross–looking ass pulled up the rug in this rank motherfucker it *might* smell better," she said, crossing her legs in the torn boyfriend jeans she wore cuffed with a pair of bright fuchsia heels with silver tips and heels that matched the words FU FOREVER across her T-shirt.

He didn't say shit as he sat forward to press his elbows into the top of the desk and continue to look at her from behind his aviator shades.

"Haven't you seen on the news that Tank is in the hospital?" she began, reaching up to trace the details of the gun with the pointed tip of her brightly covered nail.

Willie lay his hand down on his gun.

They both tensed.

Then Naeema smiled. "Tank's doing a little better—still unconscious—but better . . . *if* you give a fuck," she said.

"I don't," he admitted.

Naeema fought not to grip her gun and blow a hole in his gut. Neither his gun nor his locked door could stop that. "But I do."

Willie turned his lips downward as she nodded slowly. "And you should," he said with a one-shoulder shrug. "He didn't shit you out of nothing. My ass still sore from the way he fucked me over."

Even with the shades Naeema could see the anger in his face and hear it in his voice. "Half of a part-time business that wasn't shit before Tank took over is worth him dying, motherfucker?" she asked, her anger rising to his own. She was tired of playing checkers with his ass.

Willie reached up and took off his shades. There were dark marks on his cheeks from his constant wear of the accessories. *Him and Rick Ross's ass need to stop that shit.*

"Yo, you trying to say Fevah wasn't the bull's-eye, yo," he said.

It was Naeema's turn to remain close-mouthed. "I heard you been coming for Tank pretty hard out there about some old shit. Some old beef. It's just funny that right around the time you start to get in your fucking feelings and shit Tank got shot. That's what I'm saying."

Willie's eyes darted down to Naeema's gun before jerking back up to her face.

She thought he forgot his shades weren't on to shield that move. Her suspicion was confirmed when he slid them on and leaned back in his seat. "First off, you speakin' out of turn, Naeema, but that's nothing new," he expressed sarcastically. "Tank didn't make shit successful. I was right there with him—"

"Then why ain't *this* motherfucker thriving?" Naeema asked, looking around at his office with a smirk meant to make him feel small. "This all you, right?"

BAM-BAM-BAM.

They both looked toward the door. All Naeema could see was the top of a head and a fist but she knew it was Big Rita, Willie's boo thang. And that was the best title Naeema could think to give her.

She smiled as he swore under his breath and tapped under the desk.

Bzzzzzzzzzzzzzzzzz. Clank.

Big Rita was tall—two inches shy of six feet—and high yellow with shoulder-length hair dyed plum and an ass Willie could literally ride. Most would think she had a million ass shots or Brazilian butt lifts but she was born and bred with that ass way before bootleg versions of these procedures hit the hood and gave women the asses and hips God didn't. Big Rita's name was the most truth ever told about a woman's ass.

And like Willie she loved good shit—when it came to clothes and accessories.

"Why y'all up in here with the door locked?" she asked, giving Naeema a nasty stare when she walked past her to bend over and beckon Willie with one long fingernail.

"Ask your man," Naeema said, frowning in distaste as they kissed. Tongue sucks, licks, moans, and all. She looked away.

Back when Tank and Willie were tight she and Big Rita had done the phony friends thing but once they fell out they didn't even pretend to want to hang together anymore. "How you been, Rita?" she asked, hoping to end the show they were giving.

Big Rita sucked the whole of Willie's mouth into hers before she stood back tall and looked down at Naeema as she towered over her. "I been aight. How Tank?" she asked, and then put her hand up in Willie's direction like she knew he was about to get at her for even asking or giving a fuck.

"Better," Naeema said, her eyes shifting back and forth between them trying to figure shit out; lining up people on either side of her list of innocent or guilty.

"So what's this all about?" Big Rita asked, waving a thick finger at the guns on the table.

"She think I had something to do with Tank getting dumped on," Willie said.

Big Rita gave her a look like *Bitch, please* as she waved her hand. "It's not that serious, Naeema," she said, turning to walk over to the table and pull a bottle of juice from the fridge.

"I hope not," Naeema said.

Big Rita and Willie shared a look.

"Where were you the night of the shooting?" Naeema asked him.

"Oh you the police now?" he asked. "Just like old boy? Testifying against Mark was a bad idea. Maybe you need to take your fake detective work somewhere else."

"Co-sign!" Big Rita added with attitude before taking a deep sip of her juice and then smacking her tongue afterward.

Naeema's chest was hot with anger as she reached for her gun.

Willie reached for his as well.

"Let's be clear. The police ain't got shit to do with this because when I find out who is behind this shit 911 won't save dat ass," she said, holding her gun pointed at the dirty carpet as she backed toward the door.

"Well, what in the hell is Naeema on?" Big Rita asked, her face confused.

Willie's was not. He was a little more privy to the fact that she was willing and able to fuck shit up.

She reached behind her and opened the door keeping her back to the street as she finally holstered her gun.

"You be safe out there, Naeema," Willie said, lightly tapping the barrel of his gun against the edge of the desk.

"Same to you," she said before turning and leaving.

The heat swarmed her and Naeema rushed up the cracked sidewalk to climb onto the motorcycle parked between two cars on the corner in front of a store. The dudes posted up on the side of the building eyed her as she pulled on her pink helmet.

"Damn, she strapped yo," one of them said.

Nobody moved or fled. She wondered if she were a dude would they be that relaxed. She lowered her arms and eyed them before she flipped the pink visor down as she drove off with a sweet rumble of her bike's motor. It felt good to be back on a motorcycle even if the drive from Willie's office to her house on Eastern Parkway took less than five minutes. She felt regret to turn onto her drive and ease past Tank's Tahoe to enter her small garage that had seen better days forty years ago.

She had just parked the bike and locked the garage when her cell phone vibrated against her ass in her back pocket. She checked it. *Mook.*

"Holla at'ya girl," she said, pressing the phone to her ear.

"Got sum'n for you."

"Come thru, come thru," she said.

"Done."

Naeema walked up the broken brick path to the back door and unlocked it before entering the house. When she arrived from NYC that morning the heat that built up since her last visit to the house was stifling. She turned on the AC in the living room but the kitchen was just ridiculously hot for no reason. Frowning up at the smell of rotten trash she walked over to the can. A mouse jumped up out of the middle of the bag, landed on the counter, and scurried down the crack between the counter and the stove. "Fuck," Naeema swore with a grimace, fighting the urge to pull the stove away from the wall and fire off a round at the bootleg Mickey Mouse.

She shivered like she had the heebie-jeebies as she tied the bag and then carried it out the back door and then around the side to the large metal cans they pulled to the street every Monday and Thursday for trash collection. Back in the house she rushed through the kitchen to the coolness that had finally built up in the living room.

Naeema quickly pulled off her jacket and holster before putting the gun under her pillow as she sat down on the edge of the bed. She kicked off her heels and propped her bare feet against the rail as she looked down at the flyer for Gentlemen Only. It was Davon "Murk" Grant's high-end gentlemen's club where he ran his underground operations in dope hustling, murder, and extortion.

His reputation was well known and made him well respected. Winning his last legal battle against murder charges had to make him cocky. Stronger. More lethal.

She barely felt the discomfort of the metal's edge against the soles of her feet as she took a deep breath and tried to prepare herself to go up against a killer. She was a ballsy bitch most of the time but fear wasn't a stranger.

Her plan was laid out. She was just looking for the strength to enforce that shit.

Naeema picked up her phone and dialed Sarge.

"Yeah."

"How's everything?" she asked, glancing up at the ceiling.

"Safe. You?"

Naeema pinched the bridge of her nose. "I'm fine, Sarge."

He grunted.

She was tired of having the same old argument. "Sarge, I'm not gonna sit back and let someone—anyone—come for Tank," she said, her tone sharp.

If there was anything she could do to make sure another attempt on his life did not succeed she would. He would do the same to protect her. Ride or motherfucking die.

"I'll call you later, Sarge," she said.

"I *hope* you can."

Beep.

"I hope so too," she said, as she dialed her burner phone.

It rang several times before going to a generic voice mail. She rose from the bed and walked over to the window to look down the street at Mya's apartment building. The window where she liked to sit and look out of was empty. It was the first time since she took her to the doctor two days ago that the phone had not been answered.

Her eyes shifted again as Mook's car pulled into a parking spot in front of her house. She walked out onto the porch as he came up the stairs by twos with a cookie can in his hand. "Christmas in August?" she asked, turning sideways to allow him to ease past her into the house.

"Huh?" he asked, looking confused.

"Nothing," she said, not bothering to explain. "What you got?"

She closed the door and eyed Mook as he took the lid off the can with the tips of his long dark fingers. She turned up her nose at the Fruity Pebbles Treats. "The fuck?" she asked.

"I'll be selling weed, drinks, and snacks. Get high and kill your munchies at the same damn time," he said, offering her the can.

Naeema arched a brow. "Who baked that?" she asked, looking up at Mook.

"It's legit," he said.

"Yeah, but who baked it?"

"A company. Same place I get my weed," he said. "I ain't in no kitchen mixing up no damn cereal and weed juice."

Mook's business thrived because those states with legal medical marijuana dispensaries regulated how much weed the growers could produce per patient. The excess beyond that was big on the black market and Mook's ass was making major bank with it.

But stepping into selling edible weed, too?

"I'm offering all my clientele the first one for free," he said with a toothy grin.

Naeema picked up one of the krispies that was in a vacuum-sealed plastic. "I don't know about this but I'll try one and let you know."

"You good on weed?" he asked.

Naeema nodded before walking over to open the front

door. "I'll hit you up when I need something," she said with a little wave of her hand toward the door.

"You wanna smoke?" Mook asked, not moving toward the door.

"Nah, I only smoke alone or with my man," she said, stepping back to pull the door open wider.

"Well, try the krispie. I really wanna know if it's hitting."

Naeema eyed Mook. His eyes shifted a bit to the left before he looked at her and twisted one of his dreads. Something was up. *This fool never press me to get high with him.*

"I'm good, Mook," she said. "Now you have a good one out there today."

He came closer and his eyes dipped down to the krispie in her hand. "Well, if you not gonna try it now then let me get it back because I only got a little bit," he said, reaching to take it from her hand.

Naeema pulled it out of his reach. She held it up and then dragged it across her nose to smell. "What's in this?" she asked as she moved over to sit on the edge of her bed.

Mook laughed nervously. The whites of his eyes got big. "Weed. Shit. What you think?" he asked.

"I don't know . . . *but* I can get it tested," she said.

Mook stepped over to tower above her. "Damn, Naeema, why you frontin' on ya boy?" he asked, reaching again to try and take the krispie back.

Naeema tossed it up toward his chest with her left hand and reached under her pillow with the right. He turned and walked to the door, pulling his cargo shorts up by the back hem as he did.

"Mook," she called out to him.

He turned in the open doorway.

Naeema pulled her gun and pointed it at his chest. "You 'round here droppin' bitches to get pussy? That's your life?" she asked snidely.

"Yo, Naeema, chill, yo," he said, backing out the door.

"Forget my number, yo," she said, mocking him.

"Aight, aight, aight," he said, before turning and hurrying across the porch.

Oh shit.

Naeema looked into the face of Mya as the teen finished coming up the stairs as Mook passed her moving as fast as his baggy shorts would let him. The girl's eyes dropped to the gun still in Naeema's hand. Sliding it back under the pillow, Naeema rose to walk over to the door. "You feeling better?" she asked.

Mya looked back over her shoulder at Mook climbing inside his wheels before turning back to look toward Naeema's pillow. "Yeah," she said, walking up to the door where Naeema stood to hand her the cell phone.

Naeema took it and saw the fear and curiosity in the girl's eyes. "Sometimes a woman living alone has to protect herself," she said.

Mya's eyes showed that she had a response or a question to that but was unsure whether to ask or say it. With a little shake of her head she finally said, "My stepfather almost found the phone so I thought I better bring it back to you."

"Will you remember to take your meds? Because you have to finish the antibiotics. The big pill," she clarified.

"I will. I promise," she said, leaning a little to the right to look past Naeema's presence in the doorway at the pillow on the bed.

"It's legit, Mya. I have a permit," Naeema explained, not sure why she felt a need to do so.

"You straight," Mya said.

Naeema chuckled. "Well, I have to go," she said, already stepping back to close the door.

Mya turned on the porch with a little wave of her hand. She stopped suddenly and turned back. "You ever shot somebody?" she asked.

"No," Naeema lied.

"Would you? Could you?" she asked.

"No," Naeema lied again, even as the bodies of the people that she had shot in the past flashed in her head like a speedy picture show.

POW! POW! POW! POW!

"Bye, Mya," she said, closing the door before any more questions could flow.

Naeema looked out the rear passenger window of the taxi at Gentlemen Only. The brick storefront could just as easily have been an accountant's office as a high-end strip club. There was a lone security guard in a tuxedo posted up outside the club with his arms crossed over his massive chest. A red carpet ran halfway across the street up to the solid black door.

She paid the driver and opened the door to climb out and step up onto the sidewalk. Before the night at Club Vixen, it had been a long time since she last assumed the identity of Queen—to protect her true identity and to present as an ultra-sexy hood chick who wasn't very bright.

Walking up to the building she raked her nails through the blond lace front wig she wore with lots of body to match her elaborate makeup with inch-long mink lashes and sheer gold glossy lips. The black lace dress she wore over a black bodysuit flared at the arms and the sleeves, cutting mid-thigh and showcasing her toned legs with six-inch heels.

The whole getup was a showstopper meant to draw plenty of attention just the way she wanted.

The bodyguard eyed her as she approached.

"How you doing?" she said, coming to stand before him.

His eyes were appreciative of all the sexy she was giving but he still untucked one beefy hand to point to the building wall. She didn't bother to look because she knew it said GENTLEMEN ONLY.

"Gentlemen love eye candy and I'm looking for work," she said in a sexy vamp voice so unlike her own.

"They hire on Wednesdays. Come back then," he said.

"That shouldn't be up to you," she said.

"It ain't," he said, looking past her.

Naeema looked back over her shoulder as three fine men in tailored suits walked up to the door. "Good evening," they all said, eyeing her as they passed and entered the building.

One looked back at her over his shoulder just before the door closed.

Naeema reached in the black feather-covered clutch she carried and pulled out a couple hundred-dollar bills from the money she had gotten from Tank's wallet. She held the folded cash up between her index and middle finger. "I'm here now," she said.

"So," he said. "Either go away or I will—"

He raised his hand to press toward his right ear with his head cocked slightly to the side.

Naeema gritted her teeth, hating that her plan was going to shit before she even really got started. It was rare to run into a man who didn't let a little tits and ass distract him. *He'd be perfect for Tank's team.*

"No problem," he said, looking up at one of the black, ornate light fixtures flanking the door.

Naeema followed his line of vision. *Was there a camera?* "Excuse me."

She shifted her eyes back to him, surprised to find he was opening the door. She played it smooth as hell as she lightly tapped the money against her chin as she walked past him and inside the club. The music she couldn't hear from the street played loudly with the bass seeming to press against her body with each THUMP. He stepped inside the all-black hall behind her and although her eyes followed the length of the hall to a smoked-out glass door at the end, he pressed a spot on the wall and a hidden door opened revealing a small elevator with a metal gate with an ornate scroll pattern.

Here the fuck we go.

The bodyguard leaned in just long enough to push the button marked with an arrow pointing upward. He stepped back without another direct look at her as the automatic door closed. Her heart was beating fast as she pushed the cash back inside her clutch and stepped into the elevator that was only big enough for two. She raked her fingers through her waist-length blond hair and fixed her face to look vapid in case there were more cameras trained on her. As the elevator rose to the next level, she pulled a compact and her gloss from the purse. In the mirror she could see the apprehension reflected in her eyes. *Don't fuck up, Naeema. Do not fuck up.*

The elevator stopped and she replaced the compact and gloss before tucking her clutch under her arm. Through the gate she looked directly into a large office. It was high-end everything. Décor. Polished wood floors. Metal light fixtures. Expensive furnishings.

She eyed one man sitting behind a large wooden desk in a chair fit for a motherfucking boss. Another man sat in the chair before it and had his back to her. Naeema had never laid eyes on Murk but she knew he was the one who beckoned her forward with a quick wave of his hand.

The door opened and she stepped inside the lion's den. Her heart was beating hard and fast like she just ran a mile. "Hello," she said, coming forward. Her heels tapped lightly against the wood as she did.

Murk looked nothing like his reputation in the three-piece pinstriped suit he wore with a shirt and tie that could only be silk. The diamonds around his neck and on his watch made the look less "accountant" and everything about being a man made for money. His skin was smooth and dark. His teeth white as milk. He looked to be in his late twenties, at the most.

"How can I help you?" he said, his voice swollen with that swagger only bred on the East Coast. He leaned back against his chair to eye her.

"I was looking for a job so I wondered how *I* could help *you*," she said, keeping her voice light and airy.

"We only take applications on Wednesdays during business hours but my friend here thought such a fine bitch shouldn't have to wait," Murk said.

Naeema tried not to flinch at the insult—whether he thought it was one or not. Her instincts had been to correct his ass but instead she smiled like she was boosted up by his compliment and looked down at the man in the chair.

Her heart literally stopped as she looked at her client Diego Martinez. He rose from the chair in a bad-ass navy suit with a matching shirt open at the collar. Like Murk, his diamond jewelry had him iced the fuck out.

"Thank you," she said, turning her face away from him a little bit.

Diego reached for her hand and lifted it to press a kiss to the back of it.

His lips were smooth.

"My pleasure, Miss . . ."

She licked her lips nervously and tasted the gloss she just lathered on her mouth. "Just call me Queen," she said.

"Queen," he repeated with a little smile at the corners of his lips.

Naeema knew right then that he had clearly seen through her charade. *Did he give me up to Murk and they were just playing along for fucking kicks?*

"What type of work were you looking for?" Murk asked.

Naeema looked away from Diego as he released her hand and reclaimed his seat. "To serve drink—"

"With an ass like that?" Murk balked. "Sheiiiit."

Diego laughed and cut his eye up at her as he stroked his square chin.

What the fuck is going on right now?

"I can't really dance," she said.

"Hell, everything on you will jiggle if you just sneeze. Shit," Murk said, his black eyes taking in her body.

It was a look that would've led Tank to murk Murk.

There was a time she was young and dumb enough to be

excited by two rich ninjas eyeing her. Now she knew the shit was degrading as hell. *Thank God I grew the fuck up.*

"Banging body or not, Murk, take it from a regular there ain't shit worse than a dry-ass stripper who can't work the pole," Diego said, his accent caressing the fuck out of his words.

The men exchanged a look across the desk.

"Turn around," Murk said, sitting forward to press his elbows on top of the desk that was covered with black suede.

Go with it, Naeema.

She raised her arms high above her head to emphasize her hourglass frame even more as she slowly turned around until she was back facing Murk.

"She a stunner for sure," Diego said.

Murk swiped his hand across his mouth. "What's your number?" he said, picking up a pen.

She easily ran off the numbers of her burner phone.

Diego shifted his body in his seat. He knew her real cell phone from calling to make appointments at the barbershop.

"Bar girls work for just tips. Squeeze that fat ass in black leggings and we provide the tops. Fill out an application downstairs with my bar manager Tyrone. He'll tell you your schedule," Murk said, his tone dismissive.

"Thank you. I appreciate it," she said, giving Diego one last look before she turned to walk back to the elevator.

Naeema had just stepped in and was turning when Diego stepped in with her. He pressed the button to close the automatic door and stayed facing her with his hands in his pockets. Their eyes were locked. As the elevator began to descend he bent down a bit to press his lips close to her ear.

"I don't know what the fuck you're up to but you know you owe me now. Right . . . *Queen*?" he asked, before pressing a kiss to the top of her neck.

Naeema said nothing. She didn't know what the fuck to say.

The elevator slid to a stop and Diego waved her through as the door slid back and he opened the hidden door into the hall. They both stepped off. With one last look at each other he headed out the door of the club, leaving Naeema standing there, wondering what she had just gotten herself into.

11

Naeema turned over in bed and snuggled her body against the side of Tank before pressing kisses to his shoulder and rubbing her leg against the length of his. She reached down to trace the defined lines of his stomach before taking his dick into her hand to stroke to hardness. She enjoyed the feel of it in her hand as she shifted her body down to lick and suck first one nipple then the other.

Looking up at him she saw that his eyes were closed in pleasure.

She moved to kneel between his open legs and dip her head to take his dick into her mouth with an eager groan. "I love sucking it," she whispered against the tip before lowering her head to take enough of him in to tickle her tonsils.

"Hmmmmm," she moaned at the feel of his dick stroking against her tongue. Her free hand dipped to cup his balls and she stroked the length of him as she sucked the tip so deeply her cheeks caved.

Pleasing him excited her. Her nipples were hard. Her heart was pounding. Her pulse raced. And her clit was swollen and throbbing until it ached between her legs. She was ready. So ready.

Naeema was reluctant to let his dick go but she wanted it inside her—stroking her, pleasing her, fucking her. She straddled his strong hips and held his long, curved dick up-right as she eased her pussy down onto him with a hiss and a bite of her lip. "Tank," she cried out when she was filled with him.

She sat up straight, let her head hang back, and she rested her upper arms against her forehead as she slowly glided back and forth on his dick as she tightened her pussy walls down around him rhythmically. The feel of the root of him against her clit sent a thrill up her core and made her entire body warm from head to toe.

"I love fucking you," Naeema whimpered with her face alive with the pleasure she felt.

She circled her hips clockwise and then counterclock-wise. "Tank," she sighed. "You getting this pussy, ain't you?

"Ain't you?" she asked again, lowering her arms to press her hands down against his chest as she continued her slow wind with her hips.

She was used to Tank talking during their sex. His mouth game included more than just pussy eating and he had a way of saying just the right thing to push her over the edge.

"Ain't you, Tank?" she asked, looking down into his face.

He didn't move. His eyes were still closed.

She gasped as his body began to chill beneath her. From his dick to his hard chest beneath her hands there was a sudden icy coldness. "Tank," she whispered down to him as she pressed on his chest above his heart.

There was no beat.

She bent down to put her ear against his mouth.

There were no breaths.

She shrieked with the realization that he was dead—and had been the entire time she fucked him.

Naeema backed off him and scurried to the end of the bed as she opened her mouth to let out a scream. "Nooooo," she roared.

Naeema awakened in the middle of her bed and sat up straight with her chest heaving. She drew her knees to her chest and wrapped her arms around them as she tried to wish away the memory of her nightmare. She hadn't had one so vivid and so damn scary since she was in the throes of hunting down her son's killer.

Knock-knock.

She looked over at the door with the room only dimly lit by the bathroom light streaming down the hall. *Am I still dreaming?*

"Miss Naeema. You home? Please let me in."

Knock-knock.

"Please."

She frowned as she kicked off the covers and got out of bed. She crossed the room and opened the door. "Mya, what's wrong?" she asked, turning her head to watch the teen ease past her and into the living room. She was dressed in a tank and colorful sleep pants with not a bit of shoes on her feet.

Naeema shut the door and locked it. She reached to flip the light switch.

"No, don't turn on the lights, please," Mya whispered.

There was a tremble in her voice.

"I'm not hiding in my own house, Mya," she said, flipping the switch and bathing the room with light from the ceiling fixture.

BOOM-BOOM-BOOM.

Mya's eyes widened into miniature saucers as Naeema turned with a frown at someone knocking on her fucking door like the police about to do a raid. "Who is this?" she mouthed to Mya as she pointed one long nail at the door.

"My stepfather," Mya mouthed back, crossing her arms over her chest.

What the fuck?

She pointed toward the door leading into the kitchen and didn't open the front door until Mya was in it. Naeema was taken aback when she saw the nice-looking light-skinned dude on her porch in nothing but some jeans still unbuttoned at the waist. "Can I help you?" she asked, ignoring the ripped details of his body.

His eyes looked past Naeema. "Tell Mya it's time to come home," he said, his chest heaving like he ran across the street. *Like he chased someone across the street.*

"Mya who?" Naeema asked with an attitude. "Do you know what time it is?"

His face got stiff with anger and his thick brows lowered as he leered down at her. "I saw her run over here."

"Well, no you didn't," Naeema said, putting one hand on her hip. "But why is someone running from you anyway?"

His eyes dipped.

Naeema remembered that she was in just her purple cotton gown, which had a plunging V-neck and was way too revealing to be answering the door in. "Excuse me," she said, moving to shut the door.

He jerked out his hand to hold against the door to stop her. "You butting into my family's business right now," he said.

"No, you *brought* your family business to me right now," she stressed. "And now you need to carry that shit back with you. Ya heard me?"

"Mya," he called out, taking a bold-ass move forward.

Naeema stepped in his path and put her hand up against his chest. It was sweaty and her fingers slipped a bit. "Are you kidding me?" she snapped.

"Mya," he yelled again. "Let's go."

Naeema stumbled back when he pressed forward just across the threshold. She rushed forward and pressed against his chest with both fists. "Mo-ther-fuck-er," she said as he stumbled back onto the porch.

"I will call the police," he said, his eyes darting to any space he could see inside the house.

"Yes, let's call the police and then we can have them interview all parties involved and run whatever tests necessary to get to the bottom of the whole story," she said with clear intent that she was double talking and he needed to read between the lines.

He eyed her.

"Plus, you just tried to bum-rush my home," she said. "So yes, let's call the po-po, ho."

"I'm sure in the morning whoever you looking for will be home," she said, closing the door as he nervously licked his lips and kept looking past Naeema with urgent eyes until the door closed in his face.

She grabbed her gun from under the pillow and cut off the lights before moving over to the window to pull back the curtain and blinds to eye him still standing on the porch with his hands on his hips looking down like he was deep in thought. She stayed there with her finger on the trigger as she watched him until he finally left her porch and crossed the street to enter the apartment building with one last look back at her house.

Keeping the gun in her hand she crossed the floor to open the door to the kitchen and turn on the light. She frowned a bit when it appeared empty but then she found the young teen in the corner behind the door. "Sit," Naeema said, moving over to the fridge to pull a can of no-name soda out to hand to the girl.

Mya did as she was told and took the soda with a small smile that didn't even appear real. "Thanks."

Sitting the gun on the table Naeema took a seat. "How long has he been messing with you?" she asked, and then pierced Mya with her eyes.

"Messing with me?" Mya asked before opening the can and taking a sip.

"Yes . . . and based off what you was doing when I first met you, you know damn well what I mean," Naeema said, her voice hard and meaning to show she was in no mood to play.

Naeema had a lot on her plate with keeping up with Tank's well-being, supervising Sarge as he helped protect Tank, and investigating three possible suspects in Tank's shooting. Mya was getting to be a handful when added to all that.

"If you didn't want me involved then why did you run your ass over here?" she snapped at the girl's continuing silence.

Mya's eyes filled with tears.

Naeema released a heavy breath and tilted her head back as she rubbed the space between her well-groomed brows. She knew that her connection to the little girl—her desire to protect her—was all about her own harried child-hood and the mother she never got to be to her son. The girl's tears caused a pang in her heart that let her know she had come to care for the misguided little girl.

"Since I was eleven."

Naeema lowered her head to eye Mya in surprise and horror. "Does your mother know?" she asked, feeling her chest burn in anger.

Mya shook her head and looked away. "She didn't be-lieve me," she said.

The look of hurt in the girl's eyes was all too real and it stung Naeema to the quick.

"I want you to get rid of him for me . . . with your gun," she added softly.

Naeema's face frowned. "No, because it doesn't take murder. We'll go to the police or DSS if we have to," she said, surprised at her willingness to fuck with either agency.

"Then my mom will be mad at me for doing that," Mya said, her eyes hopeful. "If he just goes away she won't blame me. She'll think he left her or something."

The sadness of it all weighed down on Naeema's shoul-ders and she literally slumped from it. It was a world com-pletely fucked up when a child felt she had to plot the murder of someone to feel protected. She eyed Mya. Her world was already laid out on a fucked-up foundation. *She'd rather take on the big bad monster than make her mother do it.*

"I'm gonna figure out how to help you but I'm not a killer," she lied.

Mya looked hopeful and disappointed all at once.

"Murder is never the option," she lied again, even though she knew she relied on it in the past to resolve plenty of issues.

"You stay here tonight. Go get in my bed," Naeema said, rising to pour the rest of the soda down the drain.

As Mya left the kitchen Naeema wondered what to do with everything just laid at her doorstep. She could not ignore a child being molested. And if Mya had not asked Naeema to murder him she probably would have snuck and did it while leaving the girl and her mother none the wiser.

Naeema felt overwhelmed like a motherfucker.

She grabbed the gun and then the back of one of the chairs to carry into the living room. Sitting it by the window she took a seat and crossed her leg, sitting the gun on her lap. She glanced over at Mya lying on her side with her hands tucked under her head.

"First time in a long time I ain't got to worry about nobody bothering me in my sleep," Mya said into the quiet.

Naeema gave her a smile and then turned her head to look out the window to make sure the girl's stepfather didn't let his desperation of Mya telling and getting caught lead him to do something stupid. She sat there keeping a watchful eye on the girl as she waited and plotted.

Thud-thud-thud.

Naeema whirled on the chair just seconds before Mya's stepfather came bounding across the room from the kitchen and swung, striking her across the face and knocking her from the chair to the floor. Her gun fell from her lap as she did.

Shit. Shit. Shit.

Her head throbbed like crazy and she winced as she raised it enough to lay eyes on him as she pounded her fist against the floor. She hated that she slept on this fool and he snuck up on her from behind.

Disrespect?

In her home?

Hell no, motherfucker.

She fought through the throbbing pain in her head and jumped to her feet as he yanked Mya from the bed.

"Now let's go," he said, his voice a low, fuming snarl.

Naeema grabbed the toppled chair and took two large steps to reach him before she swung the chair like a bat. His head was the ball.

CRACK!

He cried out and stumbled to the left to fall against the wall before he fell on his back.

Naeema's chest was heaving as she stood over him and released the chair. It fell to the floor loudly. She winced from the throbbing in her head.

Click.

She whirled at the sound of the gun being cocked behind her. "No!" she screamed, holding up her hand as she eyed Mya standing there with the gun pointed at her stepfather. In the fray she must have picked it up from where it landed.

"Mya, please, no—"

POW!

Mya's fingers began to tremble around the gun. "I'm sick of his shit," said the little girl who had already grown up far too soon.

Naeema went to her and hugged her close with one

hand as she removed the gun from her quivering hand with the other. "Go home right now. Get in bed. Stay there. You were never here," Naeema whispered as she rocked her back and forth a bit like a child. "You were never here."

She leaned back to find Mya staring at his body as the blood continued to pool from the bullet that landed in his neck. It was hardly an accurate shot, but it was deadly as a motherfucker.

She led Mya into the kitchen. The back door was still ajar. She shook her head to see he had jimmied the door open. "Don't let anyone see you," Naeema said.

Mya nodded but she looked numb and distant.

Naeema grabbed her chin and forced the girl to look at her. "Hey," she said, jostling her chin. "You were never here."

Mya nodded as another tear fell.

With one last hug she pushed the girl toward the door.

Naeema made sure to leave the door just as it was and walked back to the living room to step over his legs to turn on the lights. The smell of fresh blood was already rising into the air. Stepping back from the scene she bit her bottom lip as she eyed the dead body.

She missed Tank more than ever. One call to him and he would have come and handled it all. The body. The traces of blood. Her.

I have to protect Mya.

She felt guilt. She had a hand in this disaster. She couldn't deny it. If nothing else, it was her gun that Mya shot him with and she never should have let it be so accessible. *Shit. Fuck. Shit. Fuck. Dammit.*

She opened a drawer and pulled out an old sweatshirt.

She carefully wiped away Mya's fingerprints and then wrapped the shirt around the barrel of the gun as she moved back to the same spot where Mya stood when she shot him. Shaking her head with regret over how Mya's life took a turn that the little girl may never overcome, Naeema fired a bullet into the wall. The shirt wrapped around the barrel muffled the sound a little bit. But most important, she wanted to make sure she had gunpowder residue on her hand.

Naeema retrieved her cell phone from where she left it on the bed and did something for the first—and hopefully last—time in her life.

"This is 911. What is your emergency?" the operator said.

"A man broke into my home and assaulted me. I shot him. He's dead," she said, her voice just as lifeless as the man on her floor.

"You got enough yet?"

Naeema paused in the doorway of Tank's room the next morning at Sarge's sarcasm. Ignoring him, she walked over to the bed and bent down to press a kiss to Tank's forehead, cheeks, chin, and then lips. "Love you, Lavarius," she whispered near his ear, using his real name, which most people didn't know.

She felt Sarge's eyes on her as she came around the bed to hand him the McDonald's she brought for him. "I know you saw the news," she said, moving to stand before the sink and look at her reflection in the small mirror above it.

The blow Mya's stepfather—Shawn Polite—landed

across her face had left it swollen and reddish in color. The shades she wore did not do much to hide that fact. Pushing them atop her close-shaven head, Naeema turned and leaned back against the sink with her arms across her ample chest.

Sarge shook his head as he took a bite out of the breakfast sandwich. "Better you got him than Tank," he said.

"Ain't that the truth," Naeema added.

The police had questioned her, checked the registration of her handgun, surveyed the evidence of the break-in and the assault before ruling she was within her rights to protect herself. She thought the comment one of them made that it was one less criminal they had to waste a bullet on was cruel and insensitive but she was just glad her plan to cop to the shooting and cover for Mya had worked.

Naeema didn't bother to tell them she knew he lived across from her. That was their job to ID him and notify the family. *Good fucking riddance.*

"How was everything yesterday?" she asked.

"No visits," Sarge said before releasing a belch that could rival a thunderstorm.

Naeema nodded. "You want to head home for the day and come back tonight?" she asked.

"No," he said.

She knew he would never admit that he felt better keeping an eye on her.

"How's it going?"

Naeema shook her head. "I'm no closer now than I was a few days ago," she admitted, hating that the truth was just simply the truth.

Looking over at Tank in the bed, she rubbed her hand up and down the length of her tatted arm. Her son's faces. She didn't fail him and she could not fail Tank.

Gentlemen Only was actually a well-laid-out and well-executed mini-paradise for well-groomed men looking for more upscale surroundings to view T & A. Naeema looked around as she waited for the round of drinks she ordered via the tablets all the waitresses used to send orders straight to the bar. Men lounged in their seats sipping high-end drinks from crystal glasses and smoked premium cigars as they watched the show. It was different from the strip clubs she had been to and she could see why the men paid their annual membership fee of five thousand and up.

Naeema had to admit that the talent was top-notch as well. Costumes. Routines. Pole work. Work the crowd. Titillate.

All of that was cool but she wanted more info than the ins and outs of the club. She looked up at the one-sided mirrors of Murk's office. She had to find out if he had retaliated against Tank and only he—or those close to him—would know the truth.

"Here you go, Queen."

The only problem was he rarely ventured onto the floor and you could never tell if he was in his office or not.

"Queen!"

She turned at being yelled at by the bartender. "Sorry," she said.

It was her first night of work and she had to get used to being called by her alias again. Besides the night she danced for Fevah it had been a long time since she drew on the made-up identity.

Picking up the square tray she held it atop one arm and held the rim with her other hand as she made her way over to her group of tables to the rear of the room. The room was set up in levels based on the fee paid. The closer to the stage the more prominent a member. Because she was new she was assigned to newer or lower-paying clientele. One of the waitresses who trained her called them the low-ballers and no-callers.

Levels. They existed in every part of life just to make somebody feel lower than the next man.

"Here we go, gentlemen," she said, setting the correct drink in front of each of the four men seated at the table. She gave the tab to the white man with red hair with a fifty-dollar cigar clenched between his perfect white teeth. He accepted the pen she offered and signed the bill to add to his tab.

She was walking away to head to another table to check on them when she spotted Diego unbuttoning his suit jacket and taking a seat at the front of the club near the stage. She was hoping he would not show up because she was not ready to deliver on her debt to him. She moved over to the next table and took their order, being sure to keep her back to the front of the club. She kept it up as she headed to the bar to pick up the order.

"Queen, one of *my* clients wants to see you at table three."

She looked over at Tyrai standing next to her at the end of the bar. The tall redhead, who had freckles across her shortbread complexion, was territorial. The levels existed among the waitresses as well. Looking over her shoulder she eyed Diego as he leaned back in his seat and looked up at the topless dancer onstage as he blew smoke rings into the dimly lit air.

She had to admit the motherfucker looked good as hell. Too good.

"Aight," she said to Tyrai, her eyes still locked on Diego's profile.

Naeema loaded her tray with the drinks and served her clients, easing the hefty tip inside her bra, before she lowered the tray and made her way around the tables to Diego. "Good evening, sir. My name is Queen. How may I serve you?" she said, pulling out her tablet.

Diego kept his eyes locked on the stage as the dancer climbed up the pole, locked her legs around it, and turned upside down with the pole now snug between her ass cheeks as she twerked. He was reluctant as hell to shift his eyes from her but he eventually did, swiveling a bit in the leather seat to look up at Naeema.

"Meet me outside when you get off . . . *Queen*," Diego said, before turning to give her his back.

She pushed her golden wig hair behind her ear before turning and walking away from him. With a look up at Murk's office she knew she had to decide if getting closer to him was worth her getting too close to Diego.

Naeema wavered back and forth on just what she was willing to give up during her entire six-hour shift. Her mind still was not made up as she changed out of the skin-tight leggings and hot-pink crop top into jeans and a tank. She left the dancers and waitresses in their dressing room counting their tips and taking pics for Instagram as she left the club through the back entrance all employees were required to use.

She paused in the doorway at the sight of Diego's convertible Benz. He sat behind the wheel with the motor running, confident as fuck that she had no choice but to honor his demand. She was about to open the passenger door but he shook his head and motioned for her to come around to the driver's side.

Confused—and relieved—she moved around the front of the whip, the lights from his Mercedes flashing across her body as she did.

"I didn't have a chance to ask you why you're doing this."

Naeema paused before she continued the steps to stand beside his door. "I need to make extra money," she lied smoothly. "I just didn't want people in my business, that's all."

Diego chuckled. "Working for the man your husband testified against. You think I'm fucking stupid or nah, Naeema?" he asked with a shake of his head.

"Never that," she assured him. *Shit.*

"Then a nigga like Murk will understand why you in his club frontin'. Right?" Diego asked, trying her.

Naeema peeped his game. "If you think I'm up to something why not snitch to your boy?" she asked.

Diego shrugged. "We do business together. That's all. Plus, there ain't shit *you* can do to Murk to hurt him. So I'm out of it. Plus I need something from you," he said, as he handed her a large Louis Vuitton box. "Inside is a package I want you to deliver for me."

"A delivery?" she asked. "That's what you wanted?"

Diego's eyes dipped down to take in the soft swell of her

pussy in the jeans she wore. He reached out with his left hand and slid it between her thighs palming it. "When I get this the way I want it you will offer it to me. I don't highjack pussy. I don't have to," he said pressing his thumb against the center of her lips deeply until he was massaging her clit.

His fingers were warm and the pressure was good. Real good.

Naeema released a soft but hot little gasp before she licked her lips. "You think forcing me to commit a crime is going to make me want to give you my pussy?" she asked, fighting for control.

"Who says it's criminal?"

"Then use a courier," she countered, hating that she had to fight not to spread her legs wider for him.

"I am. You."

Naeema felt her hips involuntarily flex as he hit the right spot and she felt herself about to cum. Shaking her head she stepped back leaving his hand in the air with his fingers stilled pursed to pleasure her.

Diego chuckled and pressed his fingers to his nose to sniff before he sucked his fingers. "Prime pussy," he said, with a shake of his head before he shifted his car into drive.

Naeema's heart was still hammering in anticipation of the nut she almost had.

"Directions are inside," he said, revving the motor. "And keep the bag when you're done."

He accelerated forward and then turned to drive around the building. Soon the sound of him zooming away down the street echoed loudly.

Naeema walked around the club and stood on the curb to hail a cab. They were few and far between at two in the morning. "Shit," she swore as one went by already occupied.

"Queen, next time call for one about thirty minutes before you get off."

Naeema turned and found the security guard standing at the curb beside her.

"One's on the way," he said, looking down the street at the oncoming traffic.

"Thanks, Capo," she said, offering him a smile. "Don't let me keep you."

He didn't say anything but he didn't move from his spot either.

The other girls said he was married to the same woman for the last ten years and had two little girls that he adored. He never once went out the way with any of the girls and was always respectful. She was really beginning to respect him. He was a stand-up guy.

As the other workers began to pull out of the rear employee parking lot in droves, Capo remained. Eventually a yellow cab pulled out of traffic and slowed down in front of them. He opened and held the door.

"Thanks," she said.

"Night."

"Penn Station," she said to the driver. Tank's Tahoe was parked there. She never wanted to give someone a chance to contact the cab company and discover where they dropped her off.

As the cabbie drove off, Naeema opened the lid to the box and moved back the tissue paper. In it there was one of the new Louis bags that slightly resembled a Birkin. She saw it online for over four grand. She couldn't afford a lot of designer shit but she stayed browsing their sites.

She lifted the bag but there was nothing underneath it. She opened it and inside was a brick of what she assumed was heroin. She closed the lid. Naeema was far from perfect but doing anything to help flood the streets with heroin was a line she wouldn't cross. *I can't.*

She looked out the window and her eyes were troubled. She would rather fuck Diego than help fuck up her city.

12

*N*aeema smoothed her hands over the leggings she wore with a GENTLEMEN ONLY belly shirt as she listened to the instructions Tyrai was giving her as she swung the length of her blond hair behind her back. When she came in for her shift Tyrai let her know Murk personally requested her to waitress a party in one of the private rooms.

"Don't make eye contact, keep a smile on your face and extra wiggle in your ass, and be like Beyoncé on the elevator to whatever the fuck they're doing. Got it?" Tyrai said, pushing her breasts up in the matching T-shirt she wore.

Naeema nodded her eyes, shifting to the door as it opened and a line of suit- and blazer-wearing men entered the large circle-shaped room with padded leather banquets lining the walls and two poles running from floor to ceiling in the center. She bit some of the gooey gloss from her full lips. Bass-filled music was already blaring in the room.

Two strippers entered in nothing but thong bikinis and thigh-high boots with their breasts swaying one way and hips another. Murk nodded and they both jumped up on the pole.

"Aight. Let's get it," Tyrai said, picking up one of the trays of flutes they filled with pricey Ace of Spades Champagne.

Even as Naeema handed out the flutes to the men with a smile in place she was feeling like her time at the club was a waste. She never even got close to Murk or saw him. He was interested in her working for the club but any plans she had of him being caught up in her physically was not happening. She was tempted as hell to walk away and find another way to get at him.

Someone lightly grabbed her wrist and Naeema was brought from her thoughts to focus on Diego sitting there in a light gray suit with a black shirt open at the collar. His grip tightened and the look in his eyes was clear as hell.

She knew what he wanted and she had yet to deliver. His package was hidden under the firebox of her fireplace. "Tonight," she lied, before trying to gently pull out of his grasp.

Diego shook his head and held on, his black eyes piercing her.

Naeema felt lightheaded that he was about to expose her but he suddenly released her causing her to stumble back and have to hold the tray tighter to keep from tipping the drinks over.

"Here you go, Blondie."

Naeema broke her stare with Diego and looked at the rough-faced dude in all black sitting beside him who reached up to take his own flute from the tray.

"Thank you," Naeema said, accepting the tip.

The way he eyed her made her feel like she was putting on a porno for him. She kept it moving. Once her tray was empty, Naeema pulled the small tablet they carried to send orders to the bar.

"Good evening, sir. My name is Queen. How may I serve

you?" she asked, going back to the first man to whom she served the complimentary champagne.

His eyes widened as he looked past her and up at the ceiling.

Naeema turned and she arched a brow at one girl standing on the other's shoulder as they twerked for their lives . . . or the tips. The dollars weren't just raining . . . there was a storm. *I ain't mad at it.*

"Good evening, sir. My name is Queen. How may I serve you?" she repeated, bending down low so that he could hear her over the music.

"Crown Royal on the rocks," he said, before standing to add to the fray by tossing money up in the air without a care.

Must be fucking nice.

As she continued taking drink orders she felt eyes on her. She knew without looking that it was Diego and when she drew near him she saw that she was right. He removed the cigar from between his teeth and blew smoke rings as he sat with his legs spread wide. There was one hell of a show before him but it was her he watched.

Naeema felt nervous.

"Good evening, sir. My name is Queen. How may I serve you?" she asked as she came to stand next to Diego's knee.

He looked up at her as he licked his bottom lip.

Naeema kept her face cool but it was fake as hell. She couldn't lie; Diego was sexy as hell.

If he wasn't hustling dope . . .

If she wasn't in love with Tank . . .

If she didn't completely give a fuck . . .

Diego's eyes looked devilish in the seconds just before he reached forward to grab her ass and pull her closer. She fought the urge to slam the tray against his face and completely fuck up his thoughts. She tried to step back but he gripped her closer and then patted his lap with his free hand.

His eyes dared her to deny him.

This motherfucker got me jammed up right now.

She perched her ass on his lap atop his knees.

Diego pressed his face against her neck as his hand massaged her exposed lower back. "You got a hard head, Naeema," he whispered in her ear.

She stiffened at his use of her name. "So do you," she said sarcastically as she looked pointedly down at his erection.

He chuckled. "Where my package?" he asked in her ear, his hand moving up under her shirt and against her ribs to palm the side of her breast.

Naeema eyed him like *Are you fucking kidding me?*

He kept his eyes locked on her as his hand continued until his finger stroked across her nipple. "Deliver my motherfucking package."

Naeema's hand came up to pry his fingers from her. She fought against the strength of his hand as his eyes filled with amusement at her. *So I'm a fucking joke.*

A different time and place Naeema knew she would straight drop-kick Diego's ass for the disrespect.

"What do you think Murk would do to you now—or in the future—if he knew the wife of the snitch who tried to take him down was working in his club?" Diego whispered in her ear as he palmed her breast.

"How do I know he doesn't already know?" she asked, looking over at the man they were talking about.

Murk's eyes shifted over to them.

Naeema was surprised when Murk's face tightened with anger. She made a move to try to rise from Diego's lap, pleased that her "boss" was upset by it. "He's looking," she said, not taking her eyes off Murk as he motioned for Tyrai.

"Who gives a fuck," Diego whispered against her neck, taking a short inhale of her perfume there. "You smell good as fuck. Maybe I will trade the delivery for the pussy."

Naeema feigned helplessness as Tyrai turned to look over at them as well. She said something to Murk and then disappeared from the room. Murk rose and walked over to them. Naeema couldn't front that she got nervous as hell.

"I bet your pussy smell just as good," Diego said, pressing a kiss to her neck as he continued to softly roll her nipple between his fingers.

Murk held out his hand to her. Naeema took it.

Diego unburied his face from her neck and tightened his hold on her breast as he glanced up Murk.

She felt caught between the two men. Diego was a hard head with a harder head down below enjoying his hold over her. *What does Murk want?*

"Not the waitresses, yo," Murk bent down to say, still holding Naeema's limp hand in his.

Diego and Murk shared a look.

The door opened and Tyrai led four girls into the room before she closed the door. The women removed their shirts and straddled some of the anxious men's hips as the women on the pole continued to twerk away near the ceiling.

Diego held up his hand releasing her.

Murk let her hand drop as well.

Naeema was free. She jumped to her feet and adjusted her bra to fully cover her breasts again.

Diego motioned for one of the girls to come to him.

"Sorry about that," Murk said to her, his intense eyes on her. "The waitresses serve drinks not ass."

"Thank you," she said.

"No thanks," Murk said, dismissing her. "It just is what it is."

Naeema nodded and opened her mouth to say something—anything—not to break the small connection they had, but Murk turned and strolled back to his seat. One of the dancers got off the pole and came over to Murk to climb onto his lap and bury his face between her breasts.

"Queen, take off," Tyrai said as she passed her.

Naeema looked away from Murk and the dancer but then spotted Diego licking away at one girl's brown nipples as she let her head fall back with a smile.

"Queen," Tyrai said sharply. "Take off. Go home, your shift is over."

"I didn't do anything," she protested, playing the role like she truly gave a fuck.

Tyrai eyed her. "So what you wanna do, argue with the man to let you work or take ya ass the fuck home like he said?" she snapped.

"You act like it's life or death," Naeema grumbled, still in her role as Queen.

"Bitch, it might be," Tyrai said, glancing over her shoulder before looking back at Naeema serious as hell.

Naeema pretended to look surprised and afraid. "Mr. Grant seems so nice though," she lied, playing innocent.

"Don't play like you ain't heard about Murk's past, Queen," Tyrai said with a tone filled with her desire not to play games.

"A little," she conceded.

"I've been here since he first opened up and he promised us all he was legit now and we shouldn't worry about our jobs," Tyrai said, looking down briefly before looking up at Naeema. "Still, it's hard to move on from your past, you know? So just go home tonight. Okay?"

With that she turned and began the hard switch of her hips around the room as she continued to take drink orders.

Naeema headed to the door just as another waitress came in to take her place. With one last glance at what would turn out to be one helluva party, she left.

It was a little after twelve when she finally got home. She had left the lights on hoping to fool any other grimy, low-life thieves into thinking she was home. She climbed from the SUV, looking over at the apartment building on the corner. Except for the black wreath on the door nothing else about it looked any different, including the dudes sitting on the stoop blazing as they listened to music blaring from someone's phone.

Tilting her head up, she spotted Mya sitting in the window. She started to wave to her but held back. She wanted to check on her. She wanted to know she was as okay as she could be about killing.

Naeema wanted to protect Mya from any possible suspicion about her stepfather's death. She watched too much of *The First 48* and the ID channel to let the neighbors see the stepdaughter of the man killed hanging out with the woman who they believed sent his no-good ass to his Maker. *Fuck him.*

With one last look back at the window, Naeema made her way to her house and jogged up the stairs. As soon as she unlocked and opened the front door her eyes fell on the large spot on the floor where she had to mop up the blood. Naeema had seen and played a strong role in murder but never inside her home before. It was just a few feet from where she slept.

The AC unit had the living room nice and cool as she pushed back to close the door. She removed her gun from the tote she carried and placed it back where she kept it hidden in the ash trap of the fireplace. Standing upright she eyed the three pieces of paper taped to the wall above it. Her eyes shifted from each one to the next. "Suspect one, suspect two, and suspect three," she mouthed.

Suspect one was Yani. Had a so-called loyal employee took out his boss? *For what motive though?*

Suspect two was Willie. Did his struggling business and envy of Tank lead to him wanting him dead?

Suspect three was Murk. His desire for revenge and why was clear.

On each sheet she had jotted down everything she had discovered about each man. She picked up the Sharpie from the mantel and worked it between her fingers before she wrote on Murk's sheet, *Sticks to the rules he sets for the club* and *Wants to go legit.*

She stepped back and eyed the papers one by one with a shake of her head that increased in intensity. None of it was enough to help her get it altogether.

Murk seemed to be the most evident candidate but she doubted he would accept the unfinished job of killing Tank just like that. Naeema didn't want to make the same mistake she made during the hunt for her son's killer by assuming it was the obvious one. Sometimes it wasn't the person most likely to do something. That was the only thing keeping her from catching Murk alone and sticking the barrel of her gun in his mouth to force him to cop to the shooting. She would have to reveal herself and she didn't want to kill anyone but the person who gunned down Tank—even if they deserved a bullet between the eyes for other dirty shit they got away with.

Naeema reluctantly turned away from the sheets and walked across the room to stick her head in the kitchen just long enough to make sure the back door was still secured. She didn't know if she would ever feel completely comfortable in the house again. *Especially with Sarge up at the hospital and my ass here all alone.*

She stripped as she walked down the hall to the first-floor bathroom. She had just turned on the shower when she whipped her head around to look over her shoulder. *You know what . . .*

Naeema scurried back into the living room and retrieved her gun carrying it with her to the bathroom to sit on the edge of the sink. She also didn't pull the shower curtain. *Fuck that shit.*

As she washed, Naeema continued to run over the facts in her head. She couldn't get over that she felt like something was staring her in the face and she was looking right past it. It was the whole not-seeing-the-forest-for-the-trees thing.

Yani. Willie. Murk. And truly her gut was telling her Yani was a punk ass but not a killer. So Willie and Murk.

And maybe someone else I don't know about?

Am I wrong and Tank wasn't the true target?

What the fuck am I missing?

She was still wondering about this long after she dried off and pulled on Tank's personalized football jersey. Naeema sat in the middle of the bed watching as much TV as she could with the picture ripped across the middle from the cracked screen and browsing Twitter and Instagram accounts of the celebrities she followed. When she got tired of the majority of them reposting inspirational quotes she dropped her phone and leaned over to open the top drawer of her dresser for her weed box.

Damn my stash is low.

She twisted up her lips at the thought of having to double back and call Mook. She preferred medicinal weed and although Mook's scandalous ass was not the only one selling it underground, he was the only one she knew. For a second— a hot-ass second—she thought about calling him to bring her a half-ounce of Night Train. It would help her sleep.

She picked up her phone and her thumb hovered over his name in her contacts. *Do I love smoking that much?*

She shook her head. Mook was not to be trusted. She deleted his contact before she changed her mind. *Fuck that and fuck him.*

Tank would know where to get some weed. He hated that she loved it so much but he loved the way she sexed him when she was blazed. It was during those times that she was her most creative. She smiled thinking of the night she first jacked him off with her breasts as she sucked the tip of his dick. "Good times," she said longingly with a shake of her head.

Tank.

A desire to be by his side hit her.

She looked over her shoulder at the sheets of paper on the wall. Was she so busy chasing the shooter that she was missing out on the chance to at least be near him? *When I sought revenge for my son he was dead and gone. Tank is still here.*

She wanted to settle the score but at what cost?

Her eyes shifted down to the fireplace where the package of heroin was stashed. Her shoulders slumped.

Just how many lines was she willing to cross?

Early the next morning, Naeema stood in the doorway feeling like sleep played keep away with her all night. She looked up and then down the street and tensed when she spotted a town car double-parked outside the apartment building near the corner. There was a line of cars behind it.

The front door opened and Mya stepped out onto the porch in a pretty black dress with a white collar. A woman in her mid-thirties soon followed in a black wrap dress with her hair pulled up into a tight topknot. Her eyes were swollen and puffy, her face already streaked with tears.

Mya looked up as they came down the stairs. Like Naeema did last night she raised her hand to speak but then made a fist and lowered her arm.

Naeema shifted her eyes to Mya's mother and found the woman staring at her with a face filled with hate. She saw Mya reach over to grab her mother's arm.

Some of the people in the funeral procession lowered their windows or got out of their cars. Those neighbors already outside in their yards or on their steps looked down the street.

Not blazing and having no clue where to get some weed, Naeema already felt on edge but she forced herself to call on the good sense her grandfather fought hard to instill in her and stepped back into her house. As she closed the door she spotted the woman noticing Mya looking over at her. She roughly pulled her daughter to her side and covered her face with her hand as she rushed her down the stairs and into the back of the car.

Too bad you weren't that protective of her before.

From her window she watched and waited until the funeral procession was gone before she left her house again and jogged down the stairs to climb into Tank's Tahoe parked at the end of her driveway. She paused and checked the rearview mirror as a blue car passed by on the street. She reversed the SUV onto the street until she was able to accelerate forward.

She was pulling off her Foxy Brown cap, retiring Queen, sending Sarge home, and just going to be Mrs. Cole at her husband's bedside. For today it was what she needed and it was more than enough.

Is someone following me?

Naeema had just gotten onto the Garden State Parkway and looked in the rearview mirror. She hadn't been able to pinpoint any one vehicle that might be on her heels but she couldn't fight the feeling she was being followed.

Is it the black sedan or that white pickup truck? Neither? What the fuck?

At the sudden blare of a horn, Naeema quickly shifted her eyes from the rearview mirror and jerked the wheel to the left to pull the Tahoe from the right lane where she accidentally drifted. The driver of a red compact she almost hit lowered their driver's side window.

"Dumb bitch," he screamed at the top of his lungs.

Your momma.

She didn't even feel like getting into it. She was emotionally and physically drained. The late night at the club. Getting up early to give Sarge a break at the hospital. Trying to stay on top of Tank's business through Grip. Hunting down a wannabe killer. Taking credit for a murder she didn't commit. She was being pulled every which way but loose.

Naeema accelerated ahead. She checked the rearview mirror and her hands tightened on the wheel to see a blue car quickly shift to the right into her lane. *Is that the car that went by my house?*

Without using her turn signal Naeema switched lanes again, sped up, and switched to another. The blue car stayed a few cars behind but it accelerated forward as well. She still wasn't sure.

Naeema eyed the upcoming exit for Elizabeth. She bit her lip and stayed in the middle lane. Her body was tensed in her seat as she waited until just before the exit ramp to slide over between two cars. Horns blared. The car behind her swerved a bit in shock as Naeema sped up around the curve and then eyed her rearview mirror to see the blue car do the same.

As she drove onto the surrounding city streets, Naeema sped the fuck up taking last-minute turns as she tried her best to shake whomever was on her tail. She didn't know if it was just someone following her and reporting her moves or someone out to do harm.

She made the left onto Frelinghuysen Avenue, a wide, long street that would lead her back into Newark. She was familiar with the neighboring city of Elizabeth but she knew her hometown better and right then she needed the advantage. As she pulled to a stop at a red light she checked the rearview mirror again. The blue car was speeding toward her. In the distance she could see the clock tower of the Elizabeth train station. She took the streets to reach it and drove into the small parking deck.

She quickly parked on the lowest level, reaching in the armrest for her gun before she hopped out of the car and ran away from it to duck down between two SUVs just as she heard the tires of the blue car squeal against the concrete. Her heart pounded. She was running off pure adrenaline. *Aight motherfucker. Let's play by my rules now.*

With the gun in her hand and at the ready she eased up enough off her haunches to see the car stop behind Tank's SUV. Through both the rear window of the SUV to her right and then the passenger window of the blue car she could see a small man behind the wheel. She was too far to make out his features but she could tell he spoke to someone on his cell phone—it was a cheap flip phone. A throwaway.

He accelerated forward and she lowered her body as she watched him slowly drive the full length of the parking deck. He passed by the two SUVs and she moved deeper into the shadows caused by the large vehicles. Her gun was cocked and pointed to put some heat in his ass if he came for her.

The car circled twice more and Naeema was able to get the license tag number. She was itching to jump in front of the vehicle and put a few bullets through the windshield. With one murder on her hands that the police were aware of she was wary as fuck at getting another one, regardless of the situation. *If I had a burner gun his ass would be fucked.*

As soon as she spotted the car turn to go up a level, Naeema came from between the cars and raced across the short distance to climb behind the wheel of the Tahoe. With the gun still in her hand she started the car and sped out of the parking deck, going fast as fuck through the streets until she was back on the parkway.

There was one thing she was sure of. They had come to take her the fuck out because someone hired to just follow her would have never exposed that fact. Now the question was whose toes had she stepped on enough to make them come for her when she didn't fucking send for them.

$\mathcal{N}$aeema had never felt so alone in her life. So unsure. So tested.

She scooted the chair by Tank's bedside closer as she lay her head atop the hand she held between both of hers. Her grandfather used to warn her that a person never misses their well until the water runs dry. She now understood that shit more than ever.

Tank was a constant and in the last week and some days since the shooting it was clear that she needed him—whether by her side or at least close enough when she called on him. First Tank was shot and now someone was on her ass.

Was it Yani?

You can believe what the fuck you want but I didn't have shit to do with this shooting, Naeema, and if you try to come at me I will stop you.

Or Willie?

You be safe out there, Naeema.

Or Murk?

What do you think Murk would do to you now—or in the future—if he knew the wife of the snitch who tried to take him down was working in his club?

She was lost more than ever.

Naeema pressed her lips to Tank's hand. Even with the saltiness of him not having a bath or shower since before the shooting, she enjoyed the feel of his skin against her mouth. A small but very necessary connection.

The bathroom door opened and Sarge stepped into the room. Thankfully his hands were still dripping wet from him—at the very least—rinsing them off. "I'm ready," he said.

Naeema shook her head. "You can't go back to the house right now," she said.

Sarge frowned.

"Somebody was chasing me today and they know where I live," she said, feeling overwhelmed. "I can't let you go back there. Not yet."

"You go too far," he said, his fuzzy silver brows furrowed.

"Not now, Sarge," Naeema said, turning her head down to press her lips back to Tank's hand as she closed her eyes. *What do I do now?*

"But I'm ready to—"

"It's not safe," she snapped in irritation at his insistence on ignoring that she was looking out for him.

He grunted.

"It's not safe, Sarge," she repeated, her tone softer. More respectful.

He grunted again.

She released a heavy breath. "Fuck," she swore.

"Not with Sarge in here."

Naeema stiffened and raised her head to find Tank's eyes open and resting on her just as he tried to strengthen his hand around hers. She felt weak with relief but she rose to her feet, his hand tight in hers, as she smiled down at his face. "Welcome back," she whispered to him, bending to press kisses to his face. She even enjoyed the feel of the facial hair that grew in lightly prickling her skin.

He nodded and closed his eyes to receive them.

Naeema didn't pray often but she wore out God's ear in those moments with thanks and pleading for Tank to become one hundred percent again.

The hospital room door opened and the nurse on duty walked in with Sarge following close behind. Naeema didn't even know the old man had left the room. "Thank you," she mouthed to him.

He nodded his head roughly and she knew he was still annoyed with her.

Sarge will be the fuck all right.

Hell, I will be the fuck all right. Tank is back.

Naeema held on to his hand as long as she could as the nurse did a quick evaluation of him and asked Tank questions to see if he was aware of the time and place. Never once did his eyes waver from Naeema's face and she didn't miss that with each passing minute his hold on her hand got stronger.

"I'll notify the doctors that he's awake," said the nurse, a plain-looking woman with bright red hair, as she raised the head of his bed a little.

"Sarge," Tank said still sounding tired. He gently lifted his chin toward the door. "Just for a sec."

Sarge nodded and actually formed his usually frowning lips into a smile. "This is good," he said, moving toward the door.

He paused with it open. "It's too soon to put too much on him, Naeema," he said, not even looking back. Seconds later the door closed behind him.

Naeema bent again to kiss Tank's mouth.

Tank averted his head. "Breath stink like dog shit," he said.

Naeema smiled and turned to look down at the tray of hygiene products that had been sitting on his nightstand. She held up a smaller tray with a toothbrush, toothpaste, and mouth sponge on a stick. She felt Tank's eyes on her as she moved to the sink. She smiled at him when she came back over to sit the tray on his chest. "This is a first," she said. "And we have done a lot of things for each other."

He winked as he opened his mouth.

As she cleansed his mouth, tongue, and teeth, Naeema wavered over telling Tank everything that had been going on since the shooting. But she bit her mouth and said nothing. Not yet. *Sarge is right. It's too soon.*

She held a cup to his mouth for him to rinse it. "I'm a barber . . . not a nurse," she teased.

He laughed and then winced.

"How do you feel?" she asked.

"Still sore."

"I'll be glad when the doctor gets here," she said, turning her back to him as she returned to the sink.

"Where's my phone?"

Naeema looked up at her reflection in the mirror. "I have it," she said. *And what?*

"Call Grip for me," he said, closing his eyes.

Naeema ran a dozen different outcomes around in her mind from having Grip clue Tank in to everything going on. "Let's talk to the doctor first, Tank," she said. "If everyone knows you're conscious they're going to flood this room with visitors and I just want the okay from the doctor first."

He nodded with his eyes still closed.

She watched him in the mirror. Soaked him up. Reveled in him. *I love that man to death.*

"Come here, Na," he said, opening his eyes to look at her.

She turned and walked over to him, taking the hand he held open for her. "I missed you," she admitted.

He puckered his lips and she bent down to kiss his lips softly. Once. And then again. She made to rise up from him but he shook his head and locked his eyes with hers. "*Kiss* me," he stressed.

And she did, tracing the bottom of his mouth with her tongue before she gently sucked it as she touched the side of his face. At the first feel of Tank's tongue she circled it with her own before she deepened the kiss with a soft moan filled with just how much she ached for him. Emotionally and physically.

Tank broke the kiss and shifted his head to the side. "Look," he said, lifting his square chin.

Naeema glanced down at him and jumped back slightly at the sight of his hard dick tenting the blanket. "Tank," she said, looking back at him.

"*Both* heads working just fine," he said with a big smile.

Naeema kissed him again.

"Touch that motherfucker," he said thickly, low in his throat.

Naeema stared down at him. "Really, Tank? At a time like this?"

He thrust his hips up off the bed a little.

She held up the blanket and slid her hand down his left thigh to wrap around the thick base of his dick. "It's hot too," she said, feeling heat rise in her as well.

His lids came halfway down over his eyes. "Let me see."

She held the blanket up with her free hand and made long strokes up and down the length of him finishing with deep pressure against the smooth tip. "Feel good?" she asked.

He glanced over at her and nodded. "Damn right. Let me know I'm alive in this joint, yo," he said, his eyes back on her hand job.

The hospital door burst open. They both looked up at the redheaded nurse standing there. Her eyes widened at the scene laid out before her.

"His monitor was . . . is . . . going off. Are you going to stop?" the nurse asked, seeming completely shaken.

"Are you going to leave?" Naeema countered.

The nurse turned and left the room.

Tank chuckled. "Bonnie," he said.

"Whaddup, Clyde?" she asked, still milking his dick.

"I fucking love your ass, Na," he said.

"You better."

Knock-knock.

"Damn," Tank swore.

Naeema kissed his mouth and then moved down to suck the tip of his dick once. Deeply. "Now *that's* love," she said, releasing him.

He laughed.

"Come in," she called, taking a seat and crossing her legs as the doctor entered with a wary expression.

"So you're up, Mr. Cole," he said. "And I see you're . . . excited . . . about it."

Naeema and Tank both laughed, but as she sat back quietly while the doctor examined him she felt tears rise up.

She was happy and sad all at once. There was so much to deal with. So much shit. Naeema was too excited about Tank to let anything worry her . . . for now.

Throughout the day the silence in the room was deafening. Everything was hanging in the air. All of the shit that needed to be said—to be revealed—was looming like a dark-ass cloud.

"Give me my phone, Na," Tank said from the edge of the bed. "I need to talk to Grip and Tina."

"Tina?" she said with an attitude.

"She's my connection in the police department," he explained. "I want a real update on the shooting."

"Tank—"

"I need to talk to Fevah," he continued.

"She fired you," Naeema admitted.

He frowned and then shrugged one broad shoulder as he nodded. "I can understand that. She must've been scared having someone shoot at her like that."

Naeema bit her mouth and dropped her head.

Sarge grunted.

She shot the old man the nastiest side-eye as she fought the urge to get up and slap the piss and shit out of him. "Tank, you need to relax," she said, turning in the seat to eye her husband.

His look shifted from her to Sarge's profile and back to her.

"Enough is enough," Tank said. "The doctors said I'm fine. They're keeping me for observation. It's time to get back to business."

"I—"

"Naeema," he said, his voice hard. He took a visible deep breath. "My phone. *Please*."

She glanced over at Sarge sitting in a chair by the window as he looked up at the game show playing on the television. He never broke his stare on the set.

"It's downstairs. I'll go get it," she lied, rising from the chair.

Tank nodded as he looked down at the IV entry still taped against the back of his hand.

In the hallway, Naeema pulled out the phone and unlocked it. She dialed Grip.

"Yo."

She walked down to the end of the hall to lean against the large metal frame of the window. "Grip, this is Naeema. Tank is awake—"

"Wow," he said. "For real?"

She nodded. "Listen. He's going to call you. Lay low on the real reason behind the shooting," she said, turning to press her back against the wall.

The line was quiet.

"Grip?"

"Tank and I go too far back for me to lie to him, Naeema," he said. "You know that."

"I'm not saying lie. I'm just saying not today. That's all," she stressed. "He will leave this hospital, bust his stitches, and fuck himself up if he knows there's a chance he's the target."

"But—"

"Just until he's released and then I promise we all will

work together to find the bum bastard who did this but he needs to be closer to a hundred percent before he even thinks about it."

Grip went quiet again.

"You can beg his pardon later, Grip," she said, her voice hard. "Dayum."

She hung up on his ass. "Grip better not fuck with me," she muttered as she scrolled through Tank's contacts and hit the DIAL button.

Naeema paced.

"Hello," the voice said hesitantly.

She dropped her head so low her chin almost touched her chest. "Hi . . . Tina. This is Naeema. Tank's wife," she said.

"Oh my God, did he die?" she gasped.

Naeema pressed her fingertip against one eye as she felt it jump in agitation. "No, no he didn't," she said. *And why would I call you if he did?!*

"How can I help you?" Tina asked, her voice cool.

Calling the woman her husband smashed during one of their many breakups wasn't easy—especially a woman whose taste she once slapped out of her mouth.

"I need your help," Naeema admitted, her stomach in knots. "Can you—"

"*My* help?"

"Yes, Tina. Can we meet?"

"No. Matter of fact. Hell no," Tina stressed.

Oh, she a bad bitch over the phone line?

"Listen, Tina, I have a tag I want you to run. Someone left a dent in Tank's Tahoe and a lady who saw the car gave me the info," she lied smooth as fuck.

"Then why not give the info to the police?"

Naeema looked pensive, her eyes darting back and forth as she thought quickly. "Because she might be wrong. I don't like tying a brotha up in the system for no reason," she said, hoping it was the right thing to say to nudge the bitch into just running the damn tag.

"What is it?" she asked reluctant as hell.

Naeema gave her the numbers and letters from memory.

"I'm at work. So hold on."

Naeema walked to the nurses' station and held the phone down out of their line of vision. "Can I borrow a pen please?"

They all eyed her oddly. One winked and gave a thumbs-up and the redhead's lips were tight as hell with disapproval. *Snitch bitch.*

Taking the pen, she turned and walked down the hall.

"Okay I found it," Tina said, her voice real low.

Naeema jotted down the name and address on the back of an old envelope in her purse. *Kevin Greene?*

"And can we keep this between us. Tank will go bananas if he knows something happened to one of his whips," Naeema said, with a roll of her eyes and a flip of her middle finger that she wished she could deliver to the bitch in person.

"He's awake?" Tina asked.

"Tank's gonna call you about the investigation into the shooting of Fevah, but I'm curious. How's it really going?" Naeema asked.

"The case is already getting cold because the detectives are still looking into the rapper's background for a possible motive," Tina said. "Are *you* sure?"

"Sure about what?" Naeema said, playing mental checkers with her ass.

"You made it seem like Tank was the intended target and not Fevah," Tina said.

"No, no, no," Naeema said. "It was Fevah. I was just mad at you being there and wanted to piss you off. Sorry about that."

"Oh."

This bitch is too naive for Tank.

Naeema walked back toward Tank's room. "Thanks, Tina. I appreciate it," she said forcing civility into her tone. "And Tank's awake so he'll be calling you in a little bit."

She ended the call. *Beep.*

Naeema erased all recent activity on the phone before she walked back into the room. She smiled but it faded because the chair Sarge had been sitting in was now empty. "Where is he?" she asked, coming over to hand the phone to Tank.

"The caf," Tank said.

I didn't see him leave.

"Will you help me take a shower?" he asked. "They want me to get up but I'm supposed to call the nurse for help."

Naeema nodded.

"I knew you would," he teased. "You don't want them to see all this."

She smirked when he flipped his hospital gown open and flashed his dick at her. "They wouldn't know what to do with it, boo," she said as she turned to grab a clean gown from the top drawer of the nightstand.

"No one knows what to do with it like you," Tank admitted.

Naeema turned and placed her hands on her hips. "Just how many have tried?" she asked him, dead-ass serious.

"Never enough to top you," he countered.

Naeema gave a sarcastic snort as she crossed the room to open the closet and pull out his shaving bag. "If your clippers in here, you want to shave too?" she asked, unzipping it.

"I need to get shot more often because in the past that would've been one helluva argument," he quipped.

"Don't ever wish that, Tank," she said, her eyes and her voice serious as hell.

He came over to drape one arm around her waist and pull her body close against his. She hugged him back. Tight enough to enjoy the feel of him but not too tight to possibly hurt the gunshot wounds that would permanently scar his body.

"You don't understand, yo, I thought I would never hold you again," she whispered against his neck. "This right here feels like the realest shit ever."

Tank pressed a kiss to her temple. "It *is* the realest shit ever."

With his arm draped across her shoulders they made their way to the bathroom. She locked the door behind them and then went behind Tank to undo the strings tied around his neck. "I should have turned the shower on first," she said, moving back around him to turn the knob so that steaming hot water flowed from the head and hit the tiled wall of the open shower.

Tank took a piss in the commode before he stepped into the shower and leaned his back against the wall, letting the water pelt against his legs. "That feels good," he said.

"You should have taken off the bandages," she warned.

Tank shrugged as he took the washcloth and bar of soap from her. "They'll change them when I'm done," he said, wincing a little as he raised his left arm to wash the right.

"Call me when you're done," she said, picking up the hospital gown before reaching for the doorknob.

"Stay with me."

Her hand closed into a fist as she looked back at him.

The soapsuds clung to the contours of his body as the steam swirled around him like a lover. Being near death hadn't done a damn thing to his sexy. As Naeema stood there and watched him lather his dick she felt that bud between her legs wake up. *Just fine as hell for no fucking reason.*

The steam started to fill the entire bathroom and press against her body causing the peach strapless romper she wore with gold gladiator sandals to cling to her.

He lowered his head as he massaged the length of his dick. It hardened in his hand. He cut his eyes over at her. "What you gon' do wit' it?" he asked.

Naeema breathed through her open lips as she watched him. It hadn't been *that* long since they sexed on the balcony the night of the shooting, but it seemed like a *really* long time. "Tank," she said, her whisper mingling with the steam.

"Nah, nah. Fuck that, Na. I'm a get this nut regardless," he said, biting the side of his tongue as his hips arched up off the wall as his stroking quickened. "You want in or not?"

Naeema stripped, double-checked that the door was locked, and draped his gown over the commode before she turned her back to him and looked back over her shoulder as she bent over to grip the seat. She shivered at the feel of the water hitting against her ass as she felt Tank turn to stand behind her. His hands held her ass and his thumbs spread the lips of her pussy as she arched her back and rose up on the tips of her toes.

They both cried out as he slid inch after delicious inch inside her. He pressed against her walls and made his presence known. There, surrounded by steam that made it all hotter, Tank stroked them to an explosive nut that made them both taste the steam as they gasped and hollered out with the sounds of their pleasure bouncing off the sweaty walls.

$\mathcal{N}$aeema kept pushing the button for the lobby as if it would make the elevator move any faster. Not that she had to lay eyes on the hospital's cafeteria to know Sarge was not in it. *He took his ass back to the house. I just know it.*

As far as she knew Sarge never ventured into the caf during any of the days she had him watching over Tank. She assumed as much because she always brought his food. Always. The fact escaped her notice until her and Tank's hot moments in the bathroom were over. She couldn't think clearly until then. His failure to return to the room after nearly a half hour just confirmed her doubts.

Ding.

As soon as the doors opened enough for her to get through them she did. She followed the signs on the walls to the cafeteria. The doors were locked.

Fuck it. Fuck this. Fuck him.

But she didn't mean it. She didn't mean that shit at all.

Retracing her steps she headed back to the lobby, flipping over her cell phone in her hand to dial Sarge's number. *Answer. Answer. Please answer.*

"I told you I was ready," he said.

"Sarge—"

Naeema looked up and spotted Grip coming through the

front doors of the hospital. She smiled at him and crossed the distance to stand before him. "Grip," she said, reaching to hold his wrist.

"I was just headed up to see Tank," he said.

"Sarge don't hang up," she said into the phone, before pressing it against her chest and looking up at Grip. "Stay with Tank 'til I get back."

She moved past him and quickly walked out of the hospital suddenly aware that she didn't put her underwear back on. "Where are you now, Sarge?" she asked.

"Almost home."

"Don't hang up," she said again as she made her way to the parking lot and eventually inside the Tahoe.

He grumbled but didn't hang up.

As she made her way from New York to New Jersey, Naeema left the phone in the cup holder on speakerphone. She focused on the road but she could tell from the noises Sarge made that he haggled with the cabbie over the fare, noisily entered the house, cursed and then threw a shoe at a mouse, stomped down the stairs, took a noisy piss, turned his television on, flipped channels, farted, and noisily chewed on what could only be chips or ice. That didn't include the dozen or so times he dropped the phone and cursed her for it.

Naeema kept her eyes focused on the road ahead and checked the road behind her in the rearview mirror to make sure she wasn't being followed. She still wasn't sure she was successful even as she turned the Tahoe onto the drive and pulled all the way into the backyard. Quickly she grabbed her gun as the sound of Sarge alternating between farting and laughing at *Martin* reruns echoed.

"I'm home, Sarge," she said into the phone, climbing

from the car and then taking the short set of stairs to the back door, which she unlocked and entered the house.

"Good."

Beep.

She stood at the entrance to the basement. "We're headed back to the hospital, Sarge," she yelled down the stairs to him. "You got five minutes."

"Not," he yelled back.

Another fart sounded off.

Knock-knock-knock.

Naeema went still as she cocked the gun and raised it as she looked around the open basement door to the back door. She eased along the wall to pull the blinds and curtain back enough to peek out.

"It's me, Miss Naeema. Mya."

With the help of the porch light her eyes locked with the teenager's through the glass. Reluctant as hell, she lowered the gun and opened the door. "Mya, you can't be here. Go home," she said.

Mya was dressed in the same colorful sleep pants she wore the night she killed her stepfather. Same pants but not the same girl. That was impossible.

"We're moving tomorrow," she said, wringing her hands together as her big bright eyes filled with tears. "I just wanted to th-th-thank you for what you did. I want you to know that I know it's a second chance and I won't fuck it—I mean—*mess* it up."

Naeema had been more of a mother to this young woman standing before her than she had to the child she bore fifteen years ago. Hearing that her mother was moving them away and knowing just how far Mya felt she had to go to be free of her stepfather was tougher than she ever thought. "You promise?" she asked, her voice soft with emotions she wasn't comfortable with. At all. "Good grades. College. Only young men worth your time. Good job. Marriage. Beautiful babies. You promise not to waste your second chance? You promise not to *fuck* it up?"

Mya nodded before she stepped into the house and hugged Naeema close enough for her to feel the girl's heart beating hard in her chest. "Okay. You gotta go," she said, giving her an awkward pat on the back with the hand not holding the loaded gun.

Mya released her and turned to walk down the stairs. She gave Naeema one last glance over her shoulder before she waved and strolled around the rear of the house. Naeema pulled the door closed and went down the stairs to stand at the corner to watch the shadow of Mya's figure move down the driveway in the darkness.

"Oh fuck me," Naeema said as the small blue car rolled by the house.

She gripped her gun tighter and raced forward to grab Mya's arm and then roughly push her back against the house. "Stay here," Naeema said to her, continuing down the drive with the gun behind her back.

She spotted the brake lights of the car just as he pulled into a parking spot up the street. *This bold motherfucker.*

Naeema looked up and down the dimly lit street. Her breaths came in short bursts as she tapped the gun against her thigh. *What do I do?*

"You want me? Then you got me, motherfucker," she said, coming up behind her neighbor's pickup truck and creeping across the street before she took off at a full run.

She came up on the passenger side of the car and with a little grunt, she gritted her teeth and jerked the door open as she held her gun steady in her hand and pointed it at the man's head.

"Don't you fucking move," Naeema said, keeping her gun trained on him. "Kevin Greene, right?"

He dropped his head as he shook it. "Shit," he swore.

"This not your first night outside my damn house, is it?" she asked, realizing she caught him off guard because it was just another night for him. Watching her.

The fuck?

"What the fuck do you want?" she asked, her voice hard.

The lights from an oncoming car flashed across their faces. She saw a hint of fear in his brown depths. She hoped he saw her capability to kill in hers.

"Miss Naeema, you okay?"

His eyes shifted past her but Naeema fought not to let Mya's sudden appearance behind her rattle her. "Go the fuck home," she said to her, never once taking her eyes or her gun off him. "Now!"

Mya's face suddenly pressed against the driver's side window.

Again Naeema had to steady herself. For one hot second she considered pointing the gun at Mya to get her to finally go the fuck home.

"That's the man that broke into your house. That's him," Mya said excitedly as she pointed her finger against the window toward his face.

He lightly pounded his fist against the wheel.

"Don't move, you thieving little bastard," Naeema said, as she climbed into the passenger seat. She reached over to pat him down from head to toe. With a smirk, she took the small gun in the ankle strap he wore and the stun gun pressed between the driver's seat and the armrest.

She pushed the stun gun under her thigh and sat his gun in her lap. "Drive," she ordered him, reaching behind her with her free hand to close the passenger door. "And you better not hit her."

Naeema picked up his gun, now holding a weapon in each hand as she eyed him with a hard stare.

He gripped the wheel with both hands and pulled out into traffic carefully, leaving Mya behind standing in the street watching them drive off.

She put one gun to his head and pressed the barrel of the other to his belly. "Make a left at the corner and then a right on Sixteenth Ave," she said.

He followed her directions as he cast her side-eye glances, revealing that he was nervous.

Good.

"What the fuck do you want from me?" Naeema asked him, not even flinching when he suddenly swerved the car. She just pressed her knee against the dash to steady herself.

She moved the gun from his belly to press between his legs. "Do that bullshit again and I will blow what little bit of a dick you have the fuck *off*," she promised him.

He pressed his thin lips closed and squinted.

He was thinking just as hard about a way out of the jam she had him in as she was trying to figure it all out.

"Make the right on Seventeenth Street and pull into the empty lot," Naeema said.

"Fuck," he swore under his breath.

"Basically," she said, agreeing with him.

He pulled into the asphalt-covered lot.

"Park," she ordered him.

He did.

"Turn the car off and toss the keys on the floor," she said.

He did that as well.

"Who do you work for?" she asked.

"He told me in advance to say 'Fuck you' if asked," he said, his voice almost as thin as he was.

"Fuck *me*?" she asked with a little laugh.

"You're playing some dangerous games," he said.

Naeema arched a brow. "You think I'm playing?" she asked.

He nodded and glanced at her briefly. "And out of your league."

"So I'm playing? I wasn't . . . but now we can. Let's play baseball. Three strikes and your motherfucking ass is out," she said, dropping the gun to the floor to press down on with her foot.

He shifted in his seat. "Put the gun down before you slip and shoot it," he said, the slightest tremble in his voice. Almost undetectable.

Almost.

"Strip," Naeema ordered him, moving the gun away from his head but holding it steady and aimed to shoot the fuck out of him.

"Listen, I was just looking out for you like I was asked," he said. "That's why I was outside your house."

Naeema twisted her full lips, picked up the stun gun, and flipped the switch. A small red light on the side came on. "Lies," she said, before reaching over to press it against his bare arm.

Bzzzzz-zap.

He released a high-pitched shout that could shatter weak glass as his body went rigid.

"Let's try this again," she said, finally removing the prods from his body. "Strip."

"You—"

She backhanded him twice.

WHAP-PAP.

"Shut your smart-ass mouth up," she snapped.

He glared at her as he massaged his jaw and mouth.

"You hard-headed motherfucker," she grumbled, reaching out to him with the stun gun again.

"Aight. Aight," he said, pressing his body back against the door away from her as he yanked the polo shirt he wore over his head. He unbuttoned and worked his shorts and boxers down over his hips and ass.

She eyed the tattoos randomly scattered on his chest. Some of them looked more like fucking Etch A Sketch than real tatts. *Hmmm . . .*

Naeema turned the stun gun and pressed it against his chest with the two prods flanking his brown nipple.

"Who do you work for?" she asked.

He raised his hand as if to grab her wrist.

"Strike one," she said.

Bzzzzz-zap.

He shouted out again from the voltage as his body convulsed.

"Who do you work for?" she asked again.

"Ask your snitch of a man," he said between deep gasps for air.

"Strike two," she said simply, now reaching to press the

stun gun against his fleshy balls so deeply that she could feel the warmth of them against the back of her hand.

"No, no," he begged.

Yes, yes, yes, motherfucker.

She notched her chin higher as she pressed the button.

Bzzzzz-zap.

He hollered out sharply in pain and rocked back and forth in the seat as he clutched at his tortured balls. Naeema calmly looked in his backseat, which was filled with takeout containers, empty wrappers from snack foods, and clothes that needed to find a Laundromat fast and in a hurry. She snatched up a musty shirt and shoved it into his mouth until he quieted down.

"Where all that smart mouth now?" Naeema asked before she raised her hand and zapped his chest again and again methodically.

Bzzzzz-zap.

He shrieked.

Bzzzzz-zap.

She didn't give a fuck.

Bzzzzz-zap.

He broke into her home.

Bzzzzz-zap.

Violated it with his presence.

Bzzzzz-zap.

Hurt Sarge.

Bzzzzz-zap.

Stole her weed.

Bzzzzz-zap.

Chased her down.

Bzzzzz-zap.

And her gut told her he shot Tank.

Bzzzzzzzzzzzzzzzzzzzzzzzzzzzzzz-zap.

She removed the stun gun and looked at her handiwork. It took nine zaps, as she put the heat to his ass, to spell out FU in large letters with the two dots the prongs of the stun gun burnt into his flesh. He writhed in pain, his face twisted with it.

"It's never, ever fuck me. It's always fuck you and you'll *never* forget that," she said, her eyes hot with anger and her power in the situation.

"You crazy," he said between pants, his eyes glazed with agony.

"You don't *even* know," Naeema said, by way of agreeing with him.

"Let's switch up some shit," she said. "Different question and different weapon."

It was clear to her that he worked for Murk and the drug lord wanted revenge for Tank testifying against him.

Ask your snitch of a man.

She turned off the stun gun and pressed it back under her thigh as she used her foot to slide his gun forward on the floor as she pressed her gun against his now-sweaty head. She picked up his small gun in her right hand and pointed it toward him.

"Should I let you live after you tried to take the life of my man?" Naeema asked.

"I didn't, I swear," he said, stumbling over his words as the smell of his urine suddenly filled the air.

"I don't believe you," she said. "You shot Tank and you

came for me earlier today and tonight you sat outside my house and were coming for me again, motherfucker. Wrong fucking move."

"I didn't—"

POW!

His blood and brain matter splattered against the glass and the door as his body convulsed before his eyes went still with death.

Fuck it.

Naeema calmly used the shirt to clean her prints from his gun. She didn't want to risk walking home with it. At least with her 9mm she had a license. She looked up and down the length of the street as she worked. There was no traffic and the two apartment buildings flanking the lot had long since been abandoned. Across the street was West Side Park. It was the perfect spot for a crime.

Leaving his gun on his lap, she pushed her weapon down into the front of her strapless bra, held the stun gun in her hand, and climbed from the car. Quickly she bent and used the edge of her shirt to clean any fingerprints from the door handle.

Humph. Murk's ass is next.

Without a fuck to give for the death she left behind, Naeema made the short walk back home.

I should have asked him more questions before I killed him.

"Na."

Murk wanted Tank killed because he testified against him. So why was he following me? Why chase me? Why break in my house?

"Na."

Murk knew who I was then, right? So why let me work undercover in his club?

"Naeema . . . Naeema!"

She blinked and turned her head to find Tank sitting on the side of the hospital bed with his eyes on her. The secrets she kept from him caused her to look away from him before he saw too much. She forced a stiff smile when she saw that Grip's eyes rested on her as well.

"Yo, what's on your mind, baby?" Tank asked.

Something ain't right.

"Nothing," she lied.

Grip pushed up off the spot where he was leaning against the counter of the sink. "Well, I'm heading home," he said, going over to Tank with his fist extended. "Good to look you in the eye again, yo."

Tank dapped the top of his fist with his own. "Damn right," he said.

Naeema looked away from them as she gently chewed on her bottom lip. "What am I missing?" she mouthed. "What *the fuck* am I missing?"

Barely an hour had passed since she branded, tortured, and killed a man. She walked away from the scene plotting on sitting outside Gentlemen Only and murking Murk before he had a chance to blink or think. A phone call from Tank summoning her back to his side was the only thing that kept Murk from joining his goon in the motherfucking hereafter.

She left Sarge behind at the house positive she had assured his safety—for at least the night—and made her way back to NYC. Time brought on deeper thinking and clarity that the heat of the moment had fucked all the way up.

Something ain't right worth a fuck.

"Did everything between us change while I was down, Na?"

Naeema stiffened as she looked back at him. "Never," she said, her voice soft.

He said nothing. He was waiting on the truth.

"I think you were the real target of the shooting and not Fevah," she admitted.

Tank scowled. His eyes shifted about the room. He was processing shit.

Just as surely as she knew her own name she knew Tank was recalling every step, every moment, and every little detail about the night of the shooting. She sat up a little straighter in her chair and didn't say a word as she watched him.

His lips moved with whatever words he mumbled to himself. His eyes were intense and focused as he stared at nothing. His face showed everything, including the moment everything clicked.

"They kept shooting even after the door Fevah was about to get out of closed. Three more shots," he said.

She nodded. "Exactly."

He locked those black eyes on her. "What you been up to, Na?" he asked, his voice hard.

Naeema opened her mouth but just released a heavy breath instead of the truth. Tank's anger at her for tracking down the killer of her son was hard to forget.

POW!

A vision of Kevin Greene's blood and brain matter hitting the glass flashed.

"What do you think about Yani, Willie, or Murk for the

shooting?" she asked instead, keeping the murder to herself for now.

He gave her a look that let her know she was pump-faking him on the truth and not fooling him. "Willie don't have the balls," he said with a shake of his head. "He's all talk. Plus, he knows I floated him the loot to start that bail bond bullshit he done fucked up."

Oh.

Naeema nodded. "And Yani? Not as the shooter but a part of the setup for the shooting."

"Nothing to gain . . . that I know of," he said.

"And Murk?"

Her heart was pounding so loudly she wondered if he could hear it. "Definite possibility."

Naeema looked down at the floor and then back up at him. "Why'd you testify?" she asked. "You had to know he would come for you."

He released a Sarge-like grunt and shook his head with regret. "I let the detective I know who worked the murder case blow it up in my head like they had him. He did so many favors for me in the past and he called me on it and asked me to testify. Everybody involved was shocked like a motherfucker when he got off on a fucking technicality. I coulda slapped the shit out of the judge as soon as he said the words that set Murk free."

Naeema's eyes took in every aspect of his handsome face. "Were you afraid of him?" she asked in disbelief. In her eyes Tank had no fear. She didn't want that to change.

He looked at her like *Bitch, please,* even though she knew he would never say the words to her. "Did I go in hiding? Hell no, I ain't afraid of that fool, yo. By going the straight route it put me in a jam where I couldn't move underground to off his ass without drawing attention to myself."

She smiled and stood up to press a kiss to his temple.

He sat back to look up at her. "Is Murk still alive, Naeema?" he asked.

He might as well have asked had *she* killed him because that's what he meant and she knew it.

"For now," she admitted, her eyes going ice cold with anger.

He reached up and cupped the back of her neck to pull her down closer to his. "I don't need you to fight my battles. I'm back. I got it," he said, his words caressing her lips before he tasted them briefly.

Too late.

"Besides there's one more mo'fucker I gotta check out," Tank said.

Say what now?

Naeema stepped back, her face filled with confusion. "Who?" she asked.

Tank wiped his mouth with his hand. "A greedy-ass, no-account, selfish damn politician," he said.

Naeema arched a brow. "Hell, could you whittle the list down for me a little more?" she asked, her voice sarcastic.

Kickbacks were the name of the game and plenty of politicians on every level wanted to know what they could get out of any deal that came across their desk. Plenty of scratched backs and kissed asses.

"I got proof of some of his shady shit but I never thought he would try to kill me for it."

Naeema crossed her arms over her ample chest. "How does he know what you have?" she asked.

Tank looked at her and then shifted his eyes away.

She repeated the question.

"I used it against him," he admitted, glancing over at her and then glancing away.

"For money?" she asked, her eyes now big as shit with surprise. "Motherfucking blackmail? Now you're caught up in all that back-scratching, ass-kissing bullshit that's had this city fucked up for decades?"

Tank was her moral compass. He was willing to put in the work to handle any situation by any means but his preference was the high road. The legal road. The right road.

The fuck?

"And to push him to do good for the city," Tank said, his face tight with anger fed by her accusations. "Trust me, it's a lot of shit going down that I had a hand in, Naeema. A lot of good shit."

Her body relaxed a little and she undid her arms.

"I could've turned his ass in and it would've led to him being forced out of office but I had a leash around that motherfucker's neck and I walked his ass where the fuck I wanted him to go, to do what the fuck I wanted him to do," he said, his voice passionate and his eyes blazing. "Sometimes the devil you know—and got control of—is better than the devil they replace him with. You get me?"

She nodded and stepped forward to stand between his open thighs, rest her hands on his broad shoulders, and settle her chin softly atop his head. She closed her eyes at the feel of his hands settled on her hips and then wrapped around her.

In that moment each needed the feel of the other.

That's the man that broke in your house. That's him.

Her eyes opened as Mya's words came to her.

It made more sense for a man to have one of his goons break into a home to find evidence being used against him. Perhaps the politician thought Tank hid the shit at her house and wanted it back. Wanted to be free of Tank. And when that didn't work murder was next.

She licked her lips and stroked the back of his head. "Who is it?" she asked, forcing her voice to be soft and innocent.

"Huh?" he asked, his face snuggled against her cleavage.

"The politician? Who is it?" she asked, before pressing a kiss to his head.

His body went stiff. Naeema grimaced. *Shit.*

"Hell no," he said, now using his hands on her hips to push her back from him. "No."

"What?" she asked innocently, pretending to look confused.

Shiiiit.

"Run that bullshit on somebody that don't know you," he said, reaching behind him to push back the sheet on the bed before he lay down. He patted the small, empty space next to him.

Naeema wanted to finish what she started and that meant finding out the name and present location of the dirty politician, but in that moment—after all the days waiting and praying for Tank to be okay and present—that little piece of space on the bed beside him won over any other desires she had.

She kicked off her heels and lay down on her side with her face pressed into that intimate nook between his chin and his shoulder. With his arm settled over her and his hand resting comfortably on her ass, she kissed the pulse of his neck. "Welcome home," she whispered, promising herself that she would make the pitiful pawns on the chessboard of their life recognize that it's the job of the queen to always protect her king.

"*W*ell, damn."

Naeema shook her head as she looked at the way Tank's living room was completely trashed. It took her right back to the night she came home to find her shit ransacked. Reaching under the sleeveless bulky sweatshirt she wore she pulled her gun from the leather holster she wore under it.

Stepping over shattered lamps and broken picture frames in her path she was all the more certain that she made the right choice to leave the hospital as soon as Tank hit a snore deep enough to shake the roof.

She headed back to Newark, checked on Sarge—who was sleeping with a bat in his hand, she parked the 'Hoe, and headed back out on the streets on her motorcycle. She could lose another fool on her tail quicker than with the SUV.

She walked through the entire house and saw the same chaos in each and every room. She didn't know how long ago it went down but it was clear the politician was looking for the proof Tank held over him.

And now I'm looking for him.

She saw the back door had been kicked in and shook her head. The door was cracked and one of the hinges was broken. She wished she had been on the inside of the door when it flew open so she could have politely fired off a round of bullets—hopefully while their leg was still high in the air. *Fuck 'em up. Balls and all.*

Before leaving the house she slid her gun back in its holster and walked over to the garage in the backyard. She was surprised to find the door still locked and secured even with the keypad on it. They made a bad assumption that his garage was just a garage. Their dumbness was her luck. She entered her birth date and walked in, flipping the switch to bathe it with overhead light.

He'd converted the small garage to a gym and her eyes fell on the heavy bag hanging in the corner. A vision of her hanging on to the bag as he fucked her from behind flashed. *If that shit could talk . . .*

Naeema moved over to his large wooden desk in the corner and sat her gun atop the scarred wood as she took the seat behind it. She smiled as she looked down at a carving of her name in a heart. She traced the grooves with the tip of her index finger. That was a new addition. *I wonder when he did this.*

As she turned on his all-in-one computer she went through the files stacked neatly next to it and the ones filed away in the three drawers. She wanted to find something—anything—to lead her to the politician's identity. Unlike her, Tank was so organized—a point of contention in their marriage—so he had made it real easy to breeze through everything. Client files. Employee records and time sheets. Receipts. Old tax returns.

Nothing stuck out.

She logged on to his computer, knowing his password

hadn't changed since their separation. He trusted her just as much as she trusted him. That was just fact.

"Follow the money," Naeema whispered, pulling up and then logging in to his bank accounts. She knew that info as well.

"Well, damn, Tank," she said at the total balance of his personal and business accounts. It was well into six figures.

She also took note that he had a safe deposit box as well. She could only pray whatever proof she needed wasn't safely hidden away in it.

Chewing on the pointed tips of the fake fingernails on her left hand, she used her right to scroll through his business accounts first. She went back nearly three months, opening every sizeable deposit. "But what blackmailer pays with a check?" she said softly, already thinking of leaving that particular trail unsearched.

"Whoa, whoa, whoa," she said, squinting as she clicked on the entry for a check in the amount of ten thousand dollars and enlarged the copy of the check.

"Looky here, looky here," she read aloud. "Councilman Victor Planter. Humph. And the memo says for security detail. Bitch puh-*leeze*."

She shook her head as she backed up and found three other ten thousand dollar deposits from the business account of the councilman's office.

She jotted down the dates and then jerked open the drawer to search the client files again going back to a date before the first check five months ago. Her pulse was racing as she did. Like a hound dog on the hunt for blood her tail was wagging. "Got you," she said, pulling out the file. She missed it the first time because it just had his name and not his title.

There was a signed contract for services on file but Naeema wasn't buying it. "Nah, son," she said, biting the side of her tongue as she pulled out the folders holding time sheets. "Naaaaah."

She frowned at them only going back the two weeks before he was shot. She sat the files atop his desk and checked the computer but there was nothing there. Leaning to the side she looked down at the large paper shredder beside the desk. She had no minutes or even seconds of her life to spare pasting together shredded papers. "No fucking way," she said.

She leaned back in the chair and crossed her legs as she looked at the gym. It was right there on those mats that Tank taught and trained her how to defend herself. Many more times than not their wrestling moves, where he easily dominated and pressed her body beneath his, led to kisses, moans, and the rushed removal of just enough clothes for him to fill her pussy and stroke them both to a hot, sweaty nut.

They could never get enough of each other. Not in love, sex, or even when they were hard down at it arguing. It was never enough. *Fuck it.*

With his injuries it would be a good minute before Tank would be able to wrestle with her on the mat . . . or in bed.

That's why I have to finish this before his enemy comes for him again while he's weak. To me, I don't have a choice. I'll be the strong one for now.

"No haps," Naeema said, logging off the computer and replacing Tank's files before she left the garage. As she walked across the yard to the house she eyed the damaged door again. Who knew how long it had sat like that. Tank was lucky he was in a decent neighborhood or his house would have been stripped completely clean. Fiends would have formed a fucking line to work together to get all his good shit out of there quick as hell.

She entered the house and jammed the door back inside the frame as much as she could. She looked around at the mess. As much as she wanted to continue to hunt down Tank's shooter, she wasn't sure which path to follow. Kevin Greene was the hit man and he was handled but who sicced him on Tank and then her? Murk or Councilman Planter?

With the blackmail angle added to the mix, Murk was no longer a definite and she wasn't sure if she pinned down the right politician. Sliding the gun into the mouth of the councilman like it was a steel dick would get her some serious answers, but it could also mean serious jail time if he was innocent. She wasn't willing to chance it. *Plus if he's a legit client of Tank's it wouldn't be good luck for the business.*

Of course killing both would erase all doubts, but taking out an innocent man wouldn't be right. All she wanted was the man who put a hit out on Tank. That's it. That's all.

"Oh, fuck my life," she said, picking up the broom from atop the items strewn from the cabinets on the polished wood floors.

Tank might get released the next day or soon after and she didn't want him to come home to the house being so fucked up. She had never been the domestic type and would much rather drop-kick an enemy than pick up broken plates, pots, and canned goods.

"This some real bullshit right here," she grumbled, dumping a dustpan filled with shattered glass into a garbage bag.

As she moved from room to room setting things right, she was still trying to process all the new shit added to the mix. Blackmail and political corruption.

Naeema didn't bother much with politics. Outside of voting for Barack to ensure his first and second terms she didn't get into the rest of the mess. Just like with the police, she didn't feel like weeding through who was real and who was fake. *Fuck 'em all* was her motto. Selfish? Yes. And she knew it. But a politician having to be blackmailed into doing what the fuck he was elected to do anyway? Proof positive she wasn't all the way wrong.

In Tank's bedroom, Naeema bent down to scoop up all the clothes thrown to the floor from the dresser drawers and closets. She dumped them on the box spring haphazardly dropped back atop the bed frame. The mattress, sheets, and covers were across the room on the floor.

One by one she either folded his massive collection of designer T-shirts in dark colors or hung his button-down shirts back on the hangers that weren't broken in half. Those were dark as well.

She didn't know what rule book said bodyguards and security had to wear dark colors but Tank stuck to that shit. She pressed one of the V-neck tees to her face and deeply inhaled the scent of his cologne and the fabric softener still clinging to it. *He does look so good in dark blue. Black too. But nothing is sexier on him than the deepest darkest blue and gray. Gray too.*

Turning with a stack of folded shirts on one arm she bent

at the hip to pick up one of the dresser drawers from the floor. She sat the shirts in it to free up her hand and then slid the drawer back into the opening of the dresser.

When she packed his bag for that weekend in New York she had been surprised to find the light gray shirt and reached for it with a desire to see him in anything but his beloved dark clothing. She thought the gray would be a good compromise. She was hella wrong.

You grabbed the wrong damn shirt.

Naeema paused in closing the drawer as she remembered how the blood from the gunshot wounds soaked the shirt turning the light gray crimson. So much blood. So many shots.

Naeema blinked with each echo of the bullets she recalled.

POW!

POW!

POW!

POW!

So much blood.

One of his beloved dark shirts wouldn't have shown the blood so much.

Naeema frowned deeply as she rose to her feet. She looked down into the drawer and then over at the bed. The gray shirt had stuck out to her because it was an oddity. It was different. It was something Tank didn't fuck with on duty. That was the first and the last. That she knew.

But she knew something else now. It came to her so easily *now*. She knew something that she should have known a long time ago. "Shit," she swore as she turned and let her body lean against the tall dresser.

She closed her eyes. "Think, think, think, Naeema. Think, bitch. Think," she urged herself, pressing her hand to the side of her face and rubbing it up and down distorting her features as she did.

"How did I miss it?" she whispered. "How the fuck did I miss it?"

Her heart pounded as she covered her face with her hands and let her body sink until she sat on the floor among Tank's things. Clarity was a motherfucker . . . especially when it proved you were wrong. Dead wrong.

"I killed the wrong man," she gasped as she drew her knees to her chest and wrapped her arms around her legs.

She felt numb. She had killed before but it was always to right a wrong. To fix shit. To make someone pay. To strike back.

Kevin Greene was dead by her hands and he was no innocent. But he did not shoot Tank. She killed the man when his crimes warranted a solid ass whipping at the most. She took his life for nothing.

POW!

She flinched at the memory of his blood and brains splashing against the window behind him. Death was nothing new to her. But killing someone who didn't deserve it was. It was like the need for revenge put up a shield that protected her from the magnitude of the violence she wrought.

But the shield was down now. She was vulnerable and she felt every bit of the guilt, the regret, and the remorse.

POW!

Her stomach moved in reverse and she hustled to her feet to run toward the adjoining bathroom. She slipped on something and fell to her knees but she quickly recovered and made it to the commode just as she hurled the contents of her stomach. It seemed to go on endlessly and she was weak by the time her stomach settled down and she slumped to the floor, clutching the toilet as she breathed deeply and winced at the taste of vomit coating her mouth and tongue.

Father God, forgive me. Please.

The rest of the night came and went as the time hit midnight. Naeema's hands tightly gripped the handles of her motorcycle as she road through the streets of Newark. She felt her cell phone vibrating against her chest inside her bra but she ignored it. It had to be Tank and she didn't want to lose focus. She didn't want her thoughts muddled and confused.

She didn't want to fuck up. Not again.

For the last few hours she sat in Tank's house and ran over everything in her head again and again. She made sure her memory wasn't fucking with her. She had to be sure that rushing and being blinded by rage didn't leave her short-sighted and confused. She had to be sure that she was gunning for the right person this time.

She had to. Her conscience—which was admittedly as changing as the direction of the wind—would accept nothing else. But not getting to the bottom of it was impossible as well.

Naeema weaved in and out of the cars lining South Orange Avenue as she headed from Newark's downtown area to the section bordering the township of South Orange. A half a block before the town she turned into the driveway of a white stucco two-story house with green shutters.

She parked and quickly climbed the steps to the front door. She had barely rung the doorbell before the door opened and Grip's tall, opposing figure filled the frame. His eyes filled with surprise at the sight of her.

She smiled, took a step forward, and pushed the button on the stun gun.

Bzzzzz-zap.

Without hesitation she pressed it to his neck and then stepped back just enough to drop-kick his big ass square in the chest sending him flying across his living room. She rushed inside and shut the door as she pulled her gun from the holster under her shirt. She sat on his chest and pressed the gun to the small spot between his eyes with both hands.

It is what it is.

"What the fuck, Naeema?" he roared, his eyes on her.

"Shut the fuck up," she snapped, looking down into the face of a traitor.

She saw a change in the light in his eyes. She knew he was plotting how to take her down. "Don't fuck with it, Grip," she warned him. "Or I will put four bullets in you the same way you did to Tank."

The look in his eyes changed again. "Me?"

"You, motherfucker!" she said.

"I wasn't even in town, Naeema."

"Yes, you were."

His body tensed beneath her.

"Don't try me, Grip," she threatened. "You will die sooner than later. I got zero fucks to give about your life, bruh. You know motherfucking well that I ain't the chick to sleep on. You were there. You know better than almost anybody that Tank trained me in this shit. I. Ain't. The. Fucking. One."

His eyes changed again and this time she saw his fear.

"Why'd you do it, Grip?" she asked, her tone softening but still menacing. Still showing that his life hung by the thinnest of threads. She pressed the gun deeper against his head.

His eyes crossed like he was trying to focus on the barrel.

"I didn't—"

"Shut up," she snapped roughly. "You told on your damn self, fool."

Grip's face filled with questions.

She nodded. "That's right. You did."

He was unsure.

"You and the rest of the crew shut Yani out when I dropped the word on him bitching out at the shooting. No one spoke to him. Not even to fire him. Even he told me that. So how did you know Tank wore a shirt light enough to show his blood?" she asked, shifting her head side to side before she bit her bottom lip.

"It couldn't have been easy seeing all that blood stain his shirt," she said, repeating his words from the day he came to the hospital.

His eyes revealed he remembered the words.

She bit her bottom lip as her eyes burned looking down at the man who betrayed a friend. "Did you enjoy seeing the blood? Huh? Is that why you pointed it out, you sick bitch?" she asked, her lip curled in anger.

"Naeema, I didn't," he said, his eyes filling with tears. "Please, you're wrong."

She shook her head softly. "No I'm not. You want to know something, Grip? You talk too fucking much. If you weren't there at the scene how did you know I left Yani behind?"

I don't blame you for leaving his ass there.

His words were unspoken but they hung in the electric air between them.

Her finger stroked the trigger and the need to fire one off in his head was so strong she could taste it. She wanted nothing more than to send his traitorous, no-good ass on to the devil.

Calm down, Naeema. Keep it cool, bitch. Get answers first.

"Did you shoot him? Were you there? Did your hit man report back? What happened, Grip, because Tank would've taken a bullet to save you," she said in a harsh whisper revealing the pain of his betrayal.

Another shift in his eyes. "I've been looking into the shooting myself, Naeema. I know how you do and I didn't want to reveal too much info to you. I did talk to someone on the scene and they told me. Th-th-that's all," he stammered.

"What else you find out?" she asked.

His eyes shifted back and forth quickly. "Not much. But I'm on it," he swore.

Naeema pretended to release tension from her body as she pulled the gun back from his head just a bit. "Why didn't you tell me that?" she asked as she rose to her feet and stepped back from him. She purposefully lowered the gun and made a move as if to holster it.

He reached out to strike her, but Naeema was ready for his ass and ducked before she quickly moved around him to kick the back of his leg and deliver a hard knuckled-up blow to the back of his head. She followed it with several wicked kicks to his side that surely cracked his ribs. Two fists to the cheek and another square to his eye. It felt good to whip his ass.

She holstered her gun before dropping down to one knee beside him lying on his stomach. "Liar," she whispered down to him harshly as she gripped his chin and jerked his head back. "If you're innocent then why try and attack me? Dumb fucker. You fell for it."

Grip's jaw clenched.

"You put me on the trail behind Murk's murdering ass so keep that bullshit about not revealing too much to me. You told me that so why not tell me anything else, you lying motherfucker?" she asked.

She delivered a blow with her left fist to his already damaged ribs. He howled in pain. "Why did you want Tank dead? Why did you shoot him? Why did you try to kill him, Grip? And you better start answering questions motherfucker because it's the only thing that will save your life. Fuck *you*. I want the truth."

He closed his eyes, squeezing them tight. "I was paid to do it," he admitted.

She looked down at him in disbelief, her disgust for him sticking in her throat like bile. "You betrayed Tank, a man that is like your brother, for money?" she asked.

"I was never his brother," he said, looking up at her. "I was his employee. Don't get it twisted. Only motherfucker in this world Tank give a fuck about is you."

"And he deserved to die for that?" she screamed.

"I needed the money."

Naeema didn't know if she had ever hated anyone besides the killer of her son so much. She was consumed with it. But she learned her lesson. She took a breath and gave herself a long ten count. "Who hired the hit?" she asked, her voice devoid of emotion. She was numb from his betrayal.

"You gon' kill me anyway, Naeema. You think I'm stupid," he asked.

"Yes, I am, Grip," she admitted with a nod. "You will never live to see the sun rise and that is no one's fault but your own. Tank may not have meant shit to you but a paycheck but he gave a fuck about you. He trusted you. Loyalty over everything, motherfucker. You know that. You disrespected that. So yes I am going to take your life and unlike you I will succeed at the job because that's how *I* do."

He glanced up at her.

Their eyes met.

"Who?" she asked again.

He pressed his lips and eyes closed.

"And since you dropped Murk's name then I'm figuring it's not him because you wouldn't chance me finding out you were involved. So *who*?" she asked, her voice low, hard, and deadly.

He remained quiet.

She pulled out her key ring and released the sharp

switchblade. "So you're more loyal to *that* motherfucker than you are to Tank. You willing to let him live while you die? What sense that make?" she asked softly.

He looked up at her.

"None at all," she whispered down to him. "You might as well serve up the one-way ticket to hell for him too."

"Don't do this, Naeema. Please," he said.

"You ain't got much choice in the matter, Grip. The queen always protects her king. Always," she spat just before she roughly rolled him over onto his back and plunged the knife into his heart with a grunt.

She stood up and walked away from him, careful not to touch anything as she calmly took a seat on his leather couch and crossed her legs. She watched his body cycle through its steps toward death. A tear raced down her cheek.

She derived no fetish-like pleasure from killing. That man convulsing on the floor as his blood stained the carpet was someone she considered a friend. His betrayal was painful but she knew she couldn't keep it from Tank. She had to let him know so that he'd never sleep on another motherfucker again.

She wiped the tears from her eyes as she rose to her feet and moved over to stand beside his body as it began to go still. A tear fell from her face and landed in the blood pooling from his mouth. "It wasn't worth it," she whispered down to him in regret. "May God forgive us both."

He opened his mouth and whispered a name in the seconds just before he took his last blood-filled gasp. She paused for just a moment before she bent to remove the knife from his dead body. She fought the urge to close his lids over his eyes but didn't want to chance leaving prints. She closed the knife still warm and sticky with his blood and patted her holster to ensure she had her gun as she looked around the living room. With one last look down at his body, Naeema used the end of her shirt to open the door and leave.

One down and one to motherfucking go.

𝒩aeema put on a fake smile as the passenger door to the Sprinter opened. "Thanks for meeting me," she said, sounding all pleasant and shit even as her hatred burnt her gut like bottom-shelf liquor.

Diego closed the door and smiled, looking around at the interior of the luxury van. "Tell your boy to get his shit customized," he said, his voice slightly mocking. "I got mine to the shop now getting pimped the fuck out, you know?"

She nodded. "How do you know this my husband's shit?" she asked, the bleach she used to wash the blood from her hands causing them to itch as the scent of chlorine filled the air. "You know him?"

Diego turned sideways in his chair and eyed her. "Nah, I don't know that dude," he said with a cocky shrug of one shoulder.

Liar.

"Let's go to a diner. I'm hungry," she said, driving the Sprinter out of the parking lot where she asked him to meet her and leaving behind his Benz.

"Cool," he said, slumping down into the seat. "Your man ain't gone like you having other dudes riding in his shit."

"I wanted to get your package back to you as soon as possible," she said as she turned a corner. "Not trying to stop your hustle but I ain't getting involved with that shit, Diego."

She motioned with her thumb over her shoulder and he turned in his seat to spy the large Louis Vuitton box sitting on the seat behind her. He looked back at her. "What up with that, yo?" he asked, licking his lips and clasping his hands.

Naeema pulled to a stop at a red light. She turned her head to look at him. "I rather fuck you," she lied simply with a shrug. "I don't hustle or help hustle dope."

His eyes dipped down to the sweet spot between her thighs in the black leggings she wore. "Who says a fuck is enough to keep me quiet?"

"A fuck from some random chick probably ain't. But with *me*," she said cockily as she pressed her hand against her chest and tapped it several times. "Trust and believe you'll owe me after *a fuck* with me."

He looked out the windshield as she drove forward. "Shee-it, well pay your motherfucking debts then. Right now. Pull over there."

That'll work.

She slowed the Sprinter down and turned into one of the openings for Weequahic Park. She parked by the basketball court and shut off the vehicle. "Let's go," she said, rising to move to the rear. She pulled the tank top she wore up over her head and patted the seat by the blacked-out window.

He rose from his seat as well and was already unzipping his pants as he did. "Trust me, you ain't the only sex star up in this motherfucka," he said, freeing his dick.

Naeema was phony as shit as she smiled and licked her

lips at the sight of it. He was straight. No doubt about it that his dick—which was plenty of shades darker than his Latino complexion—was thick and heavy. Still, any small chance he had of getting her pussy wet faded forever when Grip whispered his name to her before he died.

Diego paid to have Tank killed and she wanted to know why.

He stood before her and gripped the back of her head to guide the tip of his dick into her mouth. She fought the urge to bite as she closed her eyes and let him thrust his hips forward sending his dick back and forth along her tongue.

Revulsion for his ass made her stomach turn.

She pressed her head back against the strength of his hand on her neck to free her mouth. "I like sucking dick on my knees, *papi*," she said softly, hoping her hatred for him didn't show in her eyes. She stood up and held his shoulder to turn him and then pushed against his chest until he dropped down into the seat. His dick stood at attention.

Naeema went into Queen mode. Although he knew who she was, she needed to pretend to be someone other than Tank's wife. She had to fake herself the fuck out. *The ends justified the means.*

She grasped his dick in her hand and took it into her mouth as he gripped the back of her head and thrust his hips forward off the seat as she sucked him. She faked it well with moans and slurps and deep sucks but it might as well have been a dildo as far as she was concerned.

"Don't make me cum. Not yet," he whispered.

She looked up at him with her mouth still wet and forced a smile as she rose to sit on his lap with her hand still tightly stroking his dick. "Feel good?" she asked.

"I knew I would get this pussy," Diego boasted, his eyes hot with desire for her. He wanted it and bad.

What she had for him wasn't what he was begging for.

"You did?" she asked, rising up off his lap and undid the front latch of her bra to press his face between her breasts.

He pressed kisses to each smooth brown globe before taking one nipple into his mouth to suck deeply.

Motherfucker please.

The chill that coursed over her body was disgust not desire. She reached behind the back of the seat and grabbed the rope she had already pushed into the leather pocket. As he gripped both breasts at once and sucked both nipples she faked a hot gasp and leaned back from him as she pulled the rope forward. She crossed the ends as she jumped off his lap to come around him looping the rope again and again, pressing her knee to the back of the chair to jerk it tightly.

"Yo, what the fuck, Naeema," he said, pulling forward against the rope.

She tied a knot and looped it again so that the rope pressed his arms down against his body before she knotted it again. She came back around the chair and sat in the one facing him. Her eyes dropped down to take in his dick now lying on its side like it was deflated. She smiled and pouted her lips. "Poor baby," she said.

"What the fuck is this, a robbery, yo?" Diego asked, still struggling against the rope.

Naeema shook her head. "It's kinky sex," she lied, kicking off a shoe to extend her leg and stroke his flaccid dick with her foot.

He shook his head and relaxed his body as he eyed her. "How my dick taste?" he asked.

"Forgettable," she shot back.

"I shoulda nut in your fucking mouth," he spat.

"I woulda spit it back in your face."

"*Puta*," he swore.

"And a damn good one," she advised him, kicking his dick lightly up against his stomach before she removed her leg from his lap and crossed it over her other one.

He started cursing in Spanish and Naeema studied her nails until he quieted down.

"How's Councilman Planter?" she asked, watching him closely.

His eyes were a dead giveaway as they filled with surprise. Naeema got confirmation that Diego knew the man. She was still insistent that the break-ins at her and Tank's place were a search for the evidence that Tank had against the councilman. Diego put a hit out on Tank but the councilman was still in the mix. Question was: How?

Diego's whole demeanor changed. "You know more than I thought you knew," he said, his face arrogant and his voice demeaning.

"You not the first motherfucker to make that mistake," she said.

He shook his head.

"You're the last one left, fool," she lied. "And it's all on you. I honestly didn't even know your role in all this shit until the councilman gave you up."

Diego's eyes iced over. "I hate weak motherfuckers," he said, his voice filled with disgust. "Almost as much as I hate fucking snitches."

Careful, Naeema. Slow walk this motherfucker. Don't rush it.

"Your bitch of a husband fucked up some good money for me," he said. "He fucked up everything testifying against Murk and then blackmailing Vic. Them fuckers ran scared. Shit on the deal. I *needed* that fucking money."

She kept her face passive but she was truly confused as hell. *Deal? Them? Who?*

"Not giving away four-thousand-dollar Louie V bags," she said, knowing she had to fill the silence to keep him talking.

"There was three times that in heroin inside it though," he bragged.

"You're not a boss, not to him anyway. Or me," she said. "That's why you're here tied the fuck up."

"I'm a fucking boss, bitch. Believe that. I did what Murk ain't had the balls to fucking do. Okay? All this going legit shit and so happy that Victor help him beat the last murder case, now he gone just *let* that motherfucker walk these streets."

Councilman Planter was in with both Murk and Diego and Tank testifying fucked up whatever deal they were about to go in on. The councilman got scared and Murk was sticking to going legit. Naeema remembered her last conversation with Tyrai from Gentlemen Only.

I've been here since he first opened up and he promised us all he was legit now and we shouldn't worry about our jobs.

"I did what neither one of them punk motherfuckers had the *cojones* to do," he spat. "Fuck letting that snitch live. Fuck trying to find whatever shit he had on him to stop blackmail. Yo, murk that motherfucker and be done with it. Kill two birds with one stone. No snitching. No blackmailing. Done deal. Now let's get back to fucking *business*," Diego said, his lips curled in anger as he stared out the window and stomped his foot as he talked.

This motherfucker ain't bright worth a fuck.

He sat there tied in a chair, with her in total control, and bragged about the death of her husband—*her* king—putting a business deal his ass needed back in place. *He don't know me very well, do he?*

She uncrossed her legs.

He looked over at her. "You disappoint me, *Queen*," he said mockingly.

She eyed him as she sat up on the edge of the seat.

"I actually thought you thought Murk put the hit out and you was undercover to kill his ass or something. I wanted you to take that nigga out. Do what I couldn't do without starting a fucking war on these streets, man," he said.

Maybe he does.

"The *fuck* was I thinking, yo?" Diego asked himself before he laughed.

And then again, maybe not?

She stood up and straddled his lap again as she reached to grip his chin and turn his face toward her. She stared at him. Something about the look on her face made him fight against the ropes and jerk his head from her tight grasp. "You fucked up, Diego," she said, releasing his chin roughly only to slap him twice across the cheeks until they reddened.

He spit and it landed on her chin. Thick, hot, and clinging.

Naeema wiped it away with her hand and then smeared it on his cheek. She reached behind him again and pulled two connected spools of thin metal wire from the pocket.

He eyed them warily. "What the fuck, yo?" he asked, his voice rising more successfully than his sudden attempt to get up from the chair.

She said nothing as she unrolled the two spools and exposed a good length of wire between them. "I'm not going to kill you with this," she promised even as she pressed the wire against his neck. He struggled. She pressed her knees into the edges of the seat to brace herself. "You have helped to flood these streets with enough heroin to leave our people fucked up from it for a long damn time. For some people it will take years to get their shit back together."

"Ahh," he cried out as the wire broke his skin.

The break filled with blood.

His eyes filled with fear.

The interior of the Sprinter filled with his cries.

She did not let up. She pressed down harder. The blood reddened his neck. The gash deepened as his flesh tore from the wire.

Like with Grip she knew she couldn't use a gun to finish him. She didn't have a burner and hers was registered in her name. No, she had other plans for Diego. Something that was fitting as hell.

She dropped the wire and rose from his lap to turn and open the Louis Vuitton box. She looked down at the heroin package. She had left the purse behind at her house. She opened the knife on her key ring. Again the scent of the chlorine she used to clean it rose and stung her nostrils. Using the knife she cut a long slit in the package and then opened the edges wide.

Naeema held it with one hand and then used the other to recline the chair Diego was tied to. "You lived off it, now die off it," she said before raising the package and dumping the heroin into the opening in his neck as she pressed his head back with her free hand.

Dropping the package onto his belly she turned, grabbed her shirt to pull back over her head, and climbed back behind the wheel. His cries echoed around her as the drug infused his blood and she reached over to turn on the satellite radio.

Future's bass-driven "Move That Dope" filled the speakers.

"Hey move that dope, hey move that dope . . ."

She glanced back once and turned it up feeling like he would appreciate it as she cranked the van and pulled out into traffic.

"Hey move that dope, hey move that dope . . ."

Naeema entered the hospital room and slumped back against the door, pushing it closed. Tank set his cell phone down on the bed as he looked over at her. She closed her eyes and lightly beat her head against the door as the tears she fought hard to hold back fell.

"What the hell? What's wrong? I've been blowing your phone up," Tank said as he came over to pull her into his arms.

She slumped against him in relief and buried her face against his neck. The beating of his pulse against her lips gave her life. "I got 'em. I got Grip and I got Diego," she admitted in a rush.

Tank stiffened and pulled back to look down at her. "What?" he asked.

"This dope dealer named Diego paid Grip to kill you because you messed up some big deal between him, Murk, and the councilman when you testified against Murk and blackmailed Councilman Planter," she said.

"Wait a minute. Hold up, yo," he said, walking away from her toward the window just to turn and come back to her. "Grip?"

She nodded, tears filling her eyes again. "I'm sorry," she told him, hurting for him.

Tank pulled her to him and pressed kisses against her forehead as he stroked her back. "Baby, why you always taking shit like this on?" he asked, relief in his voice. "What if they had . . ."

Naeema shook her head. "The queen protects the king," she whispered against his chest.

"Na, baby, baby. Come on," Tank chastised her.

"I should've made them bitches bow down to me. All hail the Queen, right?" she joked before another round of tears swelled her chest. "I made light work of them fools. I got you. When you weak. I'm strong. And vice versa. It's me and you against the fucking world, Tank. Forever and always."

"Forever and always," he agreed.

She hugged him tight.

"Where are they?"

"Huh?" she asked, feeling so fucking wiped out and drained from it all.

"The bodies. Where are they?" he asked.

"Grip is home and Diego is downstairs in your Sprinter," she said.

"Lie down," Tank said, gently nudging her toward the bed as he crossed the room to open the closet. He pulled out his duffel bag.

"Tank," she said, rising from where she had just sat on the side of the small bed.

"I gotta clean this shit up now," he emphasized, his eyes serious as hell. "I'll be back in no time but I gotta handle this shit real quick and make sure you aight. No repercussions. You did the lightweight now let me finish it up. Lie down. Fucking sleep. Rest your nerves. I got this. I'll be right back."

Naeema saw the determination in his eyes and truth be told she was physically and emotionally drained from the weight of it all. She nodded and he rushed to pull on clothing as she lay back on the bed.

Her king was back and she wasn't at it completely alone anymore.

It felt damn good.

Epilogue

My city. My city.

Newark, New Jersey, was everything it appeared to be—good and bad—and much more. The city's history was rich, from it's founding way back in the 1600s—the third city in the state—to the influx of black folks in the 1950s and 1960s, the riot of 1967, and on up to the election of its first African American mayor, Kenneth Gibson, in 1970. There was plenty more during and after those highlights, but there was a lot more Naeema didn't give a fuck about. That was just truth. The history was so disconnected from the realness of Newark today—the shit about the city that helped shape her into a woman with a heart who was also willing to go all out to protect those she cared about. Growing up on the streets of Newark helped shape her and frame the way she viewed the world. She wanted nothing but the best for the city because the best is what it deserved.

Through the pink visor of her helmet Naeema eyed the Krueger-Scott Mansion as she passed it on her way down Martin Luther King Jr. Boulevard. The forty-room, Victorian home sat empty, now a historical landmark and a shadow of its former beauty. It was a symbol of the contradictions within the city. The former beauty and the ongoing ugliness. Surviving. Battling for superiority. The mansion almost looked out of place amid its surroundings. A sign of past wealth fighting to overcome the look and feel of poverty on the blocks surrounding it.

Louise Scott, said to be the city's first black millionaire, once owned and lived in the mansion from the 1950s up until her death in 1982. That was the type of history that should be told, taught, impressed. Motivation.

As she zoomed past St. James AME Church and then Whigham's Funeral Home on her bike, Naeema thought of Mya. She said a quick prayer for the teenager, hoping she was at the very least motivated to be, do, and have better thanks to her promise to Naeema. Naeema knew herself to be far from a role model but she did cop to a murder she didn't commit in order to give Mya another shot at more. Over the months Naeema fought the urge to track her down to see if the teenager was keeping her word because she honestly didn't know if she could swallow discovering otherwise. She would be beyond pissed but even more so she would be hurt. *I'd rather not know.*

The cold bite of the winter air nipped at her and the speed of the bike only intensified the chill. She welcomed it. Accelerating the bike, Naeema easily moved between cars to reach Springfield Avenue. She eyed the tops of the towering buildings of downtown Newark in the distance before she made the turn, enjoying the feel of the mechanical muscle she rode as the bike dipped a bit before she controlled it and sat upright in the seat as her ride continued up one of the major thoroughfares of the city.

The landscape changed with each mile, the inconsistencies of the city becoming more obvious. The streets more congested and unkempt. The homes less pretty. The truth. There were areas of improvement but more was needed. The "renaissance" of the city had yet to reach beyond downtown and its surrounding areas.

A thin man stumbled into the street from between two cars and directly in Naeema's path. Her eyes shifted quickly to the left. A car was coming toward her in the other lane. Gritting her teeth she braked, praying her wheels wouldn't lock up, as she tried her best to avoid hitting him

She felt the rear of her bike lift up and eased off the brakes as she turned the wheel around as soon as the car passed her. She had missed the man by inches. The squeal of the rubber against the road and the rise of smoke around her was enough to let her know she was lucky to still be seated. With her heart pounding, she turned her head and eyed the man. *You dumb motherfucker.*

Naeema drove her bike forward slowly to reach him and grabbed the back of his dingy shirt in her glove-covered fist. Lips tight, she yanked back once, pulling him off his feet and down onto his ass before she released him.

"Hey," he said, his voice devoid of any energy as he lifted his head to look up at her.

She shook her head. The dullness of his skin, the yellow of his eyes, the stench of his body and his breath, the scabs on his skin from scratching. The slow death he was bringing on himself. A heroin fiend.

Feeling frustration and disgust overwhelm her, Naeema checked for traffic before doing a U-turn and continuing on her way, leaving the man behind. She wished she could outrun the truth of the rising heroin usage in the city as well.

Naeema hated it. *Shit was mad hectic and getting worse day by day.*

She wasn't dumb enough to believe that killing Diego and destroying that hefty package of heroin did a damn thing to stop the drug game. Not with the news flooded with the arrests, the rising number of heroin and opiate addicts across the state, and the government implementing different programs and bills to help fight the battle they were losing. Killing Diego was all about revenge and she took pleasure in knowing that whatever was left of his dead body—if anything at all—would never be found. Tank made sure of that.

Grip's, too.

The ends justified the means. They had to. Their conscience couldn't rest any other way.

Grip's family held a candlelight vigil for him. Tank and Naeema attended. To do otherwise would've seemed odd. She knew the tears that filled his eyes during the vigil had been the realest shit ever. Still, she knew his grief was more for the man he thought he knew as a friend than for the traitor Grip had shown himself to be.

No one was the wiser about Diego putting the hit on Tank, Grip trying to enforce it, or Naeema executing both.

Councilman Planter was still under Tank's thumb and taking credit for programs Tank pushed him to implement. Naeema was about ready to send him to his Maker for even fucking with Diego, but Tank was handling the corrupt councilman. *For now.*

Murk's ass was living on borrowed time. Tank already assured her that as soon as he felt that enough time had passed where suspicion would not immediately fall at his feet, that Murk was outta here. As good as got. *All in due time.*

As she turned off Springfield and headed down Seventeenth Street she felt her cell phone vibrate against her fleshy ass in the back pocket of her ripped jeans.

Bzzz-bzzz-bzzz.

She slowed down the motorcycle and turned onto the same abandoned lot where she had killed the man who broke into her home. Not allowing herself to spare him an extra moment of thought, she pulled out her cell phone.

Her heart raced at an incoming text from Tank. She opened it with swipes of her thumb. "Forever and always," she read aloud with a curve of the corner of her full gloss-covered mouth.

She quickly texted him back. "Missing you. Loving you. Forever and always," she mouthed as she typed.

Tank, and a small number of his crew, including a reinstated Yani were out of the country doing security for a singer's comeback tour. She tried to not think of sexy backup dancers or groupies making a play for her man. Since his recovery from the gunshots she was trying to elevate their shit—their love. She wanted to trust him with her heart the same way she trusted him infinitely with her life. And she wanted the same from him. It was the only way they could have their "always and forever."

With a quick glance at the snow covering Westside Park directly across from her, she pushed the cell phone back into her back pocket and pulled up the zip of the fitted leather jacket she wore. She steered the bike out of the lot and continued up Seventeenth Street, making the left turn on Sixteenth Avenue once she checked for oncoming traffic.

She needed the drive after a long day on her feet cutting hair but she was ready to go home, maybe cook her and Sarge some dinner, and crash on the bed watching television. Sometimes doing nothing was the best something in the world.

"Maybe some spaghetti," Naeema said, just as she turned the corner on Eastern Parkway.

"Or we can order—"

The rest of her words trailed off as she eyed an ambulance, its red lights flashing, double-parked in front of her next-door neighbor Coko's house. "The fuck?" she whispered, slowing the motorcycle to a stop in the middle of the street as she eyed a stretcher with a body bag strapped to it. A dead body.

Naeema's face filled with confusion.

After many months of not seeing Coko or noticing any signs of activity in her home, Naeema was outside sweeping her front porch when a taxicab pulled up next door and Coko emerged from the back of it. Naeema had been so surprised that she stood there with her mouth open not even hiding her shock. She had to get her shit together when Coko turned on the sidewalk and headed toward her.

Any signs of her addiction had been gone. Her eyes clear. Her skin fresh. Clean. Neat. Sober.

Naeema squinted as she eyed the body bag. She then looked up the stretch of the street to the neighbors standing on their porches staring but not stepping up to ask questions. Show concern. Give a fuck. Bullshit rumors would fly.

Naeema rolled up closer to the ambulance just as the paramedics eased the stretcher into the back of it. She glanced up at the closed front door of Coko's house. No sign of Coko standing there with concern over whomever was just wheeled out of her house in a body bag.

How could it be?

Naeema looked back at the ambulance. It was Coko's dead body on that stretcher.

"Excuse me? What happened?" she asked.

"Overdose. That heroin ain't shit to play with," a short stocky Cee-Lo–looking dude said before slamming the door closed and disappearing around the side of the ambulance.

Overdose?

Naeema turned and looked up at the door again as the ambulance eventually pulled off down the street. There were no sirens to accompany the flashing red lights. There was no need for urgency anymore.

She felt sadness overwhelm her as she again remembered the day of Coko's sudden reappearance. She had walked over to Naeema's porch and genuinely thanked her for saving her life the previous year.

In the months since her return the two women had become friends who sympathized with each other over the plight of their relationships—or lack thereof—with their sons. Naeema's chance to do better was taken with Brandon's death. Coko was determined to reclaim her rights to raise her nine-year-old.

Naeema parked her motorcycle in the space left empty by the ambulance. As she climbed off it she spotted Sarge standing on her porch. Naeema stepped onto the sidewalk and then jogged up Coko's stairs. She peered through the window but couldn't see anything beyond the blinds.

Damn.

"What is it, Naeema?"

She turned and found Sarge standing at the foot of the steps. "They said Coko died from an overdose."

Sarge just released one of his noncommittal grunts.

Naeema crossed her arms over her chest and shook her head. "But that's bullshit," she said, glancing back over her shoulder. "Coko was clean. I just saw her this morning, Sarge. She was *clean*," she stressed, surprised at the tears welling up in her eyes.

"So what you sayin'?" Sarge asked.

"I *think* someone killed her. I *think* someone took her out," Naeema said. "I *think* there is more to this."

Sarge grunted again. And again it revealed nothing of what he felt.

"I'm going to get to the bottom it. That I *know*," she swore, her eyes filling with enough fire to burn hell.

About the Author

MEESHA MINK is the bestselling and award-winning author of more than thirty books written under three names, including the Real Wifeys series, and coauthor of the explosive Hoodwives trilogy. She was born and raised in Newark, New Jersey, and lives in South Carolina. For more information, please visit MeeshaMink.com.